How to Lose a Lord
IN 10 DAYS OR LESS

Elizabeth Michels

sourcebooks
casablanca

Published by Sourcebooks Casablanca, an imprint of Sourcebooks, Inc.
P.O. Box 4410, Naperville, Illinois 60567-4410
(630) 961-3900
Fax: (630) 961-2168
www.sourcebooks.com

Printed and bound in Canada.
WC 10 9 8 7 6 5 4 3 2 1

In loving memory of my mom, who once told me, "If you ever put me in one of your books, make me skinny." I miss you, Mom.

One

September 10, 1818

ANDREW ROUNDED A BEND IN THE ROAD AND URGED his mount into a small patch of woods. Damn the open terrain of the moors. He'd realized he was being followed an hour ago, but could do nothing about it, only push ahead in the dense fog. Pulling his knife from the scabbard strapped beneath his coat, he slid from his horse's back and waited.

Shadow's Light pawed the ground and exhaled a puff of exasperation. "Shh," Andrew breathed into the mist. "You'll have us found within the minute with all that snorting." He reached over his shoulder and gave the horse a pat on the cheek, pulling him deeper into the shadows of the trees.

For once he was thankful for the heavy fog covering the moors. There might be a terrible lack of trees this far north, but a mist could always be counted on to sweep in overnight. He'd spent the past two years cursing it for dampening his clothes every morning, the fierce Scottish winds chilling him to the bone. He was further south now, however, back on English soil and back to fleeing—or so it seemed.

Once upon a time he'd been Andrew Clifton, Lord Amberstall, famous horse breeder, gentleman of the *ton*, and all-around dashing fellow. Now… He shook his head, his over-long hair falling into his eyes. If society saw him in his current state, would they know him? Part of him hoped not. He'd pulled himself together the best he could for the journey, but this was by no means his former standard of dress.

He ground his jaw and gave his horse another affectionate pat as he led him to the thickest grouping of trees he could find—which wasn't terribly thick, considering the circumstances. Andrew sighed and wrapped his hand around the tree before him, watching. With any luck they wouldn't be seen between the tree trunks. Shadow was ready to be gone from this place, Andrew could tell. Shadow never liked standing still for long.

Andrew's gaze sharpened as two men came into focus. They'd been trailing him since he crossed the Scottish border last night. He'd thought he'd lost them when he circled back to the inn where he had spent the night. Apparently he'd been mistaken. The soft clip of horses' hooves grew louder.

"He's headed back south. Must've come this way," a deep voice rumbled. Ruffians.

Andrew had caught sight of them at first light this morning, then again just after he stopped to eat lunch. Between wisps of fog, he'd seen the men growing closer. They had the look of common highwaymen, as evidenced by their worn, ill-fitting clothes and the larger one's ruddy complexion. Andrew had increased his pace, but they'd found him in spite of his speed.

"Could've taken a different road," the smaller man replied.

"There isn't another road, you idiot," the larger man spat out, near enough for Andrew to hear the panting of their horses and smell of wood smoke that lingered about them.

Andrew pulled his dark coat tighter around his chest, thankful for the fog that surrounded him, even as it chilled to the bone. It would be raining soon. Perhaps these men would move on, seek shelter. But, even as he thought it, he knew they weren't the sort to be deterred by the weather.

The larger ruffian slowed and turned his head, staring into the woods where Andrew waited in silence, shielded from view by only a few sparse scrub bushes and scraggly trees. He worked to control his breathing. Between the fog and the stubble of dark beard shrouding the man's face, Andrew could see only the steel of his dark eyes sweeping the forest. Shadow's Light stilled, thankfully as aware as Andrew of the danger that lurked nearby. A long-held breath later, the man turned his attention back to the road.

"What's to stop him from going through farms and such?" the smaller man asked as he looked across a field on the opposite side of the road.

"Sheep? Fences and walls? Unknown lands?"

"I'm rather fond of sheep, meself."

"That, Smarth, I would believe," the large man replied as they guided their horses down the road. "Let's find this fancy lord so we can return home."

"Bet he has some coin on him to sweeten the pie," Smarth mused.

"For once, I like the way you think."

Andrew breathed deeper as the men drew farther away. "Sweeten the pie" made it seem as if robbing him wasn't their primary focus. But they were highwaymen. It made no sense. All they could want were his pocket money and any jewels he had on his person. If they found him, they would be rather disappointed, since he only possessed enough funds to get home without incident. The few items he'd kept over the last two years he'd been away were left behind at Lord Steelings' Scottish cottage, and the rest of his life was contained in a stable on his estate far south of here.

What more could they possibly desire from him? He reached up and felt his pocket, his mother's letter still folded inside.

His eyes narrowed on the two men disappearing into the fog. Was it possible that this trouble was related to her difficulties on the estate? Surely not. Her issues could all be traced back to one fact: she didn't know the first thing about running an estate. Had he learned no lesson from his father on the subject of trusting women?

"Clearly you're just as daft as he was, Andrew," he mumbled. Leaving everything he'd built to her care had been foolish, even under the circumstances. His horses were the family's only source of income, after all.

Her letter hadn't explained the root of the trouble, only that two horses had gone missing, and then some cryptic talk about their neighbor. One thing he did know for certain was he didn't want to be dodging these ruffians all the way to his home outside London.

He swung up onto Shadow's Light's back, giving him a nudge with his heel and a soft click of his tongue. A moment later, there was a spray of mud and a blast of cold autumn air as the fog bit at his cheeks. Leaning over the horse's mane, Andrew urged him forward. This afternoon, the hunted would become the hunter. He squinted into the mist.

They couldn't be far ahead. The thunder of hooves hitting solid ground sounded in his ears until he could see two dark forms on the road.

Fighting highwaymen wasn't how he normally spent his day, but he knew what must be done. He held the blade tight in his grasp as he urged his horse closer to his enemies. Drawing up between them before they could react, he slammed the butt of the knife down hard on the larger man's head, watching as he slipped sideways in his saddle and tipped toward the ground.

Andrew turned in a heartbeat, grabbing the smaller man's wrinkled shirt. He lifted the slight weight of the man from his horse, allowing the knife in his other hand to scrape against man's throat. Shadow's Light had matched his movements to the horse beside them without the need of reins as if he knew Andrew's mind. The man's drink-reddened eyes grew wide in his thin face as his gaze took in the ferocity in Andrew's gaze.

"You've been following me. I don't like to be followed," Andrew growled. His deep voice sounded rusted and tight from lack of use.

"I can see that, guv." Smarth twitched as he tried to reach for his saddlebag and was lifted higher in the air.

"Feel this?" Andrew twisted the knife so it dug ever so slightly into the ruffian's throat. "You will return to the gutter from which you crawled and remain there, far from me. Do you understand?"

Smarth gave a slight nod above the blade.

"Dismount," Andrew commanded before shooting a quick glance over his shoulder to check the other man's location. He was getting up from the road and beginning to lumber in their direction. Andrew didn't have much time.

He watched with his blade still drawn as Smarth slid to the ground with his hands raised. "Don't want no trouble, m'lord. Doin' as I was told is all."

"Do as you're told now. Leave me be." With a slap to the hindquarters of the man's horse, Andrew paused long enough to watch it sail across a wall into a pasture and disappear into the white of the fog. The other man's horse lingered behind him on the road. Andrew turned in the saddle in time to see that the large man had almost caught up with his mount.

Andrew was a sizable man and had a blade clutched in his hand, yet he knew he was outmatched when he saw the barrel of a gun rise in his direction. He spun back to the road ahead of him. His best chance was to flee—something in which he should be well versed by now. He groaned and called out a loud "Ya!" as his legs tightened around his horse.

The lone patch of woods sped by with wisps of fog chilling his skin and clinging to his clothes. He could scarcely see where he was going, but he could now hear the pounding hoofbeats of the large highway-man at his back. He sailed around a corner, urging

Shadow's Light faster as he passed a small cottage, then another.

He must be entering a hamlet. If he could make it to the center of the cluster of dwellings, he might be able to lose the man among the buildings. Perhaps if he doubled back again, he could be rid of him for good. He'd never heard of such a persistent highwayman. Wasn't there someone else to rob out here? Once again, he wondered if he was being pursued for some other reason. But he wasn't about to slow his pace to search for answers to the quandary. Instead, he flew into the unknown.

Shrouded in white, a village appeared around him, rooftops climbing free of the fog and stretching up into the clear afternoon air. If he could reach the far side of the village unnoticed, he could swing back behind the buildings.

He was almost there. Faster. He leaned closer over Shadow's dark mane.

As he rounded a corner, a tall hedgerow came into view. It was high, but Shadow had jumped higher. Andrew blinked away a memory of the exhibition two years ago—his last day at his home. This time would be different. With a last-minute tug on the reins, he was sailing with Shadow over the row of bushes and, with any luck, to safety.

⁂

Her hands slid over the mass of clay on the wheel before her. Today was the day. Today she would create a bowl. Katie pounded the clay twice with her fist, paused to consider it, and pounded it again for good measure. Or perhaps today was yet another day when she would create a lumpy plate. Judging by the fading afternoon light that peeked through the thick clouds every few minutes, she had only a few hours before she needed to rinse the mud from her hands and go inside for dinner.

The lawn around her grandmother's old pottery wheel had turned a muted gray with the mud from a week's worth of efforts in bowl making. Katie sat on the far edge of the field nearest her cottage with her back to a large hedgerow, shielding her from view on the road. It was her favorite place to sit at Ormesby Place. The scent of the grass at her feet mixed with the dust of the gravel on the road. She had a lovely view of the moors where they rolled off into the distance, and most important, she could not be farther from the stables. That was one place she never went—not anymore.

Now she had her other interests to keep her company. She slid her fingers over the clay. There was no risk in pottery. No flying across fields. No jumping over fences. And a clay bowl wouldn't leave her injured on the ground while the world crumbled around her. Katie sank her fist into the lump of mud with determination, wishing she'd remembered to bring the shaping instrument she'd almost understood how to use yesterday afternoon.

"That's my difficulty with pottery—I never seem to have the proper tool when I require it," she mused, glancing around for something that might suit her needs.

A pounding of hooves on the road made her turn,

startled, even though the thick hedgerow blocked all view. The thunderous sound still made her heart race, even after over a year of silence. Then the noise grew louder. The rider must be just behind her. She took a shallow breath. He would pass, whoever he was. He would continue riding. There was no need to panic. It wasn't as if the horse was going to come near her. The sound of hooves grew closer still as she waited. Then there was silence. She'd scarcely had time to register what was happening when the shadow of something large sailed over her head.

"Blast it all!" Katie fairly screamed as she dove for cover, the cool, wet grass slipping beneath her fingers as the horse twisted in the air above her. She crouched lower in an effort to shrink away from danger. With her hands wrapped over her head, she waited. Would it land on her? Would she be hurt once again? It wasn't until she heard the thud of the horse hitting the ground beside her that she dared to look up.

At that moment something—or rather *someone*—crashed into her pottery wheel.

She scrambled backward across the grass with frantic movements. Seeing the horse, she shifted farther from him. She needed to get away. The horse was lying down and apparently dazed, but that wouldn't last long. However, every move she made away from the horse brought her that much closer to the rider he'd thrown.

He was a lord. He must be, judging by his dress, yet he didn't belong to a neighboring estate. His blond hair was longer than was respectable and fell into his face, yet everything else about the man seemed at odds with that small rebellion. From his starched and perfectly knotted cravat to the underlying shine on his mud-splattered Hessians, the sum of his parts could be assembled into a single word: fastidious. Well, perhaps two words: fastidious and handsome.

"Who are you?" she asked, briefly distracted from her fear.

"Someone with terrible luck, it would seem," he groaned, pulling a piece of wood from beneath his back.

Her gaze fell to the ground beneath him. Splinters of wood and a heap of clay were all that was left of her newest endeavor. "My pottery wheel."

"Was an unfortunate place to land? I quite agree," the man grumbled as he rolled fully to his back, still lying amid the broken pieces of her wheel.

Before she could demand answers, however, she heard another rider approaching. Turning away from the man and his horse, she picked up her walking stick and took a step forward, brushing the grass from her breeches.

No one ever visited Ormesby Place, and now she had two men here within minutes of one another. She ducked through a hole in the hedge. Her eyes narrowed on the man rounding the corner into view. He didn't look to be the friendly sort; that was certain.

The man didn't live in the area. In fact, he looked to be one of the men her brother had warned her about when she'd last gone to London—a ruffian.

"M'lady," he offered in greeting as he drew his horse to a stop. "Did you see a man ride through here?"

She took half a step back from the horse and the man looming over her. "Yes, and riding far too dangerously, if you ask me."

"Which way did he go?" he asked, indicating the crossroads just ahead.

She could tell him the truth, but something in the ruffian's eyes told her he meant the man harm. The blond man may have smashed her pottery wheel and almost killed her, but he didn't deserve to die for the crime. "Left. When you find him, you may tell him of my displeasure."

"He will soon know the full extent of our displeasure. You may count on that," the ruffian snarled. With a flick of the reins, his horse pranced to the side a few paces. The man looked up and down her hedgerow for a second.

What did he see? She held her breath, waiting for him to be gone.

"Are these Ormesby lands?"

"They are," she replied, taken aback by his question.

"Right small world this is, then."

"Is it?" She didn't care what he was referring to. All she knew was that he and his horse made her uneasy and she wanted him to leave.

The man shifted his weight in the saddle, exposing a glint of metal at his waist with the movement. He had a pistol. "I suppose not," he hedged, pulling his hat down lower over his eyes.

Katie's fingers tightened on her walking stick. She wasn't sure how helpful it would be if the situation came to blows, but she would certainly put up a fight if she must.

He finally offered her a nod of farewell as he urged his mount toward the crossroads.

Katie leaned onto the stick with a sigh. She wasn't

sure what it was about the man that had her in knots, but she was glad to see the back of him as he cantered away.

Once he was out of sight, she ducked back through the hedgerow. She drew up short when she realized how close she was to the fallen horse. The leaves brushed against her shoulder blades as she shrank away. Taking a ragged breath, she edged around the animal. It was odd that he still hadn't moved.

She was nearing his hind legs where they lay in the grass. That was when her gaze landed on his leg. Sucking in a breath, she looked down at the wound. He must have landed horribly as he tried not to fall on her. She took a step backward, away from the horse. She ripped her eyes from the horse's injured leg to the rider who'd put him in that position.

The man was still on the ground as well, although he was now sitting up. She moved closer, watching as he brushed the grass from his coat. His back was to his horse. Did he know the animal was injured?

"I heard you direct the man on my tail down the road a bit," he said as she approached him from behind.

She bent down to retrieve what was left of her clay bowl from the pile of wood. "I'm pleased I could be of assistance," *even if you did destroy my day's work and my grandmother's pottery wheel*, she finished to herself.

"Nicely done. He's been rather difficult to lose." He pushed to his feet with a small groan of pain. "Now I can continue on without further issue."

"You're leaving," she accused, making him turn toward her. He hadn't apologized. He hadn't expressed his thanks. And he was leaving?

"I'm in a bit of a rush today," he said, his gaze meeting hers for the first time.

His eyes seemed to hold the light of the sun—golden and warm as they shined down on her. And she hated him for it. Did he think he could charm his way out of this situation? If he did, he was wrong.

"You broke my property." She held up the pottery for him to see.

He lifted the clay from her hand and studied it for a second. Then he shook his blond head and a wry grin crept across his tanned face. Handing the clay back to her, he dusted off his fingers, now marred by mud. "Yes, it is a shame to deny the world your…talent."

"Indeed it is," she agreed, even though she'd yet to successfully create a bowl. "And with that in mind, what do you plan to do to repay such a great loss?"

"Such a great loss," he repeated. "Have something sent here as replacement? I'm unsure what you want from me, but I must be on my way before that highwayman returns." He stepped around her and whistled for his horse to rise.

When the animal only shifted on the ground and tossed his head, the man froze.

She stared down at the sagging clay in her hand, trying to understand how her day had gone so horribly wrong. "You can't leave," she muttered. But he was no longer looking at her.

"So it would seem," he said as he moved forward and knelt beside his horse, leaving her to stand alone with her grass-covered, would-be bowl.

Two

A JOLT. THE RUSH OF AIR. THE WHINE OF HIS HORSE. And the shattering of wood.

Everything had slowed, then flown forward in a rush as Andrew had fought to breathe. He'd felt dazed. How had that happened? And where was Shadow now? Where was Andrew, for that matter?

He was bruised, hunted, and now reeling on a strange estate. Today had not been kind. He needed to get back to Shadow and his journey if he was to find an inn by nightfall. Andrew pushed down his impatience with the delay and tried to ignore the pain in his back. The girl he'd spoken to had wandered away but returned a moment later.

He turned, truly looking at the lady for the first time. Her manner of dress was unusual. Actually, unusual was rather an understatement. Breeches, boots, and dark red hair in a loose braid, threatening to come unbound at the first hint of a breeze; she wasn't much of a lady. And yet there was something about the way she'd spoken, the way she'd carried herself...

He couldn't become distracted by her. He had no

time for that. He needed to get to Shadow. As he whistled for his horse, he spotted the animal several paces away, lying in the grass.

He was hurt. *It could be a thrown shoe*, he told himself in an attempt to remain calm.

But as he pushed past the lady, he knew it was more than a thrown shoe. He'd seen an animal unable to gain his footing before, and it always meant the same thing—serious injury. Something tightened in his chest. *Let him be all right. He must be all right*. Andrew's pace increased until he reached Shadow's side. Pain was evident in the horse's eyes. "Damn."

He should have known better than to take a jump on unknown terrain. He'd lost the man at his heels, but at what cost? He knelt and ran his hand over Shadow's mane. "You're a bloody pain in my arse. You know that, don't you?" Andrew sighed, his gaze drifting over the animal in search of his injury. Finally spotting the deep gash on the horse's hind leg with gouges all the way up his shank, Andrew winced. "You can't be hurt. Not now."

Shadow huffed and nudged his owner with his head. His eyes were somber as he gazed at Andrew.

Andrew sniffed away the stifling emotion creeping through his limbs. "I know, boy. I know."

They'd been through some difficult times together, he and Shadow. His last days at Amber Hollow, his time in Scotland…even though the great beast was ultimately the cause of his isolation, Andrew had developed a fondness for the once grand racehorse. They were alike in that respect—former greatness fallen to ruin. At some point, Shadow had gone beyond mount and become a friend.

Andrew leaned his forehead down to meet Shadow's head as he'd done so many times, waiting for Shadow to grumble at the show of affection. When he didn't, Andrew straightened, looked him in the eye, and lied. "It'll be all right, ol' boy. We'll get you mended."

But their journey would have to end here, Andrew knew. Shadow was in no state to travel on that leg. Wounds of this sort became infected. Wounds of this sort killed.

The thought of climbing atop another mount and riding away turned his stomach, yet what was he to do? He was needed at home to repair whatever damage his mother had done. He couldn't stay.

Andrew had a lifetime of experience in making difficult decisions in the interest of good business. He sniffed and adjusted Shadow's bridle. The ritual of straightening the leather against the horse's brown coat was so familiar. It was perfectly adjusted already, of course, but it somehow gave him comfort to smooth the straps.

"It looks rather bad," the woman offered from behind him.

Andrew wiped his eyes on his sleeve before replying, wondering how closely she'd been watching him. "That it does."

"I suppose it was when he shifted in the air. You were thrown rather far. He was trying to avoid landing where you did—where I was sitting. You really shouldn't take jumps on unfamiliar grounds, you know."

"You belong to this estate?" He stood, nodding toward

the expanse of land. Shadow was in pain. He didn't want this to drag out a second longer than necessary.

"This is where I live, if that's what you're asking." She was moving closer with measured footsteps.

"Good. I assume there are able-bodied men in the stables who could assist me in…" He shot a pained glance back to Shadow, whose head was now resting against Andrew's leg. He couldn't say the words, not in front of Shadow. "They could assist me in moving my horse from this field."

"Of course. I'll send for them," she said.

Nodding his thanks to her, he added, "Are there horses available nearby? For sale?" His voice came out thick with emotion. Blasted animal.

"Nearby? Nothing is 'nearby' in this part of the country. And you have a horse. Granted, he needs to be bandaged…"

Shadow snorted behind him. He knew. Shadow always knew. Andrew stiffened his jaw against what he must do and stood to face the woman, refusing to look at Shadow while he discussed the horse's fate. "He needs more than a bandage and a pat on the head, m'lady."

"I have some experience with horses, as well as injuries that leave one lying on the ground for hours, and this…"—she paused to wave an arm toward Shadow—"this can be mended."

She didn't understand. Of course he wanted to save his horse, but that wasn't to be—not with that gash on his leg and likely damage to his muscle. "Sometimes death can be a kindness," he returned in a hushed tone.

She pulled back at his words. "Death is never kind, not for those who endure it and not for those left behind to deal with their sorrow. I don't know what you believe you know of it, but…"

"I have a schedule to keep. I haven't the time to stand about debating the ethics involved with equine medicine, Lady…"

"Lady Katie Moore. Daughter of the Earl of Ormesby and your only chance at riding from here on the back of any animal." She stuck out her hand, not a demure action of an earl's daughter, but with the force of a man.

"Pleasure," Andrew muttered, staring at her muddy, bare palm. She kept her hand hanging there in midair, encased down to her fingertips in clay from her pottery. Did she expect him to take her hand? These were his only gloves. However, he did need to purchase a horse from the woman. He sighed and clasped her fingers.

"Is it? A 'pleasure?' It must be all yours, because I'm quite certain I would recall such a thing."

She leveled a glare on him, her pale green eyes appearing to be weighing his worth and finding him lacking. The feeling was mutual, if he were to be honest. Her hair was falling from its braid and she wore no hat to keep her face from the elements; she already had a sprinkling of freckles across her nose and cheeks. No wonder her family had hidden her away in the North Yorkshire moors. Brazen chit. Best to acquire the new horse and be done with her.

"Listen, I require a horse. If there is no place about to purchase one and you live on this estate, I would appreciate your assistance."

"You have a horse. I believe we've discussed it at length."

"This one has served its purpose…" He knew his words were harsh, but there seemed to be no reasoning with this lady. He braced himself for Shadow's irritated huff of annoyance, but it never came. Andrew glanced down toward the animal.

Taking a steadying breath, he turned back to the woman. "If you will point me in the direction of your stables and identify your man of business, I'll be out of your hair."

As if on cue, her hair caught a breeze and wrapped around the pale column of her neck. "Served its purpose," she repeated as her shoulders tensed beneath the mud-smeared shirt she wore. "How so? He has an injury, but that doesn't lessen his value."

"I'm traveling. I need a horse that's able to walk, gallop even."

"And you think I might have such a galloping horse?" Her pink lips pursed around the word "horse."

This was taking far too long. He'd lost half a day already to this business. He didn't want it to drag out longer than necessary. He couldn't allow it to do so. He told himself that the urgency to get back to his estate had him out of sorts, but in truth he was becoming more anxious to be gone from this place with every huff of air from Shadow's nose.

"And what of this horse?" She raised a muddy hand, indicating the animal with a flick of her wrist.

He turned toward his mount, his only companion for the past two years, with a heavy heart. He swallowed before attempting to speak, and when he did, his words came out ragged through his tightening throat. "Shadow's Light has been a good companion, but he is hurt. He can't make this journey. Or any journey, really."

"Due to his wound. He can be mended to only have a limp, maybe less. He no longer has a place with you because of a limp?" Her voice rose, carrying across the field.

Andrew turned and stepped closer to Lady Katie Moore, meeting her narrow-eyed stare. "He needs to be put down."

"He needs to be mended and allowed to rest."

He was through arguing with her over this. He knew horses. He'd been working with them all his life. And keeping Shadow alive was a selfish action. He would stay alive today, only to have to be put down next week when he didn't heal properly. Or he would survive infection to never be able to run again, living a half life. It was difficult, but it must be done. Life was filled with difficult things that must be done.

"He's my horse, and I will make the decisions on this subject. I'll take care of things here, then meet you in the stables."

He turned and walked back to his saddlebag, finally coming up with the pistol he kept there. He needed to have it done and over anyway. Once it was done, this overwhelming sense of dread and loss would subside. No sense prolonging it. It was the right decision—she was a woman; what did she know of equine injuries?

Pulling out the gun, he heard her gasp. Squeamish. He might have guessed. But Shadow would want the same as Andrew in similar situations—a swift death with dignity, not a prolonged injury that would eventually lay him low. The correct course of action was always the straightforward approach.

"You, my lord, will not be taking care of anything." She took a small step forward, straightening up to as tall as she was able, which brought the top of her head to his nose. "You crashed through my shrubbery, broke my grandmother's pottery wheel, destroyed my afternoon's work, and forced me into a potentially threatening situation with a traveling ruffian, but you will not harm this horse."

"Are you going to pull the trigger, then? Because one way or another, this horse needs to be put down." The words were difficult to speak, but they needed to be said nonetheless.

"I saved your life. You owe me a debt." She placed her hands on her hips, drawing his attention once again to where the breeches—breeches! on a woman!—outlined her legs, curving over her hips and tapering down slender legs to disappear into her boots.

"A debt."

"Yes, and you can begin repaying that debt by sparing this horse."

"You didn't save my life. I could have handled the situation."

"Do you jump over unknown hedges often? For your own amusement? I saw his pistol. And you said he'd been following you." She shrugged. "I saved your life. Now you must do a kindness for me."

He took a breath and tilted his head to the side in the manner that had once made chits smile and sigh in

London. "Lady Katherine, we've gotten off to a bad start here. I'm Lord Amberstall. I breed horses. They're my life." At least they had been until two years ago. "My estate is near London. I'm well-respected for my equine knowledge. This horse has an injury. He's damaged. What future could he have if I allow him to live? Will he race again? Will he even canter? What kind of life would that be for him?"

"Only you could make murder sound merciful." Her lips twisted with her ire.

"It is merciful!"

"The animal doctor comes to check on things in a fortnight. You may wait for him."

"Wait? I can't remain here a fortnight. Am I to get a room at the inn and cool my heels until then?"

"There is no inn. Feel free, however, to walk to London."

"Walk? Lady Katherine, I'm needed at my estate."

"It's Lady Katie. And, perhaps I could..." She stopped, shooting a quick glance at his horse before meeting Andrew's gaze once more.

"What could you do?" What could this woman possibly do, other than the obvious: sell him a horse?

Her jaw clamped shut on any offering she'd been about to make. "You may stay here while my staff sees to your horse. We may well have him mended before the doctor arrives."

"Truly? You won't sell me a piece of horseflesh so I might leave tonight?"

"No." Her chin lifted a fraction as she regarded him with light green eyes. "I wouldn't subject anyone, even a horse, to your company for the remainder of their life."

"Yet you want me to stay here under your roof? Simply sell me a horse. I'll be gone within the hour."

"I don't want you here. But you leave me no choice."

"If this is about your pottery, I'll buy you another wheel. I'd already planned to do so."

"You owe me a debt, and I am collecting by saving your horse's life. Good afternoon, Lord Amberstall. Celersworth will show you to your room. I'll send for the stable hands to retrieve your horse."

He clamped his jaw shut to keep it from falling open. He couldn't remain here. He was needed at home. He shot Shadow's Light a dark look, knowing this wasn't his fault, yet angry in spite of that knowledge. This wasn't the first time the damned animal had caused an issue in his life. His chest tightened over the fact that it may well be the last time. But he couldn't dwell on that now. He had to return to his estate, soon.

Yet perhaps it would do him good to lie low. No one would find him here. That much was true. The man he'd escaped earlier would move on and lose his trail completely. And, contrary to his denial, she had unfortunately saved his life. He cursed his sense of honor, knowing he did owe her a debt. "Very well."

He offered her a tip of his hat and turned to walk away. "Until I see you at dinner this evening," he tossed over his shoulder as he set off across the field.

He didn't wait for her reply. Which was just as well, since she didn't seem apt to respond. Muddy hands, breeches, and a complete lack of propriety in conversation... Who was Lady Katie Moore, and how did the daughter of an earl turn out so? He shook his head and walked toward the house.

❧

Katie shut the rough-hewn oak door behind her and leaned against it, her hands still shaking. She should have sold him one of the horses and sent him on his way. What had she been thinking? After he'd disappeared over the hill toward the house, she'd gone in search of a groom to organize the collection of his horse from the far field. Her search had taken her within sight of the stables.

It had been one year and three months, almost to the day, since she'd last stepped inside that building. Even seeing it today had caused her heart to race. She pushed away from the cottage door and eased her way to the small table in the front corner of her small home. Sinking into one of the chairs, she propped her leg up on the other chair as she did every night. The effort of walking all the way to the field by the main road and back made her knee throb more than usual.

She rubbed at the side of her leg in an attempt to relax the muscles as Mr. Rumples, her squirrel, scampered up onto the table and peered into the basket left there for her. Food, candles and such were always left for her in the afternoons. She saw the footman charged with the job on occasion, but he always left as soon as he arrived, offering only a bow and a "Good day, m'lady."

Katie shrugged. Who needed company? Not her. She smiled at Mr. Rumples, watching as he let out a series of chirps and clawed at the lid.

"Patience, Rumpy. You'll get yours." She shot the squirrel a look to quell his begging. "I've had a rather bad day, if you must know. This truly awful man arrived today. He smashed my pottery wheel without so much as an apology."

With a grimace, she pulled the basket of food closer. "Then another man arrived and I had to fend him off with nothing but my walking stick to use as a weapon. Well, I didn't have to *use* my walking stick, but that's hardly the point. Anyway, I saved the first man's skin and then he tried to leave. He barely offered his thanks.

"I believe he would have ridden away if not for his horse being injured. And he was a bloody bastard about that, too. He was prepared to put his horse down right at my feet." She pulled some berries from the basket and passed them to Mr. Rumples. "Not to mention that the bowl I was working on was crushed when he fell on it. 'I am Lord Amberstall,'" she mimicked. "He's a right arse. I know that much."

She ripped a piece of bread off of a loaf from the basket and took a bite. He was also handsome, but she didn't say it aloud. Swallowing, she looked at her squirrel, perched on the rim of the berry bowl. "And now I must endure him while his horse is being treated."

The squirrel looked up with a large berry held in his paws, before skittering to the table to eat his treasure.

"I know it was foolish to allow him housing instead of sending him on with one of the horses. But I couldn't." When she'd seen the horse lying there in the dirt, pain shining in his eyes, unable to stand... It was true, he wasn't left there alone for hours as she had been, but his agony was the same. His fear.

She blinked away the memory.

Retrieving a plate of Cornish hen, she ripped a

piece with her fingers and took a large bite. "It was the right thing to do." She shook her head; it wasn't as if she'd had much choice in the matter. Treating his horse's injury cracked light on a dark place she'd rather not see. Not now, not ever. But for tonight she vowed not to think of Lord Amberstall or the trouble he'd brought on his heels. Tonight she would fill her time as she always did.

Bracing her elbows on the table, she peered into the basket and pulled free a corked bottle of wine. With a sigh, she uncorked the wine and tipped the bottle to her lips. That was the beauty of living alone. She had freedom. She could drink from wine bottles if she chose, or she could sing at the top of her lungs, and there was no one around to take notice. She nodded in satisfaction.

She'd moved to the abandoned gamekeeper's cottage when she was eleven years of age, the same week her mother left. Back then, it had been a refuge, a safe place to hide from her father's wrath over her mother's departure, a place free of blame and dark looks simply because she resembled her mother. Her oldest brother had found fault with her disappearance from the house, but her father seemed relieved at the change. So, she'd stayed. Days turned to weeks and then to years. And now it was home.

The cottage sat on the edge of the woods, nestled into the curve of the moors where they rolled off into the distance. These stone walls had saved her, protected her, and kept the world and everyone in it well away for years. She'd grown up inside this one room. Katie smiled up at the heavy timbers surrounded by cream plaster that were holding up the roof. The cottage held all that she needed: a small kitchen with a table and two chairs, a rocking chair on a thick rug by the fire, and her bed. She pulled an apple from the basket and guided her leg back to the floor. She crunched into the fruit, licking at the juice at the corner of her mouth as she went to the fireplace. Her knee twinged a bit more than usual under the strain of movement, making her grimace.

A few minutes later, the fire was stoked to ward off the chill of autumn, and she was in her rocking chair holding a set of bagpipes in her arms. With the drones thrown over her shoulder, she began blowing to fill the bags. She hadn't quite mastered the instrument yet, but she'd grown weary of attempting the violin and clearly the flute wasn't her forte.

She much preferred this large windbag to the one she'd encountered today. She rolled her eyes and puffed into the mouthpiece until a tone was emitted from the pipes. Something told her his stay wouldn't be a pleasant one for her, or a quiet one.

She lifted the chanter in her fingers and blew a loud squawk, watching as Mr. Rumples dove from the table in fright. She blew another squawk—slightly better. With a thoughtful frown, she looked down at the bagpipes. She wouldn't allow some gentleman to destroy her solitude. Lord Amberstall's stay would be a quiet one; she would ensure it. With a nod, she blew into the mouthpiece again.

❦

He'd waited on the front steps of Ormesby Place

for a quarter hour before being allowed admittance. It was unheard of. This entire estate operated in opposition to good English standards, as far as he could tell. He was a titled lord. He should have at least been shown to a parlor and offered tea while preparations were being put into place. What if he'd been thirsty?

After what seemed like a lifetime, Andrew followed the shriveled old butler up the stairs to his room. He spent the last of his patience on being shown the room as if he'd never seen a bed, writing desk, and dresser before. With a thin smile, he shut the door on the man and went straight to the washbasin to rinse off the dust of the journey.

His room was as well-appointed as the main hall and stairs—which was not well at all. It bore all the signs of wealth, with plenty of candles and a polished stair rail, yet it was twenty years out of date, with faded tapestries lining the walls and life-worn fabrics covering the chairs. How odd for Lady Katie Moore to allow her home to fall into such disrepair.

He was drying his face when a knock sounded at the door. Before he could answer, a woman peeked her round face into the room. "Mr. Celersworth told me we had a guest. Please excuse the state of the room. If I'd been informed we were expecting company, I would have had it aired out, at the least." She crossed the room and was stirring a cloud of dust from a table within the minute.

Why had he been left on the front steps if it wasn't to ready his room? "My stay is rather..." *Unfortunate and becoming more irritating by the second?* He offered the woman a polite smile, watching as she sent dust in every direction with a wave of her cloth. "Unexpected."

"I'm Mrs. Happstings." She turned back to the door and waved her hand to two girls waiting in the hall. "Mary, see to the draperies. Celia, get the fire."

"Mrs. Happstings," he intoned over the bustle in the room. "Might I ask when dinner will be served?"

She sent another cloud of dust into the air and placed her hands on her hips in satisfaction. "We shall be ready as soon as you arrive downstairs, my lord."

"Very good." He pushed his hair from his forehead and took a step toward the woman. "Mrs. Happstings, I only have traveling clothes with me. I do hope my appearance will be overlooked by the staff."

She eyed him with an assessing stare. "You look to be about the size of Lord Ayton. He left a few things here before leaving for the continent."

"Ayton. Is he the head of this house?" That would explain why his daughter was running wild in breeches with her hair streaming down her back. Her father was out of the country.

"Oh no, my lord. Lord Ayton is the heir to this estate. He is on an extended wedding trip. Lord Ormesby has the run of things around here."

"I will need to meet with him, then. Alert Lord Ormesby at once of my presence in his home." Finally, a man with whom he could reason. Andrew smiled at the solution to his problems.

"I'm afraid he is away as well. Visiting his brother-in-law down south."

The smile slid from his face. "There are no other men about?"

"Not anymore, my lord."

There was a sorrowful distance in the woman's face for a moment before it was replaced with a pleasant smile. "Dinner will be served when you are ready. I'll have some of Lord Ayton's things brought to you after dinner." She waved for the maids to leave the room.

"Much appreciated. Lady Katie will simply have to accept my improper clothing this evening." Somehow he didn't think that would be an issue.

Mrs. Happstings' eyes grew wide. "Is she coming to the house for dinner?"

"She lives here. Of course we'll be dining together."

"She hasn't lived under this roof for some time, my lord. I fear you will be dining alone."

He nodded, unsure how to respond. She didn't live here? She was Lord Ormesby's daughter. She'd spent her afternoon on the estate. If she didn't live here, where did she live?

"I'll leave you to clean up for dinner. I hope you enjoy your stay at Ormesby Place."

Andrew turned to the small mirror and began the job of straightening his cravat. He may not be dressed in proper attire, but at least he would be clean for his dinner—alone.

❧

"Rastings, Smarth, I expected you days ago." Hawkes set the papers in his hands aside and glared at the two men entering the library. "With this delay, you better have Amberstall's head on a platter for me to admire."

"M'lord, about that." Rastings shot an angry glance at the man beside him before stepping forward, closer to the desk between them. "There were some problems on the road, you see."

"Problems?" Hawkes raised one dark eyebrow. "I pay you so that there will be no problems. Tell me, what use are you to me if you can't complete a job you're given?"

"By the time we reached the cottage like you asked, he was already riding south. We trailed him back across the border, but he's a slippery one, m'lord." Rastings shifted his weight and, in doing so, took a step away from Smarth.

What happened on the road from Scotland was none of Hawkes' concern. He'd hired the men so he wouldn't have to worry about such things. He needed Amberstall gone. And he would see it done one way or another. His estate couldn't last much longer without the funds the Amberstall estate possessed, and he would not lose his home when the solution to his troubles was so close at hand.

He sneered up at the men, noting the foul odor of stables and a life lived on the road. Dreadful. He would be airing his library out for days after this little meeting. If they were to return empty-handed, they could have at least bathed.

Hawkes swept his eyes over the two men. He could find replacements, but that would take time, and time was one thing he did not possess. No, Rastings and Smarth would produce results, or he would have to see to it himself. "Do I understand you properly?" His head cocked to the side. "You let him go, and he is on his way home?"

Rastings' hands balled into fists at his sides. "Well, there was the problem on the road like I said and…"

"Fields of sheep," Smarth cut in with a carrying whisper. "Tell him about the sheep."

"No one cares about the sheep, Smarth!" Rastings yelled.

Smarth shook his head in confusion. "It explains how he gave us the slip."

"Stop it at once." Hawkes stood, glaring across his desk. "Never in my life have I seen such incompetence! You will leave here at once and find Amberstall." He braced his knuckles on the desktop and leaned over the surface. "I will be very disappointed if you don't succeed in your task. You don't want to see me disappointed, do you?"

On a murmured assent of "No, m'lord," they bowed out of the room.

Turning, Hawkes regarded his brother-in-law where he lounged in a chair, clearly pretending to read. "You think I'm too harsh? They failed."

"I said nothing," Charles stated from his armchair by the window, laying aside his book.

"You raised a brow."

"You asked for a gentleman's head on a platter."

Hawkes sighed, rubbing his eyes before leaning an elbow on his desk. "We can't very well proceed with him alive. What would you suggest?"

"I wouldn't order the death of a peer of the realm, but perhaps I'm wrong," Charles offered with a shrug of his shoulders.

Hawkes didn't understand. There was no other way than through Amberstall's death.

With that man out of the way, Hawkes would gain control. All would be solved. His niece would see to that. "The Amber Hollow stables are the issue," he mused, his eyes narrowing on his brother-in-law. "He'll return for his dratted horses. That's what I tried to explain when you had the brilliant idea to steal from him. And now he's traveling home."

"You couldn't spare the horses to send riders north. I offered a solution—replace your losses with two horses from your neighbor." Charles stood from his seat and went to the window. "I didn't think you would actually steal from his stables."

Hawkes shifted and looked down at the papers strewn across his desk. Bills, notices...he needed funds, and Amberstall's death would allow him access to the wealth that lay wasting so close to his fingertips yet beyond his reach. That wealth would repair everything—his poor investment with that charlatan two years ago, the subsequent bills, and most of all, the lord in London growing angry over the lack of payment of his gambling debts. Knowing there was no other path to be taken, he asked anyway, "What choice do we have here, Charles?"

"We?" Charles's brows rose high on his forehead. "I'm only here in an advisement capacity and, of course, for my portion of profits from good business."

"Good business we can't accomplish without removing Amberstall from the situation." Hawkes gave his brother-in-law a look, willing him to understand. "I'm doing what I must."

"And you're prepared to murder in the name of good business?"

"Charles, sometimes tragedies occur. Who am I to argue with the fate of a man in the way of progress?"

"Tragedy occurred in my family only a little over a year ago, if you recall. I don't want to see more death." Charles stalked to the fireplace, leaning on the mantel to stare into the flames.

"Trevor would have made a fine heir," Hawkes offered. "And I mourn his loss as well, but the Amberstall situation is different. We've come too far, Charles."

Charles turned back to him, leveling him with a glare. "I never agreed to murder."

"It sounds so harsh when you say it that way. Never mind this morbid discussion. I will *mercifully* see to this portion of the plan. You have no reason to worry. You simply continue your research so we are prepared when the time comes."

Charles pursed his lips in thought. "Very well. No murder?"

"Amberstall couldn't be safer." He was safe for now, at any rate. But he couldn't evade Hawkes' men forever. The dirty details of the gentleman's demise didn't need to be discussed at present. For now, Charles needed to stay focused on the end of this game and how many explosives they would require. Hawkes would deal with Amberstall.

Three

HE LOOKED LIKE A DAMNED PIRATE AND HE KNEW IT.
Andrew sighed as he crunched down the gravel path
leading to the stables. Mrs. Happstings insisted that she
would have his things laundered by the day's end, but
until then he wore a billowing black shirt and black
breeches, with no cravat. He'd never been so thankful
for a coat in his life.

Lord Ayton must be a giant of a man, because the
shirt was a bit large on him and Andrew was known
for his height and build. Every tailor he'd ever worked
with had commented on the breadth of his shoulders.
He glanced down at his shirt. Why must it be black?
Every article of clothing he'd seen from the man was
black. Between black, black, and black, the options
were staggering. He couldn't be gone from this place
soon enough.

He pulled at the lapels of his coat, willing it to cover
more of his dreadful clothing than was possible. The
improper nature of his ensemble ate at him, but he
had no choice but to wear it. He wasn't allowed much
choice in anything at Ormesby Place. The option of

hen or fish last night was the only selection he'd been allowed to make thus far, and even that had been tainted by the large, empty dining table and the place setting for one.

His solitary dinners in Scotland had at least been made palatable by the lack of good gentry about. Here, she'd left him to eat alone. It was unheard of.

Had her father failed to teach her that she must dine with overnight guests even if she didn't live in the house? He'd discovered from one of the servants that Lady Katie Moore lived in the gamekeeper's old cottage. Who in their right mind would choose to live in a drafty cottage over the main house? Perhaps she was mad. That would explain her appearance yesterday— and her actions, for that matter. But when he'd caught her light green gaze yesterday, she'd seemed alert.

He turned toward the stables across the drive from the house. The building was surrounded on three sides by pastureland where horses ran in the distance. There was wildness to their movements. His eyes narrowed on the group of horses crossing the field in a frenzy of hooves, streaming tails, and pinned ears. Did no one work with these animals?

Glancing around, he didn't see any grooms and thought they must be busy with work within the stables. It was a large structure made of gray stone, and much like the rest of the estate, it bore the look of neglect. As he neared, he looked up at a large hole near the peak of the roof where many slate tiles were missing. It was covered by boards nailed at crooked angles. He would never allow such shoddy craftsman-ship at his stables. He shook his coat further into place, as if the fine tailoring would protect him from the air of chaos about the place.

"Good morning, m'lord," a lone groom offered in greeting as he stepped into the stables.

"I do hope so." Although he doubted it, since he was stranded here, Shadow was injured, and they were not on the road home right now. He smiled in spite of his situation, taking in the shine of the horse's brown coat the man was brushing. "That's a fine colt you have there."

"Aye, he was birthed just last week."

"Let me guess. That was when the doctor was last here." One week off—his luck was spectacular, truly it was.

The man nodded and went back to his work, tending to the colt outside the central and largest stall in the stable where the mare watched and waited for her young to be returned. Andrew stepped further into the stables, kicking aside hay that should have been changed two days ago and swept from the walkways. Was there no one in charge of this place?

He moved down the aisle of stalls, peering over railings and around corners with growing concern. The horses not roaming free in the fields seemed to be in fair condition, not malnourished at any rate. Stopping before a heap of rigging piled high in one stall, with saddles tossed into the corners to land where they might, he couldn't keep his dismay to himself any longer. He would never allow his stables to be run in such a manner, and he pitied the poor grooms who were forced to work in such conditions.

With a shake of his head, he turned back to the man

caring for the young colt. "When was the last time these riggings were organized?"

The groom looked up, his face frozen in discomfort at the question. "Lady Katie always said she knew where everything was and not to touch it."

"How could anyone find a thing in this chaos?" Andrew asked as he lifted a harness from the ground and tossed it from the walkway.

The man ran a hand over the stubble of his chin and shot a glance around before answering. "No one does as of late, m'lord."

"I can't say I'm surprised." He stared down the line of stalls with his arms crossed over his chest. No young miss could be left in charge of a horse operation, even if she did wear breeches and have dirty hands. Clearly she didn't have the knowledge or experience to keep a well-run stable. "To leave the living quarters of all these animals in such a condition is appalling. Lady Katie needs to leave running stables to someone more capable. This is no place for a woman."

The groom stood and guided the colt back into the stall. "If it's only between me, you, and the stable cat, things have been in a state for months now. And the horses…" He adjusted his hat. "Most of the grooms don't know what to make of it. Not me. I've been here most o' my life."

He leaned an arm on the stall door and looked back at Andrew. "The very sight of Lady Katie nearing the door yesterday startled me right out of my boots. And now she's out in the back field with your horse." He smiled, his crooked teeth shining in the dim light of day falling through the open stable door. "'Tis a good day, m'lord."

Andrew's head snapped up. "She doesn't come here often?"

"She's been away over a year." The man turned the horse's brush over and over in the palm of his hand.

He must be missing something. There was some detail of the bizarre nature of this estate that he hadn't been told. "Why, then, is she so terribly opinionated on the subject of horses?"

The man looked up and met Andrew's eyes with something that could have been pride or offense, he wasn't sure which. "Because she knows more about horses than anyone in these parts."

"Her ways seem unconventional," Andrew hedged, wanting to know more and yet aware he shouldn't care about the answers.

"That she is, m'lord. That she is."

When the man turned to go about his work without another word, Andrew left the stables. It was the safe decision, at any rate, since the structure was about to topple down on someone's head if repairs weren't made soon. Striding through the open door, he scanned the surrounding fields in search of Shadow's Light and Lady Katie Moore. He hadn't seen anyone when he approached, which meant they must be behind the building. He rounded the corner, stepping through a gap in the fencing.

When he saw her, he froze. She hadn't noticed his presence yet. She was wearing breeches again, with boots and a loose lawn shirt belted at the waist. She leaned on a wooden walking stick and spoke with one of the men who worked for her. The man's eyes never swerved to take in her curving form beneath the clinging ensemble she wore. Andrew's eyes weren't so well trained. Did she even know what she must be doing to the men in her employ? "Irresponsible, brazen chit," he mumbled to himself.

He watched as she nodded toward the fence bordering the pasture where Shadow stood. The man stepped aside and offered her a hand. With a raised chin, she leaned on the walking stick and moved with slow, uneven steps to the fence row without assistance. She had an injury? His eyes swept her legs for an explanation as the groom reached for her waist.

Andrew was striding forward before he realized he was moving. No one should touch her when she was in a state of such extreme undress. And especially not a common groom. He was about to yell when the man sat her on the top fence rail and stepped away. One of her feet was hooked on a rail while the other hung below her, swinging gently in the chilly morning air.

Her injury still didn't explain her unladylike behavior or the way in which she dressed. In fact, the longer he was in her presence the more he wondered about her. How had it happened? Did it hurt her still? He had a pile of questions heaped higher than the mess of rigging he'd found in the stables.

"This is why ladies should simply embroider and paint," he murmured under his breath as he crossed the field toward her. Now she was lame, just as Shadow was. It was no wonder she wanted so desperately to heal his horse. That much he now understood. Yet it was still the wrong decision. Crossing the clearing at her back, he set his jaw against the inevitable argument ahead of him. He knew horses, and he knew a lost cause when he saw one.

❧

"It should be wrapped tighter," Katie called out across the pasture to the groom. How was the blasted horse going to heal and take its owner far away if the splint kept slipping to the ground? She settled into her perch on the top rail of the fence, pointedly ignoring Amberstall's approach as she watched the groom's attempts to repair the splint.

She'd been up early this morning, unable to sleep faced with the prospect of seeing the annoying gentleman again. Daybreak had found her behind the stables preparing a poultice for the deep gash on his horse's leg. The horse would be healed long before the doctor came to call—she would see to it.

"It needs to be cooled with water before wrapping it," Lord Amberstall stated as he joined her at the fence. He leaned over the top rail at her hip, bracing his forearms against the wood.

"Good morning to you, as well." She kept her eyes on the horse.

"Of course, that won't heal what is troubling him, in my experience," he mused.

"Time and patience will heal quite a bit, in *my* experience."

He cocked his head toward her, drawing her attention. "I thought Shadow was going to be given room in your stables for a fortnight until he could be seen to."

"Oh, you're anxious to stay now, are you?"

"No." He drew back in offense. "I would like nothing more than to put that horse out of its misery, purchase another, and be on my way."

"Your horse can be healed, Lord Amberstall."

"So you keep saying."

"You're one of *those* people. I understand quite well." She shot him a smile made of daggers and wrapped with loathing. "I've had dealings with gentlemen like you before. You only see a small flaw, not the whole of any situation."

"I am *not* one of *those* people. I simply have standards of health and strength." He nodded with an imperious expression of all-knowing rightness—the bastard.

She let out a small breath and looked away. "Strength isn't always found in muscles, you know."

"That's precisely where strength needs to be found if the beast is to carry me down the road from here."

"*The beast*," she mimicked. "Typical."

"My apologies. Shadow's Light."

"You named your horse Shadow's Light?" She rolled her eyes. *Poor horse.*

"Yes. Do you have an issue with that as well?"

"No, it seems rather fitting."…*for the horse of an arrogant lord whose only care is fancy titles and nothing more*, she finished in silence.

"It's apparently better than 'beast,' which I apologize for the insensitivity of using."

She turned back to him, catching the lack of sincerity in his face for a second before he corrected it with a polite smile. He was just as false as the rest of the *ton*. He was the reason she kept to the moors. Yet here he was, invading her peaceful life—which was entirely her fault. "My lord, do you want my help or not?"

He pointed to the groom. "This is not the help I sought."

She watched him for a moment as she bit at one of her fingernails. Had anyone ever told this man no? She doubted it. Dropping her finger from her mouth, she leveled him with a glare he could not misunderstand. "Sometimes there are injuries, but those injuries cannot be allowed to cease life. Shadow's Light is worth saving."

His deep voice was quiet when he spoke. "You may get him to walk, but he'll never run."

"Perhaps not." She shrugged. "We shall see."

His golden brows dipped into a deep vee as he regarded her. "To what end, my lady?"

"I don't know yet." Did he truly only care for himself and *his* convenience on *his* journey to *his* home? "Don't you have any fondness for the creature? He is your horse, after all."

"Certainly." His gaze dropped to the grass, but she still saw some emotion there. It resembled regret, but that couldn't be, or if it was, it certainly wasn't over his poor horse's condition. "He's been with me for the last two years."

"And before that? Let me guess." Her lips twisted in thought. "You won him in some game of chance or swindled him away from some poor lad down on his luck."

"Actually, I bred him back two generations." Andrew's gaze lifted to Shadow's Light with a wry smile that didn't reach his eyes. "He was to be the next prize racehorse my stables produced. Everyone in the *ton* was going to desire him…and his offspring."

Her grip on the fence rail tightened. How quickly he abandoned the creature when he proved to be less than perfect. Shadow's Light now held no monetary value to him. "And now you want him dead," she finished aloud.

He sighed, shifting his gaze back to her. "His rise to the top of the equestrian community was destroyed some time ago, my lady. I only wish for him to have peace now."

"How?"

"I think I've made my view on that point rather clear."

"No." Katie searched his face for answers, trying to understand. "How was his rise to the top destroyed?"

His jaw tightened and he swallowed, the action pulling her eyes down to his thick, tan neck where the black shirt he wore splayed open. "It's a rather long story."

She blinked, forcing her gaze to lift back to his face. "I have no place to go."

He shifted in discomfort. "If it's all the same to you, I'd rather not relive it just now, since I spent the past two years escaping it."

She found she needed to know what had happened. She wasn't sure why this was important, but she wanted to know more of his past. "It's not," she stated, taking in his agitation.

"Not what?"

"All the same to me."

"In that case, I'm afraid I'll have to disappoint you."

His shoulders were visibly tense as he turned toward her, forearms still braced against the fence. His face had hardened and his warm eyes cooled into a stony look, making her wonder even more at his secrecy. "It's not something I wish to discuss anytime soon."

"Your loss." She shrugged, allowing the topic to drop—for now. "I'm an expert listener."

He almost smiled. "How does one become an expert at listening?"

"Practice. I can hear someone approach at three and twenty paces." She raised her chin in pride.

"You've certainly put some thought into this..."

"I practiced with a cat," she explained, turning back to him. "But surely if I can hear a small animal, I can hear a gentleman quite well."

"A cat," he repeated, his eyes crinkling at the corners as he fought a grin.

"Well, yes." There was nothing amusing about it. She narrowed her eyes on him. "No one else was available that week."

"You spent a week allowing a cat to sneak up behind you?" He squinted up at her, his lips twitching as he continued to suppress a smile. "And then you measured the distance?"

"When you put it like that, it sounds silly, but it was quite difficult."

He raised his fist to his mouth and coughed, which sounded suspiciously like laughter.

"Conducting scientific experiments with a cat isn't at all simple," she continued.

"I can imagine," he said, and the words seemed forced from him as his grin widened. Finally losing some inner battle with his own amusement, he laughed out loud, his voice echoing in the field and making his horse turn to discover its source.

"The animal would try to leave or lie down when his job was clearly to scamper." She pursed her lips at the memory.

His laughter finally fell away as he looked at her. "Lady Katie Moore, you're rather unusual. Are you aware of that?"

"Yes, I've been told." She'd been told on far too many occasions. And yet, it always hurt to hear it once more. She'd been paying the price for being unusual since the day her mother abandoned her as a child. She dropped to the ground and grabbed the walking stick. Offering him a tight-lipped smile, she nodded. "Good day, my lord."

⚶

Andrew crossed the floor of the room he'd been provided and sank into the chair at the writing desk overlooking the back gardens. He stared until the scenery was a blur of green, yellow, and brown mashed together, much like his thoughts this afternoon.

The more he discovered of Lady Katie Moore, the less he understood her. Oddly, it wasn't her injury that pulled at his curiosity—it was everything else. Her dress, or lack thereof, her unusual way of living… He'd seen her bite her fingernail this afternoon and then spit it upon the ground, for goodness' sake.

"She's the daughter of an earl. It simply isn't done," he said to the empty room.

And yet there was something about her smile and

a slight sadness to her light green eyes that made him wonder. He wasn't even sure what to wonder over, but the blasted chit wouldn't leave his thoughts. He ran a hand through his hair and tore his eyes from the window. Thoughts of that particular lady would lead nowhere, and he needed to remain focused on the issues at hand.

He ticked off his list of problems with a tap of a finger on the desktop. There was trouble at his estate. *Tap*. His horse was injured. *Tap*. Once home, he would have to face all the talk he'd left behind when he went to Scotland. *Tap, tap*. He sighed and pulled a piece of parchment from the drawer.

> *Dear Mother,*
> *I hope this letter finds you well, or as well as can be expected under the current circumstances. Your letter was a welcome surprise as I find I cling to news of home like the reins of a galloping mount.*

He looked down at the words he'd written. It was a bit heavy-handed in terms of poetic references, but ladies generally liked that sort of frivolity. With a shrug of his shoulders, he continued...

> *I set out to come to your aid as soon as your news was received. Yet I regret to inform you that I've been delayed in my travels. Although I began my journey south with great haste, Shadow's Light was injured on the road once over the border into England. Fear not, for I am well.*
> *The same cannot be said, however, for my*

horse. I will continue my travels home as soon as I am able. Until then I am at the mercy of a most unconventional lady who is helping to heal Shadow. I'm quite certain this will be a tale to tell once I am away from here. You have my apologies for this unforeseen delay.

Your son,
Andrew

He penned his signature and folded the parchment. His mother would simply have to understand. It wasn't as if he could change his circumstances and leave this place, even if he desired it. *I saved your life. You owe me a debt.* Her voice echoed through his memory. He grimaced. He *did* desire to leave; of course he did. But now he couldn't. And it was true that once he arrived home, he would be back in the thick of things with his old life, society…

He pushed the hair from his face and leaned an elbow on the desk. The resolution of his mother's troubles wouldn't take long once he arrived home. He wasn't sure of the details, yet how bad could things be? He'd been gone for two years, however he'd remained in contact through monthly correspondence while away. His mother was as inept as most ladies he knew when it came to estate matters. She'd most likely made an issue of nothing.

He pushed away the thought of the highwayman trailing him on the road. Surely, that danger had nothing to do with that poor excuse for a gentleman, Hawkes, on the other side of the lake. Even his madness didn't reach this far north. No. He would have a meeting or two with the troublesome neighbor, perhaps write a letter, and that would be that.

Once that was completed...then what? He tapped his fingers on the desk with a frown. His life would return to the way it had been two years prior. His breathing sped up and he fought to steady it as his fingers now tapped a violent rhythm on the desktop. If he was to be honest, he was rather dreading that last bit of his journey—the bit with salons and ballrooms. Perhaps he had spent too much time alone in the Highlands, but he simply wasn't used to the crowds of town. That must be it. He would adapt to his old life again: the parties, the horses, his mother's matchmaking...

Would he still be a sought-after bachelor, or had the events of that day destroyed all chances there? "An outcast of society," he muttered to himself. Perhaps he was worrying over nothing. If the *ton* wouldn't accept him back into their fold, his journey home would end there, alone in his stables. The thought should please him—no society, no talk, no matchmaking.

He squinted into the light coming from the lamp at his elbow as he heated the wax to seal the missive. The image of Lady Katie Moore perched on the fence rail, with her loose red-streaked hair blowing in the autumn breeze, came to mind and he stamped it out in red wax with the imprint of his signet ring. Soon he would be gone from Ormesby Place, and she and her unbound hair would be nothing but an unfortunate memory.

Four

KATIE SANK FURTHER INTO ONE OF THE OVERSTUFFED chairs in the Thornwood Manor drawing room as she pulled one booted foot up under her. She couldn't remember the last time she'd been here. At least a year had passed by. Perhaps it had been longer. Nothing had changed, from the polished furniture to the ornate tapestries covering the walls. She'd spent the first half of her childhood within these walls.

She grinned up at the timber ceiling. Thornwood was their closest neighbor and Roselyn Grey, daughter of the late duke, her closest friend. But now Roselyn was married and on an extended wedding trip with Katie's brother. The two had become close after the passing of Trevor, Katie's eldest brother, which caused quite a stir since Roselyn and Ethan were both present when the death occurred. She glanced across the room. Katie was happy for them, even if their union did leave her alone—even more so than she had been before.

Although it looked the same, everything at Thornwood felt foreign now. It might have been the ride over in the carriage instead of on horseback, or perhaps the lack of Roselyn's laughter waiting for her, but the manor was different indeed. The Duke of Thornwood had married a lovely lady two years ago who Katie hadn't met since the couple had been aboard one of the duke's ships for most of the past year. Yet she was set to take tea with the new duchess this afternoon. Everyone had wed as of late, it seemed. Katie shook her head—not her, thank goodness. She enjoyed the freedom of her quiet life. But she was happy for the happiness of others. Happy, happy, happy.

"Lady Katie! I'm so pleased you could join me today," a tall, elegant blond lady intoned as she swept into the room.

Katie looked up and lowered her foot to the floor. "You must be the new duchess."

"That I am." Her hostess grinned as she perched on the edge of the chair across from Katie. "Call me Lily. Everyone around here does."

"Lily," Katie repeated with a nod. "I'm Katie. Are you settling into life at Thornwood? It can be a bit gray in this part of the country, but I've always thought that made the moors rather mysterious."

"The manor is wonderful. And I grew up not a day's ride from here, so the landscape is quite familiar."

"Odd that we never met," Katie mused as she bit at her fingernail.

"I...didn't visit other estates often when I was young. But now I'm here. I'm so pleased to finally meet you." Lily looked away as trays of food and tea were brought in and placed before them. After nodding her approval to one of the maids, she turned back to Katie. "Tea?"

"Yes, please. I'm famished," Katie explained as she shoveled three tea biscuits from the tray onto her plate and popped one into her mouth. "Delicious!" she mumbled around a large bite. Pointing to a slice of cake, she swallowed and asked, "Might I?"

"Of course," Lily returned as she leaned in with a conspiratorial smile. "There are always plenty of baked goods in the kitchen. The dowager duchess has a bit of a sweet tooth, you know."

Katie did know. Her Grace had stepped in as a mother to her after her own mother abandoned the family when Katie was a child. She was about to say just that when the woman herself swept into the room on a cloud of dark green skirts. "Did someone say my name?"

"Only in the best light." Lily motioned for the dowager to join them.

"I scarcely believe that. Isn't the mother-in-law supposed to be a fearsome individual bent on revenge for the daughter-in-law stealing her son away?" She crossed the room with her eyes narrowed in what she clearly believed to be a fearsome expression, but it only served to make her rosy cheeks glow in the afternoon sun spilling into the room.

"Only in the gothic novels you read, Mother." Lily laughed as she rose and greeted her mother-in-law with a kiss on the cheek.

Only then noticing who Lily was entertaining, the dowager turned with open arms. "Katie, I haven't seen you here since Roselyn was in residence." She clasped Katie's hands within her own and squeezed them for a moment. "So nice to have you visit, dear."

Lily sat once more and picked up her teacup. "You spent time here as a child? You must tell me all the family secrets."

"Don't you dare, Katie. We do have appearances to keep up, you know, with the dukedom and all."

Katie smiled around the half-eaten biscuit in her mouth. "I would never speak against your family, Your Grace." She swallowed and took a large sip of tea.

"Very good. Now tell me the news of Ormesby Place. The manor has been dreadfully dull of late. No offense, Lily dear."

Lily shrugged as she selected a small cake from the serving tray.

What news was there to tell, other than the obvious detail filling Katie's spare thoughts these past few days? "I do have a visitor at present. A rather annoying gentleman."

The dowager duchess's gray eyes widened, and she pinned Katie with an all-too-motherly look. Katie was sure Her Grace must have practiced that look before a mirror to be able to recall it with such speed and clarity. "With your father away?"

"The gentleman is staying in the house and I'm well away from there, as you know." Katie couldn't imagine being back within the confines of those walls after the freedom of her cottage.

The dowager duchess waved away Katie's comment with a scowl of disapproval. "I've never approved of your accommodations, but do go on."

"This gentleman was traveling south from Scotland when his horse took a fall. The lord was thrown through the air, landing in the middle of my pottery wheel. It was quite devastating." Perhaps it was best to leave out the bit about the highwayman with the pistol. That would only serve to upset the dowager. "Then there was the nasty wound. You should have seen the pained look about his eyes before I fetched someone to have him brought in for treatment."

"Have you sent for a doctor?"

"I made a poultice and had it wrapped by one of the grooms." Katie took a bite of her biscuit.

"I do hope you aren't referring to the gentleman."

"No, his horse. The gentleman seems quite fine." Indeed he did. He was much too sure of himself—and a proud peacock to boot.

"Does this gentleman have a name?"

"Lord Amberstall."

Lily choked on her tea and looked up with wide blue eyes.

"Do you know him?" Katie asked. "Lord Amberstall?"

The dowager duchess nodded her head with a soft cluck of her tongue. "I'm dear friends with his mother. She'll be thrilled to learn of his return to the country. Poor Edwina was devastated when he fled after that dreadful exhibition two years ago. Wasn't she, Lily? We were there, you know, when it happened."

Katie leaned forward. "When what happened?"

The dowager duchess took a sip of tea and settled into her seat, clearly preparing for a long chat. "Did you say he's been in Scotland for the past two years?

No one knew where he went that morning. His mother will be so pleased he has returned."

"Yes." Katie waved away the question as if swatting at a pesky insect. "He said he was riding south from Scotland when Shadow's Light was injured." Why was no one answering her question?

"Shadow's Light?" The dowager duchess shot a curious look at Lily, who nodded in agreement. "How interesting."

"Why is that interesting?" Katie's voice raised an octave. "And what happened two years ago?"

A maid swept through the room to replenish the tea tray and all conversation ceased. Katie stared at Lily, who smiled at the maid as the dowager duchess took a bite of a tea biscuit. What did they know of Amberstall? The man was a guest on her estate, and yet she had no idea who he was. Could there have been more to his escape from that ruffian than she realized? If they knew of some violence in his past, she needed that information now. What a mess this week had become.

The moment the maid crossed the threshold into the hall, Katie leaned toward Lily. "What did that wretched man do that forced him to flee the country? You must tell me of his crime."

"Nothing as dire as what you're imagining, I presume," Lily returned with a kind smile. "He left to avoid the full force of a dreadful on-dit, really."

"Yes, dear. He was a well-respected gentleman and champion horse breeder. No need to worry over him being on your property." The older lady paused to take a bite of biscuit before adding, "He's quite safe."

Unfortunately, Katie wasn't feeling reassured. The man was residing in her father's home. They were the only ones on the estate, aside from the servants. She could be in danger and needed details about him. This was the reason she told herself, anyway. And surely it was reasonable to be concerned for her safety and such. Yes, her safety—that was why she wanted to know about Amberstall's background. She cleared her throat to ask, "What happened to change the perception of him?"

"It all started with that silly exhibition my son coerced him into hosting."

"The duke? His troubles began with Thornwood?"

"You sound surprised, dear." The dowager duchess pursed her lips. "You know how he can be."

Lily blushed and became quite interested in the teacup she held in her hand. Was she hiding something about her new husband, or was she ashamed of his behavior? Katie wasn't sure, but she knew something was off about Lily's reaction. She would discover the truth. With more knowledge of the situation, she could better deal with her house guest.

"It is interesting that our paths would cross again," Lily said. "Perhaps this is fate. Thornwood could mend things with Amberstall. Really, it's a new beginning for both of them, with our marriage and Amberstall's return."

"Do you think he could mend things after what happened?" the dowager duchess asked, pulling back a fraction in disbelief.

"Perhaps."

Katie sighed on a puff of exasperation as she

watched the two ladies speak in what might as well have been some sort of code, for all the sense it made to her. With a roll of her eyes, she asked, "Could someone please tell me what happened that requires mending?"

Lily sighed and began, "Half the *ton* was gathered at Amber Hollow—that's Amberstall's estate outside London. It was only a day into the house party when, men being men—or more specifically, Thornwood being Thornwood—a horse exhibition was suggested. Lord Amberstall was challenged to prove the worth of his horses, and so the following day he volunteered to show his racehorses, and at the center of that event was his prize horse, the future of his stables, Shadow's Light."

"The same Shadow's Light who is now injured in my stables."

Lily nodded and continued, "They were coming down the last stretch, taking jumps and showing off all the horses' abilities, when Amberstall's much esteemed horse…got other ideas for the afternoon."

"Other ideas? What do you mean?"

"Amorous ideas," the dowager duchess cut in with wide eyes. "Shadow's Light is quite the romantic with the other horses, if you take my meaning."

"Oh…in the middle of a show?" What of his training? Something like that would never happen with a well-trained horse. And Amberstall didn't seem the sort to show a poorly trained animal. Something was amiss in this tale.

"Indeed." Lily paused to bite her lip. She didn't quite meet Katie's gaze when she began again. "Half of London looked on as the great horse breeder had to have his horse restrained by four grooms. It was quite the scene. At the end of it, Amberstall stood alone in the middle of the paddock, his precious horses running amok all around him. You can imagine the talk."

The dowager duchess filled in the rest of the story when Lily fell silent. "And by first light the next morning, Amberstall was gone. No one knew where to find him. His mother was beside herself. Such a sad tale. More tea?" she asked, refilling Katie's cup.

"He left the country because his horses didn't behave in an exhibition?" She was sure the incident had been embarrassing, but to flee the country because of it seemed a bit of an overreaction. She wasn't surprised to discover the extent of Amberstall's vanity, but it was shocking nonetheless.

"Dear, you must understand the gentleman in question to see how devastating it was for him. To be humiliated there in the dirt, before so many of his peers...it's enough to crush any man's spirit. Amberstall began his work as a horse breeder when he was just a boy. And in one afternoon, it was all taken from him. He'd worked his whole life to gain the respect of the *ton*." She shook her head.

Katie understood quite well that life could change in the blink of an eye. She rubbed a hand over her knee at the thought. But fleeing the country because of the sudden change was something she couldn't quite grasp. There was one thing she had learned from this discussion: Amberstall was as wounded as she was. Yet something was missing in this story.

She wanted to understand him, to know where he came from and why he acted as he did. If she knew how he came to be, perhaps she could find a way to manage the man he'd become. She shook off the thought. "Why has he worked his entire life to gain the respect of the *ton*? And why does he require such perfection in all his endeavors?"

"To answer those questions, my dear, we would need a much larger pot of tea. For now, know only that he is an honorable man and quite safe to house on your estate—even if I must disapprove for the sake of propriety."

"I see." And indeed she did see. Amberstall was a proper gentleman to his very core. He held himself and the horses in his care to a standard none could sustain—not Shadow's Light and certainly not Katie. At present, the man could only see his failure from that exhibition and had most likely dwelled on it for years, which was absurd. She could see that, but could he? That must be why he wanted to put his horse down. Shadow was the source of such heartbreak for him.

Or did he simply see it as the proper decision under the circumstances? She took a sip of her tea and tried to focus on the conversation around her.

"But now he has returned." The dowager duchess clasped her hands before herself and grinned. "I do hope he will return to society as well. Edwina has despaired over him for far too long."

"As soon as his horse is ready to travel, he'll be on his way home." Katie wanted him to leave, truly she did. So why was she feeling so maudlin over the prospect all of a sudden? Pity—that must be what was consuming her. She shook off the thought with a stern blink of her eyes.

"While Amberstall is here, we must have both of you to dinner," the dowager duchess offered, causing Lily's face to lose all color in an instant.

Katie wasn't sure exactly what had happened in the past between Thornwood and Amberstall, but clearly Lily was hiding something. If Katie brought Amberstall to dinner, perhaps she could get more answers. With a wide grin, she turned to the dowager duchess to reply, "We would be happy to join you for dinner, but only if your cook makes that pudding I'm so fond of."

"Of course, dear."

Katie stood to leave, grabbing the walking stick from the floor beside her chair. "I will see you again soon, then." And soon she would discover all there was to know about Amberstall's past.

❧

Lily entered the library at Thornwood Manor in search of her husband. "Devon, you will never guess who is visiting Ormesby Place."

Devon Grey, Duke of Thornwood, looked up from the journal he was reading. "If I'll never guess, why am I guessing at all?" He turned in his desk chair and motioned for his wife to come closer. "I could torture the information out of you instead. I know how to make you talk, you know."

She narrowed her eyes on him. He was surrounded by journals and maps, his dark hair disheveled in the way it always looked when he'd become lost in his work. "Are you reading of pirates and hidden islands again? I can always tell when you read about blood-thirsty pirates. Ever so demanding."

"Just wait until I make you walk the plank." He chuckled, wrapping his hand around hers. "Being a thief on a pirate ship isn't tolerated behavior, you know." She'd stolen from Devon the day she met him and he'd never let her live down the crime—even if she had only stolen her father's pocket watch back from his possession. She had no regrets. Perhaps stealing a man's timepiece was wrong, but without that theft she might not have met Devon. There would have been no blackmail, no wild schemes involving her suitors, and she wouldn't be here now in his arms.

"If I'm a thief, I could steal your ship." She laughed as he pulled her down onto his lap and wrapped his arms around her.

"Not likely," he murmured against her ear. "Now, tell me your news so we can move on to more entertaining subjects." He smiled as he pulled her closer to brush his lips across hers.

"I disagree. I believe you'll find this news quite interesting."

"Very well," he conceded as he leaned back in his chair. "Who is visiting Ormesby Place?"

"Lord Amberstall."

"He's back in the country?" The duke's eyes narrowed in thought. "He's been in Scotland for just over two years."

"Because of you, evil man that you are," Lily whispered, even though they were alone in the library.

"You weren't guiltless in that little adventure, if you recall."

"Only because you forced me to drug his horse so that you might teach him a lesson and win a bet."

Devon grimaced at the memory. "I couldn't have you betrothed to Amberstall. Drugging his horse was the only course of action that had a high percentage of success at the time. It was all about the math of it, Lily."

"All I recall is the math of you winning money from other gentlemen over it."

"I'll make it up to you tonight if you like." His hand slid down her spine to pull her closer to his chest.

"I forgave you long ago, but if you must." She grinned against his lips as he kissed her.

"Minx."

She pulled back far enough to ask, "How did you know he's been in Scotland all this time? Last I heard, he'd simply disappeared."

"He's been living in Steelings' cottage in the Highlands," Devon muttered as he tried to tug her near enough to kiss again.

"Steelings has a cottage in Scotland? Sue has never mentioned such a thing."

He sighed, clearly giving up his attempt to distract her from the conversation. His head fell back onto the chair in defeat as he looked up at her. "I doubt her husband's sordid past is at the top of her list of topics for discussion over tea."

"You don't know Sue very well if you think that." Lily chuckled. "She talks quite a bit…about everything. But that is neither here nor there. Can you believe Amberstall is staying on our neighbor's estate?"

"And with Ormesby away…" Devon arched a brow.

"It seems he had trouble with his horse."

"That seems to be a pattern for him."

She shoved his shoulder and watched as he pretended to be in pain before laughing.

"Lady Katie seemed quite curious about his past when I told her who he was. Can you imagine, a stranger staying on her property and she had no idea if he could be a murderer…"

"Or a thief."

"Devon," she warned.

"I'm not saying thievery is a bad thing. It worked out rather well for me, as a matter of fact."

"They've been invited for dinner."

"And you think Amberstall dining with us would ease his mind? Have you forgotten we are the reason he fled the country?"

She glared at him for a second before saying, "With Sue and Steelings arriving in town, it will be nice to have a dinner party. Not to mention that it's the neighborly thing to do."

"Since when have I been one to be neighborly?"

"Since I asked you to be." She smiled, knowing she would have her way. He never denied her any happiness she desired.

"Damn. I suppose I should inform the kitchen of our plans."

"They already know of it." She leaned closer to run her fingers through his hair. "Now, about that pirate business with the plank…"

"Anything for you, my little thief."

Five

ANDREW WIPED HIS BROW AND SAT BACK ON THE slate roof of the stables, watching as the two grooms he'd pulled up onto the roof with him continued to patch the hole. From this height, he could see out across the low scrub brush and thick grass of the fields. There seemed to be another residence in the distance, a dark stone structure that loomed over the moors to the west.

Perhaps he should seek out some sensible gentleman of that residence to gain a horse for his ride home. The Mad Duke of Thornwood lived somewhere in this vicinity, as did Lord Bixley. However, he didn't wish to see either man, not when he'd fallen so far from the last time they'd spoken.

"What do you think you're doing?" The question was screeched from the drive. Lady Katie must have finally found him.

He pivoted and looked down the ladder to where she stood leaning on her walking stick. Wasn't it obvious what he was doing? "Repairing your stables. Where have you been all afternoon?"

"At tea." Her hair was mostly trapped in a braid that fell over her shoulder, but long strands still whipped across her face in the breeze blowing in from the moors. She was wearing boots and breeches again.

He grimaced at her over his shoulder as he began descending the ladder. "At tea dressed as a man?"

"Her Grace doesn't mind." She stepped back, shifting the walking stick in her hand. "She's seen me in worse."

"Her Grace?" He had a sudden sinking feeling about the home he'd spotted while on the roof. There was more than one dukedom in this country, but how many could possibly be in this desolate area? He stared down at her as he found the ground. If Thornwood did live nearby and she'd alerted him to Andrew's presence, he may well murder her. "You called on a duchess in breeches. Have you no knowledge of propriety?" he asked with more anger than he'd intended.

"Why ever not? I'll have you know that the Dowager Duchess of Thornwood is as good as a mother to me, and the new duchess seems quite nice as well. I'm sure they don't think a thing of..."

"Thornwood?" Damn, it was true. The shred of hope he'd been holding on to vanished. "You visited Thornwood today?" Of all the rotten luck, his had to be the worst.

"Yes. I..." Her cheeks turned pink as she choked on her words.

"You're neighbors with Thornwood." He choked out a laugh, even though it wasn't the least bit humorous. "Of course you are."

"My closest neighbors," she confirmed with an odd

tilt to her head as she watched for his reaction. She must know.

He stepped away from her and leaned an arm on the ladder as he looked out across the moors. That stone structure beyond the line of trees must be Thornwood's residence. Two years of hiding from society, and his past was within riding distance. His cheek twitched with a smile at the irony of his situation. Turning back to her, he asked, "Did you say 'the new duchess'?"

"Yes. Thornwood was wed two years ago. She's quite nice. I believe you know her from a gathering at your home. Lily? Tall and thin, blond hair, lovely if you like traditional English beauties."

"Lillian Phillips?" His mouth twisted into something resembling a smile. "Yes, I know her." They'd been on the edge of courtship when he left home. Now she was married to the man who had ultimately caused his demise. "She's now wed to the Mad Duke? I suppose my assessment of her judgment was a bit off. No one in their right mind would consent to such a thing."

"She seems happy. And I've never liked the name 'Mad Duke.' He's quite nice, you know. We're related now through my brother's marriage to his sister. He's done nothing to deserve such a name, and neither did his father, for that matter."

"Nothing except to be mad and a duke." He scowled at the horizon. "It seems rather fitting, if you ask me."

"I didn't ask you." She practically yelled the words before turning away from him on a string of murmured curses that he couldn't quite hear.

He shrugged and trailed after her. He didn't want to have cross words with the girl, but he couldn't seem to help himself when he was around her. Was it the mention of Thornwood being nearby, or was it simply the wildness of this particular female that had him at odds this time? He didn't understand why he was now following her to continue their conversation. Perhaps he'd addled his mind when he fell from his horse.

He rubbed a hand over the back of his head, knowing that wasn't the issue here. If only he could put his finger on the source of his ire... "Have you seen to Shadow's Light today? Your groom mentioned a poultice."

"Yes, I made the poultice this morning and had his leg wrapped in fresh bandages." She glanced up at him with a pert expression crossing her face. "Perhaps if you woke before noon, you would have known of it."

"I awoke at daybreak," he grated. "Of course, I have no horse for my daily ride, so I saw no reason to hurry to the stables."

She stopped her lumbering progression down the fencerow leading to the garden. Turning, she pinned him with her pale green-eyed glare. "Why were you on the roof?"

"I was undertaking repairs of a leak." He crossed his arms. "Perhaps if you hadn't been at tea on the neighbor's property, you would know of it."

"But why are you repairing my roof?" Her eyes were wide with some emotion he couldn't quite place.

"Your stables are in great need of improvement. I am here, unable to leave. I need something to fill my days." And he owed her a debt, but he didn't want to see her gloating expression so he kept that part to himself. At least he would know they were even. He didn't want to owe her anything. Though did she truly not see the need for upkeep around the estate? She should be thanking him.

"My stables are fine." She bit her lip and glanced away across the pasture.

"Your stables are a mess, the likes of which I've never seen. I plan to see them repaired."

Her gaze snapped back to meet his. "That isn't why you're here. I don't need your help."

"Nor do I need you to heal my horse, yet here we are," he replied, not daring to look away from her.

"Yes, my lord, we indeed…are here." The sprinkling of freckles across her nose and cheeks caught the afternoon sun as it made a brief appearance from behind the clouds.

The moment stretched out between them as they remained locked in a silent war, with neither wanting to declare defeat. He finally sighed, dropping his hands to rest on his hips.

She exhaled and pursed her lips.

This would get them nowhere. Like it or not, he was here on her estate until Shadow healed, and it would do no good to bicker the entire visit. He searched for the right words to make her see reason, which seemed unlikely, but he needed to try. "If you would only come and look at the plans I have drawn up to make your stables function the way they should…"

"That won't be necessary." She turned and walked away—and this time he let her go.

✦

Andrew made his way out to the road, not with the intent of leaving, but to put some distance between himself and Lady Katie Moore. Somehow the air only a few paces from the entrance to Ormesby Place seemed easier to breathe. Maybe beyond the bounds of the estate, he could clear his head. He would have to return soon, but for the next few minutes, he was free. Leaning against a low stone wall on the opposite side of the road, he looked down the drive with a sigh.

"What are you doing back so soon?" a voice called out.

Andrew turned toward the frail voice, seeing an older man round the bend in the road. Had they met? He didn't seem familiar and Andrew had only been in the area a few days. It wasn't long enough to know anyone, much less to be missed by one of the locals.

"Apologies. I thought you were Lord Ayton from a distance," a farmer offered with a smile as he neared. The flock of sheep the man was guiding toward an open gate baaed as they moved around him. "My eyes are going," he further explained.

"His clothing was loaned to me for the duration of my visit." Andrew shook the cuffs of the coat into place, discomforted by the reminder of his current appearance. "It's not what I would wear under normal circumstances, but it will do. It is rather"—he paused in an attempt not to offend the neighboring farmer with talk of Ayton—"dark. My personal tastes are a bit more traditional."

"Most tastes are. I remember how the late Lord Ayton would tease his brother about his looks, God rest his soul."

"The late Lord Ayton?" Andrew's eyes narrowed on the man. No one in the house seemed open to discussing the subject, so he was anxious to hear someone speak of it now.

"Yes. He was taken from this world at far too young an age. Terrible times for the family. But enough of that. How long is your visit?"

"I wish I knew the answer to that question." There was no way of knowing when Shadow might be healed enough to even walk to the next village, and if repairing the stable roof didn't count toward repayment of the life debt, he could be here quite a while. He settled further onto the wall. When had he become so comfortable conversing with sheep farmers? The years spent in Scotland must have soaked deeper into his bones than he'd realized. He tried to collect himself but couldn't summon the vigor to do so—a fact he blamed entirely on the lady of this estate.

A moment of silence passed while the farmer guided the sheep through the gate at his side. "I heard tell Lady Katie's been seen down at the stables the past couple days. Don't suppose you have anything to do with that?" The older man shot him a smile cloaked in some deeper meaning that Andrew must have missed. He'd forgotten what it was like to have neighbors who hung on every bit of talk in the area. Although he couldn't say he'd ever chatted with one of the farmers back home.

"I believe Lady Katie wants nothing more than to avoid me." Avoid him or annoy him—*or, at the moment, both,* he finished to himself.

"Oh?" The hint of some secret was still lingering in the man's eyes.

"We don't agree on many things," Andrew tried to explain. If he could get the old farmer to speak openly, perhaps he could gain some knowledge of the mysterious Lady Katie Moore.

"She's always been of a strong mind," the man offered with a shake of his head.

"It goes beyond being strong-minded." She drove him to madness. "And it seems I am the only one bothered by her behavior. She runs roughshod over the entire estate and no one says a word."

"There are a great many things that bother me in this world. But Lady Katie isn't one of them." The farmer adjusted his hat over his eyes and glanced around before continuing. "In all honesty, she's more of a worry to me and the missus than a bother. We've known her since she was a babe. She's not ours, of course, earl's daughter and all, but she's like one o' my own."

Andrew likened her more to a bee flitting about his face or an itch on the bottom of his foot when wearing boots, but he understood the man's feelings on the matter. "I find it concerning as well. She's allowed to live alone in a cottage, wear her hair unbound, and walk about the estate in breeches? It's unheard of."

"She has her reasons. Of that you can be sure," the farmer offered, leaning on the gatepost with an eye on his sheep.

"Reasons," Andrew scoffed, allowing his ire to get the better of him. "What reasons could a woman possibly have for such a life? She has a house guest and doesn't even deem it necessary to join me for dinner. I find it most unsettling. She's allowed far too much freedom."

"Freedom is exactly what she doesn't have, if you don't mind my saying." The farmer sighed. "No matter what she may believe to the contrary."

"Do you mean her injury?" Andrew raised a brow. "That's no excuse for such behavior."

"No, m'lord. It's m'lord, isn't it? By the look of you, I'm guessing as much."

"Lord Amberstall," he confirmed.

"Very well, m'lord. The troubles for this family began long before Lady Katie's riding accident last year." His eyes darted toward the drive to ensure they were indeed alone before he continued. "It all began when the lady of the house vanished one night some nine years ago."

"Vanished?" Andrew settled further onto the top of the stone wall to listen. "What do you mean 'vanished'? Ladies don't simply disappear."

"Lady Ormesby did just that, m'lord. It was rumored she fled to France with a lover, but Lord Ormesby had no proof of such a thing. Had no proof to the contrary either, though, if you see my meaning."

"Quite well," Andrew replied, his eyes widening at the implication. The news of such an occurrence would have been on the lips of everyone in every salon in the area when it happened. He was quite familiar with on-dits, unfortunately.

"Anyway, Lady Katie was only eleven years old. You can imagine the effect it had on her. She spent all her waking hours on horseback…trying to run from life, if you want my thoughts on it."

Andrew leaned forward, searching the man's face for understanding. "Don't tell me she moved from the house into an old cottage when she was but eleven years of age."

"She needed to be away from that place. She'd always been one to do things on her own, but when her mother left…"

"And her father let her go?" Who would do such a thing to a child? She would have needed her family more at that time, not less.

"He had more immediate issues on his mind at the time. From what I've heard tell, it was a kindness. Lady Katie may have been spared the brunt of her father's anger over Lady Ormesby's disappearance by living in her cottage. Don't know how bad things became since I wasn't in the house, but I've heard things. It's said that he wouldn't even look at the girl—all because of her likeness to her mother. But even living in the cottage, Lady Katie would still return for dinner and to visit with her brothers. That is, until last year…" He closed his eyes against some memory. "She hasn't crossed the threshold into her own home for some time now. Not that I'm one to tell stories out of turn, mind you."

Lady Katie Moore hadn't set foot inside what should be her home in a year and hadn't slept there in nine years. The information held logical significance, yet it was still unfathomable. "Lord Ormesby has allowed nine years to pass in such a manner?" Andrew's voice came out in a rough whisper. "She lives in the woods and acts like one of the horses running wild in the pasture."

The neighbor chuckled. "She has a wild spirit. I'll agree to that much."

"She wears breeches."

"Aye, always has, ever since she sat atop a horse." He smiled for a moment before glancing out across the pasture, watching his sheep.

He was clearly done divulging the Moore family secrets, but Andrew wasn't done discussing them. "I simply cannot understand it. She leaves me to dine alone. And breeches…on a lady."

The man turned back to him. "Lord Amberstall, if you don't mind my meddling, have you wondered why you might find such fault with the lady's hair, clothing, and absence?"

"Because it's improper."

"Is that all?"

Andrew exhaled with annoyance. "She has more flaws than correct parts."

"Sometimes it's the flaws that make something lovely."

Andrew narrowed his eyes. "Beauty is achieved through perfection of body and mind."

The farmer chuckled. "You fancy lords and your thoughts on beauty. You do amuse me. Now, if you will excuse me, I see one of the sheep wandering away. Enjoy your evening, dinner and all. It's going to be dark before long."

"My solitary dinner," Andrew grumbled.

The man paused at the gate, turning back to him. "You know Lady Katie has a solitary dinner every evening in her cottage—always has. If it bothers you so to miss her company, you could ask her to join you."

He jerked back a fraction at the suggestion. "I don't seek her company."

"Don't you?" The old man grinned, his wrinkled skin crinkling around his eyes.

"I…" Andrew began, but he wasn't sure how to answer. He pushed the hair from his forehead and sighed.

"Good evening, m'lord," the farmer offered, stepping through the gate.

"Good evening," Andrew whispered in return after the man was already long gone.

❧

The path from her cottage wound past the edge of the garden at the corner of the fields where the horses grazed. Katie paused at that corner every morning. The trees that her great-grandfather brought in decades ago to please her great-grandmother had matured into the dense forest that now surrounded her cottage on three sides.

She lifted her face to the canopy overhead, breathing in the sweet, wet scent of the woods around her. The leaves, bright with color, would fall in another week or two. Would Lord Amberstall be gone by then? She blinked away the thought, unsure where it had come from. She would not think about that man while enjoying what could be the last of her solitude for the day.

Bracing her hands on the stone wall before her, she watched the animals move about the pasture in the distance, serene and enjoying the morning air. The mind was a funny thing. Even Katie realized the absurdity of feeling safe on the opposite side of a low wall that the horses could easily jump, yet she did feel safe here.

Ever since her accident, her heart would race when she saw a horse. Her love had turned into a fear she could never release. She pushed off the wall and picked up the walking stick from where she had left it propped against a tree. Her new life was fine. She filled her days with her hobbies and interests, and her evenings in the cottage were quiet, allowing her to live a simple life. She was happy, truly she was. She looked back out to the horses in the field; she didn't miss them.

She moved down the path through the trees, twirling her walking stick. She'd almost perfected the ability to spin the polished wooden stick around her fingers twice without dropping it. She'd been working on the feat for a month. Her life was full.

As she stepped out into the weak morning sun, she placed the end of the stick back on the ground and slowed her pace to lean on the piece of wood at her side. She'd perfected the limp over the past year as well. It was true that her knee still ached if she walked great distances, but she'd healed long ago. She tightened her grip on the walking stick. With the stick in hand, no one challenged her avoidance of the horses. No one asked difficult questions, and no one set hopes that she would one day leave her little cottage in the woods to join society. It was the best way—the only way she knew to survive.

She leaned on the stick and took an uneven step. The path where she walked led to the edge of the east garden and skimmed its border before ending at the drive near the stables. There seemed to be a great deal of activity at the stables this morning.

Amberstall. Her eyes narrowed on the building.

Although she couldn't see him, she knew he was involved with something at her stables. She paused, glancing out into the garden to the bench where she could sketch and the gazebo where she could read a book, before her gaze landed back on the stables. Shadow's Light would have to be seen to. Surely her grooms had done a fine job, and yet...

She was walking in that direction before she could think further on it. Moving out across the drive, she took measured steps toward the stables. She could see Amberstall entering the nearest paddock. He was dressed in Ethan's black clothing again, but he couldn't look less like her brother. Amberstall appeared to be made of gold—gold hair, golden skin, a golden gaze. He probably ate only golden food and pissed gold coins. She snorted.

She stopped her progress to lean on the walking stick as her favorite groom passed by.

"Good morning, Lady Katie," he offered with a smile as he led one of the horses to the far paddock built for her training exercises years ago.

"It seems to be." She tensed as the horse passed, only releasing the breath she held when they were gone. The gravel crunched in uneven rhythm beneath her boots as she moved toward the stables.

Amberstall appeared to be alone in the paddock with Shadow's Light. She moved closer. Would he shoot the horse right there and then demand another? Or do something to damage the medicine on Shadow's leg? She wouldn't put it past the vile man. Staying close to the stone stable wall, she tried to get close enough to hear.

"Easy, easy there, old boy." Lord Amberstall laid a hand on Shadow's cheek to calm him. He looked into the horse's eyes as he spoke. "I only want to check your bandaging. I won't hurt you."

Katie wasn't sure she believed him so she hung back

to see what he would do. Yet, there was something calming about the deep rumble of his voice as he spoke to Shadow. She walked closer.

At the animal's huff of agreement, Amberstall knelt down and went to work on the splint. "I'm sorry this happened, Shadow."

Katie stilled, not wanting to intrude on Amberstall's private moment with his horse, yet unable to look away.

"When I took that jump…you know I would never wish you harm."

Shadow grumbled and stomped his front hoof on the ground.

"What? That bit about putting you down? I was only doing what was right. You're hurt. I don't want to see you in pain. An injury is worse than death, you know that."

The horse huffed and tossed his head.

"It looks like you'll live another day, thanks to the lady of the estate. I'll still shoot you if you worsen… or if you get into the garden."

Shadow snorted and looked at the ground.

"You thought I'd forgotten that little adventure of yours in Scotland? Not likely. I never heard the end of it from old Mrs. McDougall. Flattened her vegetables, you daft old beast." He laughed and ran a hand over the horse's mane. "I know. I know. She wasn't very kind. But it was wrong of you nonetheless."

The sound of his laughter made Katie smile. She'd heard it once before when he laughed at her, but this time was different. She relaxed her stance and leaned against the wall.

"We've had a time of it, haven't we? Remember when

we jumped that wall only to find the family of angry badgers on the other side?" Amberstall threw his head back in more laughter. "I've never seen you gallop so fast. I should have set an angry badger on you much sooner."

Katie knew she should leave, yet she couldn't. For the first time, there was no guarded exterior—only a man and his horse. There seemed to be a bond between the two, one that had grown over time and was deeper than the words spoken. It was unexpected, to say the least. Amberstall had been more of a beast than his horse could ever be, yet here, alone, he seemed almost...kind.

He continued speaking to his horse in a low tone. "And now we're here at the mercy of a lady to mend you and let us be on our way."

The horse nudged Amberstall in the shoulder.

"Oh, you like her, do you? I'm sure you'd be partial to anyone trying to spare your worthless life, you great waste of good horseflesh." He chuckled and gave Shadow an affectionate pat.

Shadow tossed his head and took half a step away.

"I'm only teasing. No need to get fussy over it," Amberstall admonished. "Perhaps she's not all bad. She's far from perfect, but maybe..." He looked up as a groom approached him.

She should go. She shouldn't have listened to his conversation, and she certainly shouldn't stay to hear more. What had he been about to say? *Far from perfect, but maybe...*what? She couldn't stay to find out.

She made a slow path around the corner of the stable, nearing the entrance.

A year and three months. She took a shaky breath. It had been a late spring.

She ground the walking stick into the dirt just out-side the stable door, her heart pounding as she stood listening to the sounds of the horses and the scrape of a pitchfork against the stone floor. It was dark inside the building and filled with memories—good and bad.

She took a step forward, edging her way into the structure, yet clinging to the shadows as if the build-ing itself would know of her return. Nothing had changed, yet everything had changed. It bore the look of abandonment. It had fallen into a cluttered mess of disrepair since she'd last been here.

"Damn. Amberstall was right," she whispered.

"What was that?" A deep voice sounded at her back, the sound sliding down her spine to sink into her stomach in a pool of heat.

"Amberstall." Her voice was breathless as she turned to look up at him. "I thought you were outside with Shadow's Light."

"I checked on him. But I'm overseeing the sorting of the tack this morning," he returned.

She shifted, looking up at him. "Thank you."

His eyes flew to hers, wide with surprise. "You're welcome." He nodded toward the depths of the stables and held out his arm for her. "Come in and see the results of your grooms' hard work."

She stood rooted to the spot for a minute, grip-ping her walking stick with a white-knuckled grasp. Finally, she offered him a wary smile and slipped her fingers around his arm. His muscles twitched beneath her hand, and she glanced up to see he was watching her. Heat rose in her cheeks. No one had ever looked at her with such intensity. Was it simply the amber of his eyes? Perhaps he looked at everyone that way. She didn't know why it affected her so, but it did.

He led her in slow steps across the straw-strewn floor. "We repaired the roof already. But the damage from the opening still needs to be mended. The rigging is being sorted today."

Her eyes fell on the pile of tack being straightened, currently strewn across the floor. "What a tangled mess," she muttered. "It reminds me of my hair after a fretful night of sleep."

"I can't imagine that your hair could ever look this bad."

"Clearly, you haven't seen me when I first wake in the morning." She regretted the words as soon as she spoke them. Had she just asked him to imagine her hair while she was in bed? She wasn't much for manners, but even she knew that was most likely wrong.

Her breath caught when he laughed, and she found herself smiling up at him.

His eyes twinkled like stars in the night sky as he leaned toward her with a conspiratorial grin. "Would you like to know a secret?"

"Yes.

"My hair stands on end every morning." He gave her arm a tug and propelled her farther into the stables.

"Aren't we a fine pair?" She laughed as he led her down the aisle.

"Indeed." He paused to grasp the door to the nearest stall, checking the security of the hinges with a shake of the wood. "Some of the stall doors need to be reinforced. Others simply need adjustment, but I'll see to that later."

"Why are you overseeing repairs to my stables?"

The words were out before she could think about them. She knew it was most likely because she'd told him he owed her a debt, but for some reason she didn't want that to be his reason for assisting her. Perhaps she didn't welcome an answer to her question, but blast it all, she did want an answer.

His hand dropped away from the stall door. "I've overstepped my bounds. When you were upset by the roof, I should have known…"

"No, I'm glad of it, and the grooms seem pleased with the improvements. I was upset by the roof because…" She broke off, not wanting to discuss her careful dance of fear and the protection she felt for the stables—not with him, or anyone else for that matter. "Never mind that now." People didn't show generosity such as this, not to her. She glanced down at her hand on his arm. It was the most prolonged contact she'd had with anyone in years. Why was he doing this? Any of it? "I was only curious as to why."

He frowned at her question. "I didn't consider the alternative, I suppose. It needed to be done."

"I haven't come here in some time. If I had known…" She broke off, all too aware of the truth. Even if she had known, she wouldn't have come here. She wouldn't have allowed anyone else near to make the repairs. She wouldn't even be here now if his presence hadn't drawn her in this direction.

He took a step forward, continuing their stroll through the building. "Your grooms are happy you've returned, no matter the time it took."

She nodded and looked straight ahead, unsure how

to reply. How much did he know of her past? Perhaps the grooms had told him everything and he was only being nice out of pity for her. Or perhaps the kindness in his eyes was genuine. Either way, a few days ago she wouldn't have thought him capable of it.

My lady, would you join me for dinner this evening?"

His question startled her out of her thoughts, her slow footsteps stopping as she looked up at him. "Dinner…where?"

"In your dining room," he supplied with a smile. "Within the walls of your home."

"Since there's no formal dining room in my cottage, I assume you mean Ormesby Place."

"Yes, your home."

"It's not my home." She began walking again, practically dragging him along. The door at the end of the row of stalls was now in view. Her heart was pounding. She needed air. This had been too great a leap for one morning.

"Why don't you live in the house, truly? I've heard you've been gone some time. It must make your father sad not to have you about."

She shrugged in an attempt to feign nonchalance. "I suppose I prefer the simplicity of my cottage." Never mind that she hadn't set foot inside Ormesby Place since the awful day of her riding accident. She wasn't prepared to discuss that today, and certainly not while touring her stables.

"What of your safety, staying alone as you do?"

"I'm well within our lands in the cottage." She stepped out into the weak morning sun, already feeling better about things now that the stables were at her back. Tossing a smile up at Amberstall, she added, "And I have a blunderbuss."

"You know how to operate a firearm?" He looked at her with dismay. "Who thought it was a good idea to teach a lady such a thing?"

"I taught myself, and I'm quite a good shot." She released his arm and turned toward him. "You were the one concerned for my safety a moment ago, and now you find fault with my solution?"

"You do know you would take out an entire wall of your cottage if you needed to fire that thunder pipe at someone."

"Amberstall, if you were sneaking into a lady's cottage and you were greeted with a blunderbuss, would you need it to be fired in your direction? Or would you simply leave?"

"I would never sneak into a lady's cottage," he returned with his usual highborn arrogance.

"Then why are you so concerned about it?"

He laughed, his shoulders relaxing a fraction. "I look forward to our dinner conversation this evening. Blunderbuss indeed." He offered her a nod as he turned away, heading out across the field.

"I haven't agreed to have dinner with you," she called after him.

He stopped and turned back to her. "I wasn't aware you had such a busy social calendar. My apologies."

"I don't. I always dine alone."

"Good. Then you can join me and no one will be disappointed by your absence."

"I suppose," she said, unable to argue with his logic.

He smiled and walked away, tossing out, "Until this evening," over his shoulder.

Had she agreed to dine with him? She shook her head, trying to restore order to her thoughts. She wasn't even sure why he had asked her. She could pull herself together and attend. She turned and looked up at the large stone building casting a shadow across the drive. It was only a house—a house filled with one too many bad memories.

She sighed and looked back to Amberstall's retreating form, already growing smaller in the distance. If there was a reason for his interest in dinner with her, she could not guess at it. His improvements to the stables, the dinner invitation…what were his intentions? He could be attempting kindness to overcome the rough start they'd gotten off to. He could be looking for a way to repay her for saving his life. He could simply be weary of leisure time spent alone, or he could be doing it all out of pity. Her mind refused to leave out that last option.

She gripped her walking stick as she ground on the thought, turning it to dust, then packing it back together into hard stone reality. He most likely saw her as an unfortunate case—an injured lady shut away from her family, choosing to live out her days alone in a cottage. He wanted to repair her life over a few dinners, as he had repaired the roof of her stables. Well, she was not made of rotting wood, and she would not be attending any dinners.

She was happy with the life she'd chosen, and she didn't need his pity or his help. And he wouldn't truly miss her company anyway. No. She turned and began the slow walk back to her cottage. Lord Amberstall would be dining alone this night and all others.

Six

ONE HOUR AND EIGHT MINUTES LATE. HE'D PACED THE parlor for over an hour with a drink in his hand, waiting for her. He'd changed his clothes for dinner, taking extra care with the only shirt he'd arrived with. He'd attempted to style hair that was in desperate need of cutting. He'd even arrived in the parlor a few minutes early so that she wouldn't have to wait alone.

Andrew should have known better than to count on her. He'd always been let down by the females in his life—why should she be different? And yet he'd thought she was different. This afternoon, Lady Katie had agreed to dine with him. Something must have made her change her mind, though. Had he said something to offend her?

It made no sense because they'd left on good terms, perhaps for the first time ever. He raised the glass to his lips, tossed back the contents, and turned to the footman. "I'll wait for her ladyship in the dining room now."

"Yes, my lord."

He gave up on sharing a drink with her, but they

would still be having dinner. His boots sounded thunderous in the empty hall as he proceeded to the dining room. It was too quiet. He'd grown weary of silence in recent months. But somehow the subdued nature of his Scottish solitude hadn't been this unbearable.

As he sat at one end of the long dining table, he watched the *tick, tick, tick* of the clock on the mantel. He rapped his fingers in unison with it on the arm of his chair. *Click, click, click, click. Click, click, click, click.* Making a fist, he almost growled.

The footman moved in, clearly trained to act if a dinner guest showed signs of unrest. "Would you like the food to be served, my lord?"

"No." He ground the word out between clenched teeth. "Lady Katie Moore will join me for dinner this evening, and I will wait for her arrival."

"Very well, my lord." The man moved back to his post in the corner of the large room with uneasy steps.

Another ten minutes ticked past in silence. The table stretched out before him, silver and crystal glinting in the flicker of candlelight. His plate sat empty, as did Lady Katie's chair. She wasn't going to join him. She was actually going to abandon him to eat alone after promising her company. His left brow twitched.

If she was not concerned with polite behavior, why should he be concerned? She was certainly at ease in her little cottage in the woods. And she wouldn't be easily offended by his lack of decorum, so why should he sit here alone in the dining room? Andrew slid his chair back from the table with a loud screech. "Package all of the food and fetch me a lantern."

"Yes, my lord."

A few minutes later, Andrew was striding down the path to the old gamekeeper's cottage with a basket of food in one hand and a lantern in the other. A cool wind whipped at the lapels of his coat, but he pushed forward into the dark of night. He finally rounded a bend, and a small stone cottage came into view. The thick smell of smoke from the lit chimney filled the air.

The structure couldn't be more than one room. How could she live in such a place? There were no servants' quarters, no butler attending the door for her. He took in the old, worn roof and the cracks in the mortar as he moved between beds of half-dead flowers riddled with weeds. Raising his hand, he knocked on the door. Like it or not, Lady Katie would be dining with him this evening. No one left Andrew Clifton, Lord Amberstall, waiting alone— and certainly not her.

The door creaked open a moment later. Lady Katie blinked up into his face, surprise warring with some other emotion he couldn't place and freezing her pink lips into a perfect O.

"I believe we had dinner plans this evening." He lifted the basket of food and braced it against the open door, awaiting an invitation inside, yet refusing to be told no.

❦

Katie couldn't believe this was happening. "You walked all the way here carrying your dinner?" She eyed the basket and braced her hand against the half-open door.

"Our dinner," he corrected with a pointed look, his golden gaze flaring with his ire.

She shrugged and opened the door, attempting nonchalance while her heart pounded in her ears. No one ever came to her cottage, and when she did have a visitor, it was only a servant sent down from the house. She couldn't remember ever having someone come to call on her here, much less dine with her. "What will we be having tonight?"

He ducked his blond head under the doorway and moved past her into the cottage. "I'm not sure, but I could smell it on the entire walk here. We'd best eat it or I'll start chewing on my own arm."

"I would almost like to see that." She closed the door behind him and stood with jangling nerves while he assessed her living quarters.

She was all too aware of her possessions piled high in the corners and the bed sitting in plain view. "My cottage isn't large, but it is home," she squeaked out as she took a step away from the door.

"It's…" He paused to investigate a painting she'd worked on last week. It was supposed to be the moors in the morning, but it looked more like leftover soup. "Lovely," he finally muttered. Walking to the table, he set the basket of food on the wooden surface before strolling around the open room, making the comfortable space feel small and intimate.

She began to perspire. "You can move my watercolors out of the way if you need to do so. There's room for them on that pile of books over there." He was a tall, broad-shouldered man. She'd known this before, but now he seemed even larger. Perhaps it was because she'd only seen him outdoors. All she knew was that he seemed to take up all the extra space in the room, leaving none for her. She wrapped her arms around her waist, trying to shrink smaller, but to no avail.

"You certainly have things decorated to suit you." He picked up the violin she'd cast aside yesterday and set it back down to investigate the drying herbs hanging from the rafters near the fire. Turning, he moved past her bed. His eyes rolled over the patchwork quilt made of every color imaginable as his fingers trailed over the wooden frame, far too nice for the little cottage.

It had been the one piece of her life she'd brought with her when she moved out of the house. She'd wanted an escape, a small piece of life that was her own, but her feather mattress was one indulgence she couldn't leave behind. Now her cheeks were heated, thanks to Amberstall's proximity to it. When her mother abandoned her, plenty of lessons in ladylike behavior had been left untaught, but she was certain that "Don't invite a gentleman you met only a few days ago into your bedchamber" would have been fairly high on that list.

"I've had time to be settled here, it's true." She begged him in silence not to comment on her bed, or her cheeks may burst into flames.

He glanced at her and paused, watching her. Could he guess her thoughts? Clearing his throat, he moved back toward the basket of food. "Where are your plates?"

She released the breath she hadn't realized she'd been holding. "What? Oh, here." She turned around and pulled two plates from the cabinet against the wall.

"And cutlery, forks and such?" He was already pulling food from the basket.

She hadn't realized how hungry she was until she saw the feast before her. She'd forgotten how large the meals were when served in the dining room. "I only have one fork. We could share, I suppose."

He looked at her as if she'd sprouted another head from her shoulders. "You only have one fork in your possession. But you're female."

"And like all females of my acquaintance, I only have one mouth."

"That's true, but it surprises me. Never mind, though, I can make do." He grinned and took a bottle of wine from the basket and set it on the table. "It will be like when my father took me out into the woods to sleep on the ground and live off the land. We killed our food and ate with knives. He said it would make me into a man."

"Did it?" she asked around a smile as she pulled the chair out from the table.

He held his hands out to the side and glanced down at himself before nodding. "It must have worked."

"Pleased to hear it." She eased into the empty chair opposite where he stood. "I wasn't expecting a guest this evening, or I would have acquired some things from the kitchen."

"You weren't expecting a guest?" He raised one eyebrow in question as he carved a piece of meat and placed it on her plate.

"No…" Having him in her cottage was the last thing she'd imagined. "I thought when I didn't arrive you would eat without me."

He slid the plate across the wooden surface, his eyes locked on hers. "You were mistaken."

She didn't spare a glance for the food before her—she couldn't, not when his eyes seemed to be taking her apart piece by piece. Finally, she found her ability to speak. "Why did you come here?"

"Why didn't you meet me?" He threw a hand into the air with a wince. "Apologies. Don't answer that. It was inconsiderate of me to ask such a thing."

"Was it? Inconsiderate? It seems like a reasonable question to me." It wasn't a question she looked forward to answering, but he was within his rights to ask. She had broken her word to him today.

"Clearly you were having some difficulty." He leaned over the table as if someone would hear him speak if he spoke the words too loudly. "I shouldn't point out your troubles with the path to the house."

"I walk that path every day." She'd rather he know the truth than to feel blasted pity for her. It was his pity that kept her within the safety of her walls tonight—for as much good as that had done.

"Oh." His brows drew together. Some emotion lingered around his eyes as he tore a bite of bread and popped it into his mouth.

She couldn't read his thoughts, but the emotion appeared to be sadness of some degree, and something tightened in her chest at the sight of it. She looked down at the food on her plate, unable to meet his gaze any longer. "I didn't think you meant it." She chanced a glance up at him. "The invitation, that is."

"Why would I extend it if I didn't mean it?"

"To be polite. You seem concerned with such

things." It was as close to the truth as she could bear to speak.

"I meant it."

"I can see that now." Although she still didn't understand it. Whether or not he was stranded on her property, he was still a handsome, titled lord. He was the sort other ladies would swoon over, so why would he even look twice in her direction? He loathed everything about her—he'd made that much clear.

"Good." He grinned and took another bite of meat. "Wine?"

"Yes, please."

"I don't suppose you have glasses."

She shook her head and watched him hesitate, then shrug one shoulder, pop the cork, and tip the bottle to his lips. His tan throat worked to swallow the liquid. She couldn't look away from the sight. She tried to jerk her gaze away when he returned the bottle to the table and slid it over to her with a knowing smile, but she couldn't. More for something to do with her hands than actual thirst, she lifted the bottle to her lips, placing them where his mouth had been only a moment ago. *This must be what he would taste like.*

Where had that thought come from? She swallowed and pushed the bottle back into his hand. "Why? Why did you ask me to join you?"

He pursed his lips before answering, drawing her eyes there once more. "I don't enjoy dining alone. I've been alone for two years now." He spun the bottle in a slow circle between his fingers. "Well, I was with Shadow, but he doesn't talk much."

"No? You talk to him a good bit." She tore off a

small piece of bread and tossed it into her mouth. "I must admit, I saw you with him this morning. I tried not to listen, but…"

He drew back. "I hope I didn't say anything to offend your sensibilities. When I talk to Shadow… is that why you didn't join me for dinner? Did I say something?"

"Do I look like I have sensibilities that are easily offended?" she asked, taking a bite of meat.

"Perhaps you keep them well hidden. I think you hide a great deal under the surface."

Her breathing sped. She could feel a blush creeping up her neck. What did he know? She cast him a casual smile and lifted the loose neck of her shirt and peered down into it. "No, nothing hidden in there," she teased.

"I disagree." His tone was almost wicked.

Surely he couldn't look at her and see more than anyone else saw—a broken girl who didn't fit in anywhere. And why should he see more than that? After all, that was all she was. Her life was contained in this cottage, and this was where she would spend the remainder of her days, alone. It was the way she wished it to be, and nothing he said would change that.

She grabbed the bottle of wine, lifting it to her lips to take a sip. "Lord Amberstall, would you…"

"Andrew. My name is Andrew."

She wrinkled her nose at the notion of calling him Andrew. "No."

"No? Are you in disagreement over my name?"

"Andrew doesn't suit you. An *Annndrew* would

never stoop so low as to speak to horses or eat dinner with his fingers. No. You are Andy."

"End my name with a Y? Absolutely not. You might as well put braids in my hair and teach me to giggle."

"What?" She laughed.

"Emily, Amy, Polly, Daisy…no."

"Fine, I'll call you Ande—with an E. It's very masculine." When he studied her in silence for a moment, she added, "Or Lord Horseybritches. You have your choice."

His mouth drew up into a smile, crinkling the corners of his eyes. "When posed in that light, I suppose Andy isn't so terrible, even if it does end in a Y."

She smiled and extended her hand across the table, trying not to fall victim to the charm of his smile. "Katie."

"Very well. I've enjoyed eating dinner with my fingers in your company, Katie." He leaned across the table and took her hand in his.

As his warm hand wrapped around hers, she felt his strength, his calluses, his warmth, and some of the gravy from their dinner. She gave it a sturdy shake and began laughing. "Your hand is sticky, Andy."

"I can imagine so." He released her hand with a lingering smile from which she couldn't turn away. After a moment, he cleared his throat. "Tell me, do you truly play all the musical instruments in the corner over there?"

"Yes, I do." She turned and looked at the pile of instruments beside her bed. She rose from her chair. "And no one complains of the noise, so I take that to mean I'm quite talented."

He stood as well. "You live alone in the woods. Who would complain? Rabbits? Squirrels?"

"Yes, and like I said, no complaints." She lifted her chin. "And I don't live completely alone. I have Mr. Rumples, my squirrel. He's asleep in the corner."

"You have a pet squirrel?"

"You talk to horses."

"Touché." He grinned and began putting the left-over food back into the basket. "You keep busy, by the looks of your cottage."

"I try to keep moving in life." It didn't quite explain her unending search for something more, something at which she could excel, but it came close.

"I try to do the same. I spent every day of my life in the stables. I began my work when I was only ten years of age, and I didn't stop until two years ago."

She'd moved out of her home at eleven. But she hadn't left to work; she'd left to live. Still she asked, "Ten is rather young, isn't it?"

"I didn't have a choice in the matter. Sometimes you don't think about your actions. You simply do them because they must be done."

"The past few years must have been quite the change for you." She gathered the last of the food and placed it in the basket.

"And not a welcome one," he admitted.

"How did you fill your time in Scotland? Surely you took up some hobby."

"I raised sheep."

"Sheep?" She tried to imagine him herding sheep, but couldn't. He seemed too large and powerful for that, and she wasn't only referring to his size. He had a presence when he entered a room that only influential lords seemed to possess.

"Well, the sheep were there. I had nothing else to do." He shrugged. "So, I streamlined the profitability of the land. I'd increased the size of the flock by forty percent by the time I left, but it was nothing really." Sadness crept into his eyes for a moment before he turned away from the table with his plate. He continued speaking, but she could only hear the pain in his voice as he said, "They weren't horses. Nothing can replace horses."

"I understand."

He set his plate down and turned back to her. "When was the last time you rode a horse?"

"One year, three months, and a day ago," she bit out.

"Was that when you were injured?"

She nodded as she gathered her plate from the table and prepared to take it to the small dish basin below the front window.

He took the plate from her and laid it in the basin. He didn't say anything further as he went back to the table to cork the wine and put it away. A long silence fell between them as he moved around the small kitchen area.

She wasn't sure what to do or say. Should she speak? Was he hesitant to offend her with a discussion of her injury? It hung like a thick fog in the air between them. And then in the next second, she couldn't make conversation for an entirely different reason. Her mouth went dry as she realized he was shedding layers of clothing.

He removed his coat, draping it over the chair he'd

vacated only a few minutes ago. Rolling up his sleeves, Andy turned back toward her, apparently intending to wash the plates. His tan forearms stretched the fabric of his shirt.

She couldn't make herself look away. "You don't have to do that," she muttered, watching the muscles work in his arms in fascination and hoping he wouldn't listen to her.

"We have no servants here. I can assist. It's rather novel, actually." He laughed as he dipped one plate into the water and lifted it up for inspection, splashing water all over his shirt in the process. "I can't say I've ever washed a dish."

"I can tell." She moved to stand beside him, as he appeared to require some assistance. "Try it this way." She reached across him and wrapped her hand around his wrist in an attempt to guide the plate back into the water.

His muscles jumped under her fingers.

Perhaps this was another of the lessons her mother would have taught her, had she stayed at Ormesby— "Don't grab a gentleman's soapy hand when he isn't expecting it." Her heart was pounding, however, and she had little choice but to follow through with the action now that she'd started. She didn't let go, only tried to think of the china he held and not the warm skin under her fingertips.

"Is this right?" His voice rumbled near her ear, setting her nerves further on edge.

She twisted to look up at him, which was clearly a mistake since she grazed her arm across his damp shirt in the process, pressing it to his chest. He was made of hardened muscle. There was nothing soft about Andy except the warm gold of his eyes locked on hers. For a moment she didn't move, only stared. What was she doing? Her mind was screaming for her to run, but she remained.

Finally, she came to her senses and released his wrist, untangling her arm from him and stepping away. It wasn't far enough. She could still feel his eyes on her as she walked to the fireplace. Warmth was the last thing she needed at the moment, but the fire was in the opposite corner of the room. She lifted her hands to the flames, feigning a chill.

"You're standing without your walking stick," he stated.

She felt the heat rise in her cheeks. She turned back to him, searching for an excuse. Damn. In her flustered state, she'd forgotten to limp. "I'm not walking at the moment. I'm standing. It's different."

"If you can stand, you can ride a horse."

"No, I can't," she said a bit too quickly.

"You could try to overcome your injury." He dried his hands on the towel at his side before turning to lean a hip on the worktable at his back. "I could help you."

She swallowed. "I've had a lovely evening, Andy, but I find I'm quite tired."

"Very well, then." He pushed his sleeves back down as he crossed the room to her.

Why was he approaching? There was an intensity about the way he moved, the way he looked at her, that made her breathing turn shallow. He stopped in front of her but said nothing. Was he going to kiss her?

Did she want him to? She had nothing but unresolved questions as she looked up into his face. His lips hovered above hers, so close that if she were to rise to her toes, they would touch. But she didn't dare. She was frozen under the heat of his gaze.

"If I'm to leave and let you rest, I'll need to retrieve the lantern from the hearth."

"Oh." She glanced behind her at the lantern he'd brought. *You are such an idiot. Did you really think he would kiss you? You?*

But a second later, he gained her attention once more when he trapped her fingers within his grasp and brought her hand to his lips. "I enjoyed your company this evening," he said over the top of her hand, his breath heating her skin.

A muttered, "Yes," was all she could manage in return. Her knees went wobbly at the brush of his lips across her knuckles.

"I look forward to our dinner together tomorrow night." He still held her hand for a moment, keeping her close to him. Then in the next breath he dropped her hand and turned away to retrieve his coat.

"Could we meet here again?" She knew it wasn't wise and probably sounded rather brazen, but she said it anyway. "I think I would like that more than going to the house."

His eyes flared for a second, but just as fast, the expression was replaced by a smile. "I will consider that an open invitation to dine with you. Although I may bring a fork next time."

"I look forward to it." She stepped to the side so that he could gather the lantern for his journey back to the house. Another dinner with him—she must be mad.

He paused at the door before leaving. "Thank you for a most entertaining evening, Katie."

She nodded in response. What was happening to her? Perhaps this was why it wasn't wise to allow handsome gentlemen entrance into one's bedchamber. For once she was glad her mother hadn't stayed in her life to teach her such lessons. She grinned and bolted the door. If she knew better, she might miss the thrill of this experience. Thankfully, she didn't know any better.

∝

Dear Mother,

The delay on my journey is taking a bit longer than I'd envisioned. I cannot tell you when I will arrive as I don't know how much longer I will be in this place. Shadow's Light seems to be recovering, yet it will be a few days still before he's seen by the doctor. He is currently under the care of a quite original lady. I found her most disagreeable when we first met, but the more I see of her, the more I find her a curiosity, a riddle to be solved. In the meantime, I'm trying to be of use around the estate. The state of the stables made me cringe when I arrived, but they improve a bit each day under my supervision. It does feel proper to be back in the company of horses.

Andrew lifted the pen, watching a drop of black ink pool on the metal tip. It *was* nice to be in a stable again, to feel of use. He curled his hand into a fist where it lay on the desk. The repairs had been small, not like the challenges that faced him every day at his home. It was much the same as it had been in Scotland.

"A hundred head of sheep," he muttered and laid the pen aside. He'd spent two years of his life expanding a flock of sheep that didn't belong to him. If any of the *ton* ever got news of what had become of him, he would be at an even lower level of shame. When he left, it had been to avoid the talk in town, as well as his own staff looking askew at him every time he passed in the damn hall.

He had once been great. He was Amberstall! Could he ever get that back? Perhaps the real Amberstall was gone forever, buried in the Highlands amid the sheep. Now, the best he could do was to straighten a stable, so much so that he sought to brag about it in a letter? He scowled at the written words on the page and pulled the sheet into his grasp, crumpling it into a ball he then tossed into the fire. Leaning over the desk in his room, he tried again.

> *Dear Mother,*
> *My delay is extended here a day's ride north of Great Ayton while I wait for Shadow's Light to heal. I will inform you when I am able to continue south.*
>
> *Your son,*
> *Andrew*

He gave the parchment a satisfactory nod and began folding it. It was the perfect letter—much improved from the original. Glancing over to the place in the fire where the ball of parchment was only a minute ago, he took a breath. It wasn't like him to pen maudlin letters.

The first letter had discussed Katie, for goodness' sake. His words had been true. He did find her more intriguing now than disagreeable, but one didn't speak of these things.

What did it matter what he thought of Katie anyway? He was here on a task. He was here for Shadow. He shouldn't be thinking of her at all. It wasn't as if she would make a suitable wife. He released a bark like laugh. Lady Katie Moore was quite possibly the most flawed individual he'd ever met, and that wasn't taking her injury into the equation. No, she was certainly not what was expected of the next Lady Amberstall. Yet she was never far from his mind.

Perhaps his trip to her cottage had been unwise. It was true he'd known better than to go to the private rooms of a lady, but tonight he couldn't be more pleased that he'd decided to toss propriety from the nearest window. Furthermore, he planned to promptly ignore all signs of knowing better in the near future, because in all of this mess, he knew one thing: he would not miss dinner with Katie for all the manners and proper behavior in the world.

Seven

KATIE STEPPED INTO THE STABLES, STILL UNSURE OF HER place. A few years ago, she would have been there at daybreak exercising the horses and brushing them. But now she didn't know what purpose she served within these walls. She didn't ride and couldn't allow herself to even get close enough to assist in their care, yet she was here.

Taking a step further inside, she heard a scraping sound and peeked around the corner of a stall, watching Andy push at hay with the blade of a shovel. He'd abandoned his coat and had the sleeves of his shirt rolled up to reveal his forearms like last night. She tried not to think about what his skin had felt like beneath her fingers. His muscles flexed against his sleeves as he moved the hay to the side. She was staring. She needed to stop.

In the time she'd spent in London, she hadn't met a gentleman who looked as favorably upon work as Andy did. Of course, she also hadn't met a gentleman who possessed the strength for such work. Katie shook herself. She couldn't stand here and gawk all day; she needed to say something. "I think a pitchfork would help your efforts."

"How silly of me." He turned and leaned on the handle of the shovel, a smile tugging at his lips. "And here I thought there was a distinct lack of forks of all kinds around here."

"No. Only the kind that goes in one's mouth."

"Then I think I'm safe." He reached up and pushed the hair from his face with a sigh.

"I should hope so." She laughed as she retrieved a pitchfork from where it hid behind some other tools in the corner and handed it to him.

"I searched everywhere for this earlier." He nodded toward the next stall over as he set the shovel aside. "Shadow is growing stronger already. He's looking at me again."

"I'm glad he's forgiven you for drawing a pistol on him." She leaned against the side of the stall door with a smirk.

"Perhaps. I like to think he's enjoying his care here." There was a twinkle in his eyes as he glanced in her direction. But a moment later it was gone as he turned back to his work. "Shadow was never pleased with his life in Scotland."

"Why not?"

"I don't know." He shrugged. "I took him for rides every day. I think he was lonely with only sheep for company."

"And you?" she asked as she pushed a clump of hay around with the end of her walking stick.

"Me?" He stopped tossing the hay in the stall for a moment to ponder her question. "I made the best of the situation…such as it was."

He hadn't answered her, but she didn't comment

on it. She already knew the truth. Of course he'd been lonely. He was used to London life. "Quite different from a life lived among society, I would imagine."

"Indeed. Have you been to London?"

"Yes." She rolled her eyes at her memory of the insufferable city. "My debut season was just over a year ago."

His brow furrowed in thought. "I never saw you there, and I'm certain I would remember."

"I could walk normally then, if that's what you're thinking," she replied as she bit her fingernail.

He stilled and looked at her with that intense stare of his. "No, that wasn't what I was thinking."

"Oh…good." The heat of a blush rushed up her neck, and she looked down in hopes he wouldn't notice.

When she heard the scrape of the fork across the stone floor, she glanced back at him to see he was now turned away from her. His shirt clung to his broad shoulders in the heat of the afternoon, shifting with his every move. She tore her eyes from his body and cleared her throat. "I received a note this morning from Thornwood Manor. We're invited to dinner there."

The scrape of the fork ceased with a loud screech. "That sounds like a delightful evening filled with laughter and enjoyment for all."

"I knew you would feel that way," she said, tilting her head in sympathy. He would have to be mad to view an evening with the man who made him flee the country as an enjoyable affair.

"What way?" He hadn't turned back to her, but she could see the tension held in his shoulders.

"You don't want to spend the evening with

Thornwood. But the family won't be the only ones there, it seems."

"Splendid!" He finally turned toward her, his eyes piercing her like golden knives. "Who will be there to witness this event?"

"Lord and Lady Steelings. Apparently they arrived for a visit yesterday."

"Last I heard from Steelings, he was in France with his new bride." He laid the fork aside and dusted off his hands. "I wonder what brings them back."

"You know Steelings as well?"

"Steelings is a friend."

"And his wife?"

He pushed his hair away from his face and glanced away. "I know her as well."

"Andy, do you have a past with every lady in the neighborhood?"

"It would seem so."

"This *will* be an evening to remember," she remarked, narrowing her eyes on him. He wasn't the only one dreading an evening spent with neighboring gentry. Two ladies, the second of whom was no doubt as perfect from her hair to her toes as the first, and they both had pasts with Andy? Damn, she was going to have to change out of breeches for this.

"And you will be fortunate enough to experience it with me."

"It should be amusing," she offered, trying to lift her own spirits as much as his. "And I suppose I've had less entertaining evenings."

"That can't be true. You live with a squirrel for company, after all."

She gave him a withering glare and shoved him on the arm, making him laugh. They stood in silence for a moment after his laughter died away. She twisted her fingers together in a knot. She needed to say something, but what? "About Thornwood…it won't be all bad." Lifting her gaze, she tried to offer him a reassuring grin, but she feared it looked more painful that supportive.

"I can't avoid the man forever." He wrapped his arms across his chest. "I just hadn't planned on dining with him under his roof…ever, but certainly not so soon."

"I'll be there with you, by your side all evening." The words left her mouth before she could stop them. She'd meant to offer him comfort in the form of her company, but the statement left her feeling exposed and awkward. Katie did want to support him, to help him through this difficult situation, but what if he didn't take comfort from her presence? Her heart raced in her chest as she shot him a wary glance.

His thoughts were unreadable as he tilted his head to the side and looked at her. Then, in an instant, his eyes narrowed. "Wait, you *are* planning to wear a gown, aren't you?"

"I suppose we shall find out the answer to that question together as well." She turned and walked out of the stall, grateful for once for the walking stick to lean upon.

❧

Andrew had never seen anyone so visibly uncomfortable in a gown. He smiled up at her as he helped her down from the open carriage. Although he didn't want her to be in such discomfort, in some dark corner of his mind he was happy to not be alone in his distress. He set her down on the ground and retrieved her walking stick before turning back to her with a grin.

"What's so amusing? It's my gown, isn't it?" She pulled at the lace-trimmed neck and tugged on the skirt where it fell over her hip. "I look ridiculous. I knew I would."

"Katie." He stilled her hands within his own. "You're beautiful." The statement seemed to shock her as much as it did him, yet it was true. She was radiant in the light green gown. Her pale eyes shone in the fading light of the afternoon. Her hair was even half bound, with only a few fiery curls falling over one shoulder. He left his hands covering hers for a second longer than was appropriate before pulling back to offer her escort into Thornwood Manor.

"Beautiful in this? Not likely," she muttered, laying a hand on his arm.

"I assure you it is quite likely." He nodded toward the front door where a butler awaited their entry. "Let's be done with this evening, shall we?" He sighed as he looked up at the dark stone structure looming over them in overbearing arrogance, just as its owner was prone to do.

She leaned close to him to whisper, "I believe you are as thrilled about this evening as I am about wearing a blasted gown."

He raised a brow at her. "Do you know you are the only lady of my acquaintance who doesn't enjoy getting dressed?"

"You make it seem as if I go about naked." She crinkled her nose, making her freckles dance.

"You might as well. Those breeches don't hide anything."

"Really?" She slowed her pace. "I hadn't noticed. Perhaps I should wear skirts."

"No!" He cleared his throat and turned his attention back to the butler awaiting them at the door. "I wouldn't want you to change into clothing that doesn't suit you."

"Gowns, weighty jewels, and itchy laces don't suit me, that much is true."

Andrew glanced down at her bare neck. She wasn't wearing any jewelry except for the small ovals of black jet on each ear. She was so different.

His mother had come close to sending his father to debtors' prison with her taste for finery when he was a boy. Her greed had forced Andrew into his role as a horse breeder at age ten, all to pay for her shopping habits. The strain of it had killed his father, months too soon to see Andrew's ideas and hard work achieve the first hint of success. Even if his father hadn't passed away in debtors' prison, his mother had ended his life and ripped him from Andrew's in the process.

It was rather refreshing to find a lady who didn't desire to spend all her money on frivolous matters.

His eyes narrowed on her. Katie must have different interests on which to spend all her father's funds. Her cottage was full to the rafters with such things after all. But…surely her paints, books, and musical instruments didn't cost that much. Having interests wasn't such a crime.

He led her into Thornwood Manor. The butler left after taking their hats and such and went in search of their hosts for the evening. Andrew turned back to Katie. No matter how much he discovered about her, he still wanted to know more.

Everything in life should sort easily into categories to be filed away in an orderly fashion. Katie was a lady, but she defied every rule of the female persuasion and refused to be filed away anywhere. Therefore she remained sitting on the desk in his mind, unfiled, uncategorized. This was what he'd decided last night when he lay awake, at any rate. It would explain why he kept thinking of her—she was unfinished work, a project from the day left to complete.

"Why are you looking at me like that?"

"I wasn't aware I was looking at you in any particular fashion."

"You're scowling."

"Was I?"

"Indeed."

"It must be the atmosphere here," he grumbled, pulling his gaze from her.

"I've always thought of Thornwood Manor as misunderstood." She smiled as she trailed a finger over the carving on the dark wooden staircase leading to the upper floors. "It seems a dreary place, but there's an understated pleasantness."

"Quite understated," he muttered as he glanced around at the portraits of angry-looking Thornwood ancestors lining the walls.

Moving farther into the main hall, he was squinting up at the heavy-timbered ceiling when he heard laughter coming from a room down the hall as a door was thrown open. Lady Lillian Phillips—or Her Grace now, he supposed—came to greet them. She didn't look as he remembered her, yet he knew her all the same. Her hair wasn't bound so tightly that it looked painful anymore. She had an ease to her smile now that she hadn't possessed before. Could she be happy with Thornwood? He must have greatly misjudged her two years ago if that was true. He offered her a nod.

"Lord Amberstall, we were so pleased to hear you were in the neighborhood," she greeted as she moved closer.

The last time he'd seen her had been the day of the blasted exhibition. She'd been under consideration as his wife. To the victor went the spoils, it seemed. It was just as well; he had no true desire to wed beyond duty to his title, and there was no rush on that score.

"Your Grace." Andrew bowed over her hand.

"Do come in." With a smile, she motioned to the open door behind her. "Everyone has gathered in the parlor."

"What wonderful news," he muttered, as Katie wound her hand further around his arm and gave it a slight squeeze.

❦

This had been a terrible idea. Andy moved beside her like one of the tiny soldiers her brothers played with when they were children—made of wood with a painted-on smile. Thornwood would most likely be equally uncomfortable, and his poor guests, Lord and Lady Steelings, would have to witness the entire event.

Worst of all, the damned lace trim on her dress was itchy. She wiggled in an attempt to not touch her skin to it, which was completely hopeless as it lined the neck and capped the short sleeves.

"Katie? Lady Katie Moore?" a lady asked as she crossed the room.

Did they know one another? She had brown hair and was not beautiful in the typical sense of the word, but lovely in a different sort of way. Katie couldn't place her, yet she knew she'd seen the small lady before.

"We met in London at a garden party," the woman supplied with a smile. "Lady Sue Green, although I became Lady Steelings not too long after that day. You can call me Sue, though."

"Oh, yes! You assisted me back into my dress."

"Why were you out of your dress? Or perhaps I shouldn't ask," Andy said.

"It was hot," Katie explained with a shrug. She glanced back and forth between Andy and Sue for a second. Was she supposed to offer introductions? Details like this always left her feeling befuddled. She'd had the most basic of training in society, but as it didn't interest her terribly, she'd promptly forgotten every word of it as she rode away from London. Was Andy supposed to do the introductions because he was a man? Perhaps Sue should, as she was the highest-ranking lady in the conversation…

"You do know one another, don't you?" she finally blurted out.

Sue smiled and dipped in a slight curtsy. "Lord Amberstall, we were surprised to hear you were in the neighborhood."

"It certainly wasn't a planned stop on my journey, but Lady Katie has been a perfect hostess."

"Have I?" She raised an eyebrow in his direction. He complained a great deal for someone who thought her perfect in any regard.

His smile turned genuine for a second before he glanced across the room but then it slipped from his face. "If you'll excuse me, I need to go greet our host. Lady Steelings," he offered with a nod.

"It's Sue. I said that only a moment ago, didn't I? I've never understood why we can't speak more openly among friends. It is true I've always been a proponent of chatter. Some even think I speak too much, but I've always thought..." She continued to talk about talking, but Katie's thoughts were with the gentleman who had just left her side.

Katie watched Andy go. He would either make amends with Thornwood, or the rug in this parlor could forever be stained with their blood—only time would tell.

"He seems well," Sue mused, gaining Katie's attention once more.

"Do you think so?" Katie glanced back toward Andy in concern. "He looks rather pale to me."

"So does Thornwood," Sue whispered.

Katie smiled at her. "I suppose you're right."

"I'm so pleased to see you again. I knew when I met you that we could be friends. I told my husband that very day... Well, he wasn't my husband at the time, but he is now..."

Katie looked past Sue to where the men were gathered near the fireplace. Thornwood did look a bit pale this evening. She wished she could read lips and know what was being said. She would have to work on that. Surely she could teach herself to read lips, just as she had taught herself to throw pots, play most musical instruments, and paint murals. Of course, once they went into the dining room, she wouldn't be as far from Andy and would be able to hear what was said between the two men.

When she saw Lily return to the room, Katie grabbed her chance. "I'm famished! Aren't you simply starved?" she pronounced rather loudly to Sue, causing all conversation in the room to cease for a second as everyone turned to stare.

"I couldn't agree more," Thornwood chimed in. "Enough of these dreadful pleasantries. Let's move to the dining room."

Lily covered her surprise at the abrupt change with a small nod. "Yes, I believe everything is ready. Only, have you seen…"

"Without me? Thornwood dear, where are your manners?" The dowager duchess swept into the room, scowling at her son.

"My manners became hungry while you took an hour to repair your hair…and it still looks the same to me. Lily, has my mother's hair changed from this afternoon? Not a single strand has moved."

Lily shot her husband a narrow-eyed glare in response while the dowager duchess turned her back on her son to greet their newest guest. "Lord Amberstall, how lovely it is to see you again. Your mother will be ever so envious that I was able to dine with you this evening."

"Your Grace." He bowed over her hand. "The invitation was very kind of you."

"Now, may we dine?" Thornwood asked, clearly annoyed by the delay.

"Certainly, dear. Lead the way," the older woman offered with a wave of her arm.

Andy fell into step behind Steelings and Sue. Katie stood watching the commotion for a moment before noticing Andy had his arm extended to escort her.

"I can walk to the dining room. I do have my walking stick and it's not that far," Katie complained.

"I meant no offense to your abilities," he leaned close to whisper. "I'm supposed to escort you to the dining room."

"Why?"

"Because that is the way of things. It's what you do."

"Perhaps it's what *you* do," she mumbled under her breath.

"Along with the rest of gently bred society." He wrapped his fingers around hers and placed them on his arm.

"It seems silly when I can find the dining room just fine on my own. I *have* been there before, you know."

"Then you can assist me." He grinned down at her and gave her hand a brief pat.

With a roll of her eyes, she began moving down the hallway after the others. Seeing that it was pointless to carry it, she left her walking stick leaning against a door frame in the hall and wound her other hand around Andy's arm as well.

"You're practically hanging on my arm, you know. I thought you could walk on your own."

"I thought you were strong, but here you are complaining of a lady's weight on your arm," she retorted.

"I'm not complaining." He looked down at both of her hands before sliding his eyes back up to her face in a way that made her blush. "It just isn't proper."

She tightened her hands on him, drawing him closer to her side as they walked toward the dining-room door. "I'm not proper."

"I've noticed." His deep voice rumbled near her ear.

She glanced up, expecting to see a scowl on his face, but was met with a warm grin that lit his golden eyes. Her breath caught in her throat, although she wasn't sure why. She stopped for a moment in the doorway to the dining room, unable to look away from his gaze. The rest of their party moved ahead and were reaching their seats when she finally unwound her hands from his arm and fled to the other side of the table.

What sort of spell was he casting on her with his heated looks and teasing grins? She found her seat next to Sue and flopped into it with her pulse still racing. She studied her empty plate for a few minutes, not trusting what she would find in Andy's eyes if she looked up.

"Lord Amberstall, did I hear rightly that you've been in Scotland all this time?" the dowager duchess asked from farther down the table.

"Yes, Your Grace. Steelings was kind enough to lend me his cottage there."

"You've been living in a cottage? Really, Amberstall." The dismay written on the dowager duchess' face was akin to discovering he'd been living with a family of wild jungle cats.

"What's so terrible about living in a cottage?" Katie asked as she attempted to adjust her gown so that the lace didn't touch her as she leaned forward in her seat.

The dowager duchess sent her a stern look over the rim of her wineglass. "You know my thoughts on that matter, dear."

"Perhaps the word 'cottage' is deceiving in this case. Steelings has a livable home with two servants there." Andy sent a knowing glance at Katie from across the table.

Her soup spoon clattered to the table. She usually had such nimble fingers. What was wrong with her this evening? She retrieved her spoon before anyone could comment on her clumsiness.

"Oh, perhaps we should visit while we're traveling," Sue suggested from Katie's side. "I would like to see my husband's lands. And I've never been to Scotland."

"Anything you wish, my lady." Steelings grinned at his wife.

"Oh, Sue, you can't possibly wish to go to such a damp and hostile environment," the dowager duchess argued. "No offense, Steelings."

"None taken, Your Grace."

"I think it would be lovely. Sometimes the harshest environments inspire us, if only to simply enjoy the warmth of a fire. Don't you think so?"

"But there's nothing there, dear. Lord Amberstall, tell her the truth of Scotland. However did you fill your days? Two years in such a place—I can't imagine."

"The rest was needed," Andy answered as he stared into the depths of his soup.

"How much rest can one stand?"

"Mother," Thornwood warned, causing a distinct silence around the table.

"I trust all was in order in Scotland, Amberstall?" Steelings asked, finally redirecting the conversation. "Were the sheep where I left them?"

Andy lifted his gaze to Steelings with a thoughtful frown. "There are a few more of them now."

"Are there?"

"I'm sure your man of business will inform you of the details soon. I made quite a few improvements, offset by the increase in the numbers of your sheep, of course."

"You grew that weary of the sights? You do know there's a little inn nearby with decent lager and a brunette barmaid who will..." Steelings broke off with a sheepish look for his wife.

"Oh, don't stop on my account. Please, continue your story."

"She brings lager to your table and sings songs about the sanctity of marriage," Steelings concluded with a smile.

"I don't think you're being entirely truthful, darling."

"You're right." Steelings laughed, taking a sip of his wine.

"Really, Steelings," the dowager duchess admonished as Thornwood chuckled from the head of the table.

At the older woman's continued scowl, Katie thought a change of subject matter was in order. "Amberstall is quite good at overseeing improvements. He has already seen to several repairs at my stables."

"That was nothing. You're seeing to my horse. It's the least I can do."

"We heard of the difficulties you've had with your horse, Amberstall," Lily said, looking down the table with a sympathetic smile.

"Yes, Shadow's Light took quite the fall."

Thornwood leaned forward, meeting Andy's gaze. "If you need to continue your journey faster than Shadow's Light can heal, you can use one from our stables."

"No!" Katie and Andy said at the same time. They shared a guilt-ridden glance, then both turned their attention back to their food.

"That won't be necessary," Andy added after a moment. "Thank you for the offer, though."

Katie glanced up the table to where Thornwood sat looking terribly amused over something.

"Amberstall, now that you've returned to the country, will we see you in London?" the dowager duchess asked with a joyful gleam in her eye that Katie didn't quite trust.

"Yes, I should have things sorted on my estate in time for the season." He attempted a smile, but it didn't reach his eyes. He must be focused on management of his estate, not London life. She felt quite the same about London, which was a bit ironic.

"Perfect! And Katie, I assume you will be returning to town as well?" the dowager duchess asked.

The question caught her off guard. Was anyone expecting her to make another trip to London? Surely not now. Her place was on Ormesby lands, within her cottage. She had a limp, only wore a dress when she absolutely had to do so, and had deplorable manners. One of those issues alone should have kept her safe from outings in society, but she'd been sure the collection of faults would keep her home for good. "I hadn't planned on it, Your Grace."

"Don't be silly. Of course you're coming to London. If your father doesn't plan to attend, you can come with us. Roselyn will be home by then, and I'm sure she will want to visit town."

"I don't think I should…"

"Of course you should, dear. You already missed this season. And I'm sure Amberstall here will want to renew his acquaintance with you. Won't you, Amberstall?"

"Of course."

"Will you continue the tradition of the party at Amber Hollow?" Sue asked.

"I'm not sure I should, under the circumstances," Andy hedged.

Lily coughed, choking on the sip of soup she'd just taken.

"What a shame. Lord Steelings and I have fond memories of the last gathering there."

"Oh, come now, Lord Amberstall. The party always proves entertaining," the dowager duchess said, glancing over to Lily, who was still trying to recover from the soup. "And clearly Her Grace agrees with me."

"Oh, indeed," Lily managed to say.

"The degree of entertainment is what concerns me."

"I found it quite entertaining," Sue mused, clearly misunderstanding Andy's meaning.

Andy's grip on his wineglass threatened to shatter the crystal, but when he glanced up, it was with a pleasant smile. "Are you expecting a harsh winter here on the moors?"

The dowager duchess pursed her lips and studied Andy over the rim of her wineglass as she took a drink. She might allow the subject of the party to die for now, but it was far from over. Katie had seen that look in the woman's eyes before, and it never boded well for the recipient.

"I do hope not," Lily replied. "I'm already looking forward to working in the rose gardens when the weather warms."

As the footmen came around to retrieve the soup course, Katie leaned back to give him room to lift her bowl from the table. But when she moved, the lace trim across the back of her neck scratched across her skin, making her squirm within her gown. This would be the last time she would ever let Mrs. Happstings choose a dinner gown for her. She arched her back in an attempt to find comfort within her clothing, bumping the footman's arm with her head in the process.

She gasped and looked up, hoping the dregs of her soup would not find their way into her hair. The young man was fumbling to regain control of the silver platter. But just as he did, offering her a small nod, her spoon slipped from the edge of the platter.

There was a clatter of china on silver as the footman tried to grab the utensil before it fell. Her eyes closed in silent anguish as the pea-soup-covered spoon slid down her spine, trapped within her itchy gown.

The footman gasped and made to reach for it. His fingers were a breath away from reaching into the back of her gown when he must have thought better of it and pulled away.

"Is everything all right?" Lily asked from down the table.

"It's fine." Katie turned to look up at the footman. "It's fine," she repeated.

His face was bright red as he paused beside her, clearly not wanting to leave her side when she had a dirty spoon in her dress.

Her eyes flared at him with a silent plea that he leave, and he finally fled the room with the platter in his hands.

Had anyone seen what had happened? Her gaze slid around the table. Only Andy was staring at her in wide-eyed horror. Of course. He would have to be the one to know she now sat with a dirty spoon down the back of her dress. She bit her lip and looked down at the table. She had done the proper thing, hadn't she? She couldn't very well strip down to remove a spoon from her dress in the middle of the Thornwood dining room.

The next course was served just as Sue leaned close to whisper, "You know you have a soup spoon in your gown, don't you?"

"Do I?" Katie tossed an innocent smile at her.

"At least soup is warm," Sue whispered. "I once spilled elderflower ice down my dress. I don't recommend it—quite cold, you know."

"Ice does tend to be cold." Katie was having difficulty making idle chatter under the circumstances.

"Perhaps I can help," Sue offered.

"I know I loosened my dress in public before, but I'd really rather not…"

"Did you know," Sue announced, gaining

everyone's attention, "that it is customary in France to stretch one's legs between courses of a meal?"

"No it isn't," Thornwood argued.

"Oh yes, it is indeed. Steelings, tell them, darling." She looked at her husband with an expectant smile.

Steelings studied his wife for a moment before saying, "The French stand between courses, just as my wife proclaims."

"What?" Thornwood narrowed his eyes at his friend.

Sue cleared her throat and stood. "So, in honor of our recent return from France, I think we should all stand. I feel refreshed and ready for the next course already."

With a screech of chairs sliding away from the table, everyone stood. But the spoon was still lodged in Katie's stays against her back.

"The French have such interesting ideas." The dowager duchess chuckled as she stood, looking up and down the table at everyone. "Standing…it's so foreign!"

"Where did you eat in France where they did this?" Thornwood asked Steelings, finally rising to his feet.

"The question is where did we eat where they did not." Steelings shot a questioning glance at his wife, but supported her lie all the same.

"It's not working," Katie whispered to Sue with an extra wiggle.

Sue pursed her lips for a moment before announcing, "In France, when having a truly abundant feast with beloved friends, they also hop…to show their gratitude for the hospitality. I'm grateful for the company this evening." She bounced on her feet. "Aren't you pleased with the food tonight?" She looked at Katie.

Katie hopped on her feet, trying to dislodge the spoon. "I'm quite grateful for the hospitality, as you can see." Her eyes flared as she looked across the table to Andy for support.

He gave her a tiny shake of his head before finally rolling his eyes and bouncing once on his toes. "I, too, am pleased to be here."

"And I'm the one they call mad..." Thornwood mused from the head of the table. "The French do not bounce, hop, or in any way jump between courses."

Lily leaned toward her husband. "If our guests say this is French custom, then so it is."

"If Steelings told you the sea spilled into a great teacup on the horizon, would you believe him?" Thornwood grumbled in response.

"It doesn't, just so you know," Steelings cut in. "That teacup business was nonsense, but bouncing in France is fact."

"Thank you for your honesty," Lily replied with her eyes narrowed on her husband.

Katie was still bouncing and squirming at her place at the table. The damned spoon! With a final shake of her bodice while arching back over her chair, the spoon fell to the floor with a loud clatter. She smiled at Sue. "I believe we can sit now."

"Yes, let's sit. We wouldn't want our food to grow cold."

"Oh, that was fun. I should like to travel to France—such a festive people," the dowager duchess said with a smile as she sat down.

Andy was studying the food on his plate, refusing to meet Katie's eyes, although his shoulders shook with silent laughter. Well, at least her discomfort was serving some purpose this evening. She sighed and took a bite of her food.

"I'm so pleased we met again," Sue offered with a chuckle.

"I still find it hard to believe that you remember me."

"Some people are unforgettable."

"I agree," Andy added with a smile.

Steelings lifted his glass to his lips with a frown as he looked down the table at her. "I believe we met once in London as well. Your family's home in town is across the street from Rutledge House, is it not?"

"It is." Katie tilted her head, studying Steelings' face. He did look vaguely familiar—tall, thin, but not overly so, with dark green eyes. She had seen him somewhere before. "Did we meet there?"

"You actually beat me soundly in an impromptu horse race down the street."

Thornwood let out a great round of laughter from down the table.

"She what?" Andy asked, leveling her with a glare across the table. "You raced through the streets of London?"

"Yes." She looked down at her plate. "That was before…"

"She beat you, Steelings?" Thornwood was still laughing.

"Go on and laugh. Lady Katie is a talented rider."

"Was," she corrected, lifting the glass of wine to her lips with a shaking hand.

"And will be again one day," Andy added. He was watching her in that intense manner he had that made her squirm more than any itchy lace could accomplish.

She didn't know what to say. She couldn't argue with him with this many neighbors and guests watching them. She could feel heat rising in her cheeks and everyone's eyes on her, assessing her injury, assessing her. She looked down at the food on her plate and did the only thing she could think to do. Taking a large bite of beef covered in a rich butter sauce, she exclaimed, "Mmm…this is delicious!"

"It's my favorite as well," Lily replied with a smile.

"I could help you ride again, you know, if you wish," Andy stated, clearly not deterred by her change of subject.

"I don't wish." She met his gaze across the table in silent challenge. Her heart was racing. There seemed to be something akin to hope in his gaze, but she'd given up on such fruitless emotions long ago.

His jaw tightened as he said, "The food is quite good, Thornwood. I'm glad I was able to attend this evening. Perhaps there is reason to our paths in life, a reason why Shadow's Light was injured here, of all places." He raised an eyebrow at her.

Was he implying that he was here to teach her to once again ride a horse? What arrogant rubbish! "Or perhaps your visit is pure coincidence. You could have just as easily been tossed from Shadow's back at the next town over and you would be dining with the local gentry there." Katie raised her glass to him and drained the last of her wine.

"Either way, we are glad to have you in the neighborhood for a time. Although I think you're better off here than with the Dunley family down the road a stretch—insufferable people," Thornwood said with his usual irreverent tone.

Andy nodded to Thornwood with a grim smile before turning back to Katie. He seemed to be daring her to make a move, as if this were a game of chess.

Damn, that was something else she would have to put on her list to learn—chess. Not that it would help in this circumstance. Still, there had to be something she could do. Lifting her knife to her lips, she stuck out her tongue and took a giant lick. "Delicious," she stated, licking the buttery sauce from the corner of her mouth.

With a satisfied smile, she watched Andy's face contort in shock, mixed with some other emotion she didn't recognize. All she knew was that look in his eyes seeped heat through her body and into her bones. Just when she was sure she'd won their game, she had the oddest notion that in truth, she'd lost.

Eight

KATIE SANK INTO HER CORNER OF THE COACH, WRAPPING her arms around her body in an attempt to warm herself. While they were inside the manor, it had begun misting, which turned into a steady downpour by the time they stepped out into the drive. So, they were now riding back to Ormesby in one of the covered Thornwood rigs—propriety tossed out the window in favor of warm, dry clothing.

Out of the corner of her eye, she glanced at Andy, sprawled out on the seat beside her with his arms crossed as well. She suspected his posture was more for brooding than gathering warmth. He'd conducted himself well in Thornwood's company with smiles and polite comments, but now that the evening was over and they were alone, he wasn't quite so buoyant. And in his angry state, he seemed larger than before.

Surely he hadn't sat this close on the ride to Thornwood. The conveyances were roughly the same size, yet now she could almost feel the heat of his body next to hers. The smell of the starch on his shirt mixed with his shaving soap and filled the air with an entirely male scent, which she found both intoxicating and annoying. It was mostly annoying because it was intoxicating, but it irritated her nonetheless. She rolled her eyes at her desire to take only deep breaths and glared out the window covered in rain splatter.

He shifted beside her on the bench seat and stretched his legs out even more, brushing the side of her thigh with the movement. "At least the evening is over," he grumbled.

It was shameful, but she didn't wish to move away from him now that he was so close to her. She told herself it was simply because he was warm and she was chilled, but that was a lie. She saw the manor begin to disappear as they rolled down the drive. "They aren't bad people, you know."

"Steelings isn't, I agree." He shrugged. "And his wife is pleasant enough, even if she does talk to no end and makes up ridiculous stories about France." He nudged her with his knee.

"Sue was only trying to assist me. I like her."

"How did you manage to get a spoon inside your gown anyway? I've honestly never heard of such." He shook his head as he studied her. "Perhaps if you hadn't squirmed about in your seat…"

"I was itchy," she complained.

His eyes narrowed on her. "You do know that you can't scratch things while at dinner, don't you?"

"Now I do. And now I also know the reason behind that little rule." She tried to sound as innocent as he considered himself, but her comment came out as guarded and guilty. She grimaced and glanced away.

"I thought everyone knew the rules of society," he mused. "Did you not have a…"

"A mother?" She turned back to him to finish his thought, her throat tightening around the words. "No, I didn't."

He shifted to look her in the eye as he said, "I was going to say 'a governess.'"

"Oh," she replied in a breathless whisper. She shouldn't have jumped to conclusions, but she was far too accustomed to criticism. "I had several governesses, but they always quit rather quickly… I don't know why."

"Mmm, I can't imagine."

"Why does it matter?" she asked as she elbowed him in the arm. She should be pleased he was recovering from their dinner, but did he have to find such fault with her? "If I desire to lick sauce from my knife—or my plate, for that matter—I should be able to do so. It was delicious sauce, not to mention a compliment to the Thornwood Manor cook. She will be quite pleased when she hears of it—if she hears of it."

"I'm sure she already knows of it," he said, his brows drawn together.

"And I'm glad if she does."

"Order and proper behavior are all we have, Katie." His gaze softened as he tried to plead his side of things. "I am a viscount, and you are the daughter of an earl. There are certain expectations for us."

"My way brightened a cook's evening. What did your proper behavior do?" She leveled a glare on him and refused to look away. He could keep his perfect conduct; she wanted to live her life. "Order and proper behavior are not all I have. And they are not all you have, either."

He ran a hand through his hair, rumpling it and pushing it from his eyes. "Does nothing have a sorted time and place in your life?"

"Why?" She searched his face in the dark carriage, seeing only the glow of his eyes on her. "Do you want to sweep in and fix *my* life now, Andy? I'm not a stable. I can't be mended with boards and nails."

"No, I want..." He sighed. "I want to know you, to understand anything at all about you, because you are the most maddening lady I have ever encountered." The intensity of his gaze there in the darkened carriage singed her, making her flinch.

"You didn't seem to mind my company last evening over dinner," she hedged, returning his gaze even though her body screamed to pull away, to look away.

"I don't mind your company now as we bicker in a damp carriage. I actually enjoy it, which is most disconcerting."

Had he shifted closer to her, or had she imagined that? She didn't move away, only straightened her spine to face him down. "It was never my intention to trouble you so."

"Wasn't it?" he asked, searching her face for some clue hidden there. "You could have sold me a horse and sent me on my way nearly a week ago."

"And I didn't because you didn't apologize for breaking my pottery wheel, and neither did you thank me for saving your life," she spat back. "Now who has poor manners?"

"I believe you still hold that honor this evening, my lady."

All because of a silly spoon? She'd done all right other than that mishap, hadn't she? None of the people there seemed offended by her actions, only him. "They are my friends and neighbors. And I wore a dress."

He sighed and leaned back against the seat, breaking the connection between them. "Other than friends, they are also a high-ranking family among the peerage, Katie. In this world we live in, we can't forget the part played by rank in society. I'm sure the spoon incident will be overlooked, so not to worry. Their family is known for madness, after all. What's a mistake at dinner in the face of such a reputation?"

"Thornwood is not mad! I've never understood how people can be so cruel!"

They fell into silence for a moment with only the crunch of the carriage wheels turning to punctuate the quiet. She didn't know what else to say, and he didn't seem inclined to apologize.

After what seemed an eternity, he turned back toward her to ask, "Are we to argue about everything tonight?" There was an edge of emotion to his voice that almost sounded like fear. But that couldn't be—he was arrogant and strong. People like him didn't feel fear, did they?

"It seems we will," she stated, even though she didn't want to fight with him any longer.

He pulled a white handkerchief from his pocket and waved it above his head before leaning in and flinging it back and forth in front of her, almost brushing her nose with it.

She leaned away. "What are you doing?"

"Waving my white flag in surrender of this battle. I'm weary of fighting with you, Katie. You win. Have deplorable manners. What business is it of mine? Soon I will be gone."

She nodded and fell silent for a moment, watching the raindrops slide off the carriage window as they moved down the road. Turning back to him, she begrudgingly offered, "You handled Thornwood well. I know you don't care for him after…"

"You did well, befriending Her Grace and Lady Steelings," he cut in before she could finish.

"You look nice in formal dinner attire," she countered.

"You are beautiful this evening in a gown, with your hair pinned up."

She glared at him. "Now I know you're only stating platitudes."

"It's true." He lifted his hand and touched a lock of hair where it fell over her shoulder, skimming his knuckles across her collarbone in the process. He pulled his hand back with what was clearly a sudden awareness of his actions.

She couldn't move. A groom or two had brushed against her while working plenty of times by accident. She'd been lifted from carriages and she'd been escorted into rooms, but this was different. Andy's touch was unlike anything she'd ever felt, scalding hot, yet she desired more of it. Her eyes met his in the dark as she fought to keep breathing. Finally ripping her gaze away, she managed to squeak out, "I believe we're back to my cottage."

"No, we're not," he replied, glancing out the window. "We've barely left Thornwood grounds."

"Oh, damn. It never used to seem so far away when I would ride over to visit Roselyn." She could feel her cheeks turning pink in spite of the cool weather that had her teeth almost chattering.

"You were cutting across fields, jumping fences…"

"Yes," she whispered.

She didn't realize she was shivering until he slipped an arm around her, pulling her close to his side. "You're freezing," he explained when she jumped at his movement.

Surrounded by his warmth, she relaxed into him a fraction. He laid his hand over the exposed skin below the capped sleeves of her dress. She didn't know what was happening between them or what she was about, but she knew she didn't want him to stop.

"Was that how it happened? Your accident? Jumping can be quite dangerous if you don't know the terrain well," he mused as he rubbed her upper arm to warm her, his rough skin sliding across hers.

"A fact you discovered only recently."

"Indeed," he agreed, but said nothing further.

"I knew the terrain," she finally stated. "I knew my horse…or I thought I did." She looked down at her lap. Even in the dark, she didn't want to look him in the eye when discussing her accident.

"You can know the animal well and still things happen…things beyond your control."

"Yes. The risk is great."

"And sometimes when you risk, you fall," he returned. She'd never discussed her fall before, but somehow the steady movement of his hand on her arm and the warmth of his body beside hers in the dark loosened her tongue. "I don't want to ever fall again," she admitted. "I don't think I would survive it."

"I haven't survived it."

"But you rode this afternoon." She twisted in his embrace to see his face, searching for understanding. "I saw you. And you're still here."

"There's more than one way to fall, Katie." His breathing was ragged and she could feel his heart pounding against her shoulder.

"You know, we have a great deal in common, you and I."

"Impatience with carriage rides and a fondness for animals?" His mouth quirked up in a grin, clearly trying to lighten their conversation.

"No, we had riding accidents that changed our paths in life. But we can still find happiness, Andy." She lifted her hand to his cheek, the rough stubble of beard scratching against her palm. It was brazen of her, but she needed to touch him, to let him know he wasn't alone. She smiled up into his face as she said, "The sun continues to shine after tragedy."

"For both our sakes, I hope you're correct. I've been in darkness for some time now."

"Happiness is a choice." She nodded and pulled her hand from his cheek, laying it back in her lap. She was already missing the contact with him as the embarrassment of touching him began to sink in. She was about to lace her fingers together to keep from reaching out again when he slipped his hand around hers, engulfing it within his.

Her gaze flew to his, but he continued to talk as if nothing had changed. "Did you choose happiness then? Are you pleased with your life, alone in your little cottage?"

"Of course." She was the strangest combination of at ease and on edge, sitting within the comfort of Andy's arms, his hand wrapped around hers, his other hand holding her close.

"As dark as my time in Scotland was, I learned something while there. All the musical instruments, art projects, and books—or in my case, piles of wool and heads of sheep—won't fill gaps in the heart."

"Neither will anger with the world."

"You think me angry?" His eyes narrowed on her.

"You think me unhappy?" she asked in return.

He grinned. "I'm not angry at the moment."

"I'm not unhappy at the moment." A silence hung between them, weighted by smiles and watchful eyes. The carriage slowed. His grasp tightened on her arm to keep her steady while the carriage came to a stop outside her cottage.

Only a few minutes ago she'd cursed the ride for being so far, and now she wished it didn't have to end. His hand was curled around hers, and he was slowly stroking her wrist with his thumb. She didn't want to move away from him—ever.

When was the last time she'd been held like this? Even as a child, had Papa embraced her? Had her mother? She couldn't remember. All she knew was that no other connection had ever felt this way. In his arms, she was strong and weak at the same time, and she wanted more. More of what, she wasn't sure, but she certainly didn't want it to end.

Neither of them moved until the carriage door was opened. She blinked, forcing her eyes to face forward. "I should…" She broke off as she sat forward, leaving his embrace. She moved to the door where the driver stood waiting for her in the rain.

"Until tomorrow evening, when we will be pleased and happy together over dinner," he said as she climbed to the ground.

"Until tomorrow." She wasn't sure if she called the words out or simply said them to herself. But hopefully by tomorrow she would have sorted out her thoughts on what happened between them in the carriage and be able to speak once more.

❧

Sue laughed and looked up at Lily as they strolled down the road. "And there we were with our mouths stuffed with chocolates, unable to reply."

"Which certainly didn't help matters," Steelings added.

Lily turned to respond, since Devon and Steelings trailed behind them. But before she could say a word, she caught the concerned look in Devon's eye.

"Who is that?" Devon asked, his eyes narrowed on a point just ahead off the side of the road.

Lily turned to see who her husband had spotted, scanning the garden of the small stone cottage on the edge of town. "I'm not sure," she murmured as she spied two men dressed in dark clothing treading upon Mrs. Mitchell's broccoli crop.

"One of the neighbors you've yet to meet, perhaps?" Sue offered in explanation.

"No, that's the Mitchells' house. He told me not a

month ago they had no family left." Lily glanced back to Devon. "We should go and introduce ourselves."

"No," he warned. "Steelings and I will go talk to them."

"Do you think they're the criminal sort?" Sue asked, clearly excited by the prospect.

"Well, they don't look like a couple of local vicars out for an afternoon jaunt, that's for certain," Steelings stated as he stepped around Sue to go investigate.

"Stay here," Devon murmured as he passed, giving Lily's arm a brief squeeze. He walked toward the garden gate with Steelings at his side.

"Be careful," she whispered after him, although he was already too far ahead to hear her. She knew Devon had faced enemies at sea and was no stranger to peril, but what if these men were armed? And what of the Mitchells? She searched the white framed windows of their cottage for signs of life. But the cottage was too far away to be seen with any clarity. She sighed. At least she and Sue were well enough back to not be in any danger.

A moment later, there was a tug on her arm as Sue moved forward and urged her to follow suit.

Lily didn't move, only whispered, "We were supposed to stay clear of the ruffians."

"I only want to be close enough to hear," Sue pleaded. "Don't you?"

Lily sighed. Of course she wanted to be closer; she was curious, after all. What if there was some sort of brawl or a foot chase? "All right, but we can't be seen."

Sue shot her a withering look and pulled her toward the base of a large bush, for once not going into the many reasons for hiding or the benefits of having a bush with thick foliage near a garden wall. It was most disconcerting to hear her friend this quiet.

"What are you doing in these parts?" she heard Devon ask as they crept to their hiding place.

Lily pulled a branch toward her to create a gap in the leaves to look through. The two men certainly were not locals, with their hardened features and tattered clothing. They would be at home on the streets of London, but they couldn't have looked more out of place in the Mitchells' vegetable garden.

"My friend here is looking for his cousin," the larger of the two men said. "We got word that he was staying in these parts but don't know our way around." There was something almost sickeningly sweet about the way he spoke that gave Lily chills. Who were these men?

"And you were looking for *your cousin* inside the Mitchells' chicken coop?" Devon asked as Steelings shifted to the side to block the garden gate.

The larger man adjusted the chicken under his arm and smiled. "Of course not. We were passing by when we saw this chicken had escaped the fencing and was pecking away in the road."

"That's not where we spied him," the smaller man corrected, turning toward his friend with a look of confusion crossing his face. "You said…"

"What I said isn't important," the larger man spat back at his friend.

"I'd say it's important. They're stealing that chicken!" Sue's urgent whisper drowned out all sound from inside the garden. "Who steals a chicken anyway? Jewels I understand—they would fetch a price. But why take the risk of being caught for the theft of a piece of poultry?"

"Perhaps they're hungry," Lily replied, trying to follow what was happening in the garden.

"Then go into town and steal from the bakery," Sue continued. "The cakes we had yesterday are much more valuable than anything those two could accomplish with a chicken."

"Let's listen and find out," Lily replied.

"Who is this cousin you're looking for? My home is just up the road. Perhaps I can help," Devon suggested as he took a step to the side to block their retreat.

The larger man eyed Devon. "We don't need anyone to take us in, if that's what you're offering."

"We don't?" The smaller man seemed disappointed. "Oh, no. We don't need that."

"Good, because I wasn't offering." Devon glanced to Steelings, who shrugged. He began again, speaking in slow, deliberate words. "These people from whom you're currently stealing a chicken are my neighbors. I suggest you find your cousin quickly and leave the area."

"Stealing this chicken? That's not at all what we…"

"Find your cousin if you must and leave this area," Devon cut in.

The men shot dark looks at one another for a moment before the larger man stated, "Finding that man is why we're here. As soon as we locate him, we'll be gone. Have no worries on that score." He ground the words out through a clenched jaw in a manner that gave Lily chills.

"I'm pleased I'm not your cousin, as you don't appear to be on very friendly terms with the man," Steelings mused.

"I quite agree," Sue said at Lily's side.

Devon seemed to be of the same mind. "What are your intentions once you find your cousin?" he grated, his voice sounding threatening as he stared the man down.

The smaller man glanced to his counterpart just in time to see the larger man drop the chicken to the ground in a puff of feathers and clucks and take off running. "I'm not sure what got into him. I'll just see…if he…um…" He turned in an instant and fled after his friend.

"I would wager that man doesn't have a happy reunion with his cousin in mind at all," Sue mused.

Lily was still looking through the leaves as she replied, "A bet I would not take since I would like to keep my pin money in my pocket."

"I thought I said to keep back to a safe distance," a deep voice rumbled near her ear.

"Devon!" she exclaimed with a little jump, bumping into his chest as she did so. "We were perfectly safe until you scared the wits out of me."

"Safer than whoever they are searching for, it would seem," he said as he steadied her.

"Do you think they're dangerous?" Lily asked. "We're terribly close to Ormesby lands here, aren't we? We should warn Katie of the threat—she lives alone in a cottage after all."

"Not yet." Devon was still staring off in the distance where the two men had disappeared.

Lily turned to look up into her husband's face, not

understanding why they would not warn their friend of ruffians in the neighborhood. "But someone could be harmed. Katie's cottage is off in some awful forest, according to your mother."

"Mother exaggerates."

"They'd be shot to bits if they neared her to steal a chicken," Sue stated. "She has a blunderbuss."

"Does she?" Devon asked.

"Yes, she promised to show it to me soon. I hope she lets me shoot it."

"Sue, that firearm would be larger than you are," Steelings cut in.

"None of this makes me feel any better about keeping this information from our neighbor." Lily looked up at Devon for answers. "She could be hurt. Or one of her staff…and what of Amberstall?"

"Not if Steelings and I discover what they're after first." Devon tossed a grin at his friend.

"You let them go on purpose, didn't you?" Lily looked from Devon to Steelings and back to Devon. "So that you could track them."

"What do you say, Steelings?" Devon rubbed his hands together in anticipation. "Up for a hunt this afternoon?"

Steelings glanced off in the direction the men had run with a gleam in his eyes. "Always."

Andrew dismounted and stepped through the gate, trudging over the thick grass into the field with one of the horses from the stable trailing behind him. Shadow was resting in the shade of a lone tree while Katie motioned to a groom with her hands. If he could hear her words, perhaps the motions would make sense. As it was, she seemed to be instructing the man on how to stir something in the kitchen or possibly how to twirl a lady about a dance floor. The groom appeared as lost as Andrew was. Andrew concealed a chuckle as he neared them.

"Good morning." His eyes drifted over Katie's standard ensemble of breeches and a loose shirt belted at the waist, hiding nothing from his view. Perhaps dresses on ladies were overrated. "You seem more yourself today."

"Yes, I was feeling a bit off last night on the carriage ride home. All that talk of happiness and anger. I must have had too much wine at dinner." It seemed a likely story, if not for the panic visible in her eyes.

He grinned, knowing all too well that something had passed between them last night. He'd sensed it, too, the change in the air. Whether she was planning to deny it today or not, he knew the truth. "I was referring to your clothing. You're back in your breeches."

"Oh, yes." She looked down at her ensemble and smoothed the shirt over her hip. "That I am." A blush spread up her neck and crept onto her cheeks.

He cleared his throat and looked over at Shadow, running a hand across the back of his neck. "That deep gash will take more time to heal, but are his abrasions healing at least?"

"Yes, I'm told he's healing quite nicely. There's no pulling at the wound. And my poultices work miracles," she stated. "The salve I concocted must be working."

"Haven't you seen it?" He took a few steps toward Shadow.

"Of course. But I'm not the one who changes his bandages."

"It's true, that is no place for a lady. You could get kicked. Better to leave the managing of the horses to a groom."

"I could change your horse's bandages if I chose to do so," she snipped at him. "I've done it plenty of times."

He turned to look at her. Clearly he'd hit a nerve. Could she not even stand to touch a horse? He knew she no longer rode, but he wasn't aware her fear went this deep. He tried to remember a time when she'd touched Shadow's Light or any other horse, but couldn't.

He'd been told by that groom that she no longer went to the stables, but he'd assumed that was due to lack of interest. Could Katie be that fearful of something she once enjoyed? She used to race through the streets of London. She was known in the area for her work with horses. She was able to make a salve that could heal the worst of equine wounds.

"Yet you keep your distance now," he murmured.

"Indeed. I was going to have Shadow's Light exercised today. His leg is well braced and he needs to keep up his strength." There was sadness in her eyes as she glanced at the groom who was checking the animal's bandaging. She pulled her gaze away a second later to ask Andrew, "Would you like to walk Shadow?"

"Only if you join me." He said the words before he could think of the possible outcomes of his offer. He held his breath, hoping he hadn't pushed her too far too fast.

"I can't do that." She blinked up at him, her eyes wide as she clearly searched for an excuse. "My injury."

"Shadow has an injury as well, if you recall. I doubt we will race through any fields today." Her fears had ruled her life for too long. He wanted to see her happy, smiling at him, laughing with him. He ignored the fact that in his mind she was happy at his side. He simply wanted her to be contented for her own sake—he had nothing to do with it.

"Surely you don't require my presence."

"No, I don't." He took a step closer to her. "But I would enjoy it."

She stepped back from him, restoring the void that had been between them a moment ago. "Why?"

"I wish I knew."

"You do know flattery is not your best ability."

He shrugged and held his arm out to her. "It's a useless ability. Flattery has never put food in anyone's mouth."

"Neither have proper manners at dinner," she retorted, taking his arm.

"That has a value. One must be a good dinner guest, or there will be no invitations to dine or attend any other event." He took slow, measured steps toward Shadow's Light. It did not slip his notice that while she never said she would come with him for a walk, she was at his side.

"Why do you need invitations to events?"

"Because business is done in those places." Did she have no knowledge of how things were done? She was the daughter of an earl, but she might as well have been the daughter of a farmhand for all her knowledge of society. "Dining and talking is simply what gentlemen do."

"If that's true, then you haven't done business in some time."

He sighed and gathered Shadow's reins in his hand, giving them a gentle tug to make the horse move. Glancing back to Katie, he saw that she was watching him, waiting for his response. "No, I haven't," he finally confirmed.

"And your estate is still in one piece," she added, clearly trying to make her point, even though he was feeling rather low about it as a result.

"That is debatable, if my mother is to be believed," he grumbled.

"You don't believe your mother?" She raised her eyebrows as she walked beside him with Shadow at their backs.

It was a complicated question. He believed that his mother was worried over perceived danger, but he could not be entirely sure that danger was real. It was like her to overreact, yet the thought of the men on the road made him wonder. He stared out across the moors. "Whether she is right or wrong, I will still have to return to my life soon."

"You mean your business."

He turned back to her and said with a nod, "I do."

She smiled and pointed in front of them with the walking stick in her free hand, waving it across the horizon. "I've always liked the way the moors seem to stretch on forever into the distance, as if none of the world's problems can travel this far. They are there and we are here." She turned back to him, the noonday sun catching the dark red of her hair as a lock blew across her face.

He frowned in thought. "Hiding from the troubles of the world is tiresome work." He would know. It was how he'd spent the past two years of his life.

"Couldn't it be delightful play?" she asked, glancing up at him. "Isn't it all in how you look at it?"

"With art projects and enough musical instruments to start your own orchestra?"

"There are no bagpipes in an orchestra," she replied with her chin raised in defiance.

"And I, for one, am thankful for that fact." He laughed at the look of outrage on her face, her nose wrinkling in little lines of freckles as her mouth fell open.

"Bagpipes are misunderstood," she stated, turning her attention back to the open field.

"Like gloomy castles and misfit animals?" He tugged on the arm that was wrapped around his. "Do you think ill of anything?"

"You." She shot him a green-eyed glare even as her pink lips curled into a smile. "I think ill of you."

"I feel ever so fortunate."

"You should. You're quite special in that way. See? I'm as talented with flattery as you."

"I must admit, I'm beginning to see the benefit in this flattery business." He shot her a teasing grin before turning his attention back to the field ahead.

A silence fell between them as they picked their way across the field, step by step.

"Andy, what exactly was the nature of your relationship with Sue...Lady Steelings?"

He jerked around to look her in the eye. Where

had that question come from? "That was many years ago, Katie."

"Yes. Tell me of it."

He shrugged. "There isn't much to tell. Our families desired a match, but we found we didn't suit."

"Really? What fault did she find in you?" she asked, laughing.

"Why? So you can add it to your tally of dislikes? Pardon me if I don't help you on that score."

"It's only curiosity," she complained.

"If you must know, which it seems you must, I ended things with her."

"She's quite talkative. Is that why? Too much chatter? Or was she not the exotic beauty you pictured hanging on your arm?" She leaned her head against his upper arm and batted her lashes up at him.

She was teasing, yet right now, he couldn't imagine being pleased with some exotic beauty on his arm. After all, someone else wouldn't possess Katie's dark brown lashes that brushed over freckled cheeks with every blink. He shook off the thought. "No, that wasn't the reason."

"Then why did you end things with her?"

He clenched his jaw around the words, knowing Katie would take offense. "She was always dirty."

"She isn't dirty." Katie scrunched her nose up in confusion.

"Now, I believe it was paint, but at the time..." He shrugged.

"Sue's an artist," she stated, as if this finally proved what a dreadful person he was. "Surely you didn't hold her interests against her."

"She had smudges all over her arms. It was quite disconcerting."

Katie pulled her hand from his arm to study the appearance of her own skin. Spotting a speck of mud splatter from where she had rested against a tree earlier, she began rubbing at it. "I should have guessed you would prefer perfectly clean ladies, like Lily. You were fond of her."

"I like your dirtiness." He stilled her hand with his until she lifted her gaze.

She bit her lip for a moment. He longed to smooth the crinkle between her brows, but even touching her arm seemed to startle her. It was like working with a wild horse—he didn't want her to run.

"Andy, I'm not perfect. Far from it."

"I know." In an impulsive moment, he bent and placed a kiss on her wrist where the dirt was smeared. He heard her intake of breath, but she didn't move. "I'm beginning to wonder if I was mistaken in my earlier thoughts on perfection."

Shadow's Light huffed behind him and nudged his shoulder.

"I think someone agrees with this new view of life," Katie breathed.

"He would, the great beast." He grinned and tucked her hand around his arm as he retrieved Shadow's reins.

"Come along." She pulled on his arm, sounding more herself. "Let's see if we can find some dirt to roll about in."

"Let's not get carried away. I'm only *considering* a change of view on the dirtiness issue."

"Which is a large, dirty, flawed, imperfect step for such a fastidious lord with old-maid tendencies like you." She grinned at him as she delivered the barb.

"Are you calling me an old maid?"

"If the overly starched shirt fits…" She broke off with a shrug and an innocent smile.

"As if you would know anything about the proper care of one's wardrobe. This is a perfectly pressed shirt. I met with Mrs. Happstings to discuss the care of my garments just this morning."

"Exactly." She laughed and dropped his arm, stepping out of his reach, clearly fearing retaliation—as well she should.

"What do you mean exactly?" He stomped off after her in search of answers. It was surprising how quickly she could move when she chose to do so. At times it almost seemed as if she had no injury at all. He'd wondered about the extent of her injuries on several occasions since he'd met her. He shook his head, adjusted the reins in his hand, and followed Katie across the field back toward the stables. He would sort out the truth of her injury soon enough. If only his own troubled thoughts could be sorted as easily.

Nine

KATIE LEANED ON THE FENCE, SPINNING THE WALKING stick between her fingers to draw small circles in the dirt at her feet. She'd been here since early morning, watching the horses in the field. They seemed at peace with their surroundings. They were bound by fences on all sides, and yet they somehow gave the impression of possessing freedom.

Could one live within constraints and still have freedom? She'd never found a way to do so.

She turned at the sound of horse hooves approaching. "Good morning. I borrowed one of your horses for my morning ride," Andrew explained, patting the horse on the side of the neck. "I hope you don't mind."

"Of course not." She tried to smile, but the sight of him, with his hair messy from the wind, the flush from the sun on his face, and his commanding posture on horseback, didn't allow it. Instead, she feared she gave him a slack-jawed stare, which she quickly remedied by looking away.

"I trust you're feeling well today?"

"Yes, my apologies. I wasn't feeling up to dinner

last night." She could feel the heat rising in her cheeks. "I must have pushed myself too hard with the walk yesterday."

"Hmmm," he replied with his eyes narrowed on her. He knew she was lying.

The truth was that she hadn't been hurt. She'd needed time to sort out her thoughts. She could feel herself changing, bending into something new, the longer she was in Andy's presence, like the clay she worked at the wheel—but what would she become? Even after a night alone, she didn't know the answers. "It is unfortunate. I was looking forward to our dinner together."

"As was I, but I'm glad you're feeling better today after an evening of rest."

"Oh yes. I'm in fine form this morning." Resting had been the one thing that hadn't happened. Sleep had eluded her. Instead, she'd spent the evening trying to fill her time with books, music, anything but thoughts of Andy. She stifled a yawn.

"Good. I'm on my way to return this one to the stables." He gave the horse a pat. "I'm going to retrieve Shadow's Light for a short walk. You can join me."

She glanced down at the walking stick in her hand. She'd come too close to exposing her secret shame yesterday. She couldn't take that chance again. "I can't," she murmured.

"Yes, you look terribly busy," he scoffed before adding, "And ill. Don't forget ill."

She met his eyes, attempting a convincing excuse. "I could be waiting to meet someone here."

"Are you?"

"No." She shifted her stance against the fence. So much for convincing excuses. She couldn't think with him looming over her on horseback like he was.

"Then come with me." He nodded toward the stable. "I'll change horses and meet you at the gate to the far pasture."

She nodded, unable to form words as she watched him canter away.

"Idiot," she mumbled to herself as she set off toward the gate. So much for avoiding him until her mind was clear. She might as well have had her blasted dinner with him last night, for as much good as the time alone with her thoughts had done her.

A few minutes later, he arrived with Shadow's Light following him. "I thought we would follow the boundary of your property. I'd like to check the fences while we're out."

She glanced ahead to the low stone wall stretching off into the distance. "This is the side bordering Thornwood's lands."

"All the more reason to check the fences," he stated, holding his arm out to her.

She looked up at him as she wound her hand around his forearm. "Do you still not trust him?"

"Hmm." He busied himself with straightening Shadow's reins.

She dropped his arm and stepped in front of him to gain his attention. "What do you think he will do to you here?" She gestured to the moors. "We're alone. There's no one to speak ill of us, no one to ridicule us, no one to hurt us…"

"Is that what happened to you in London? You did race a horse through the streets…" He broke off with a shrug of his shoulders.

"Not London in particular." She took a few steps in silence with her arm looped around his again, hoping he would move on to another topic. But when she chanced a glimpse at him, he was still looking at her, waiting.

Katie rolled her eyes and sighed. "Society as a whole has never quite accepted me into the fold. Shocking, I know."

"Quite."

"I'm better suited to a life here."

"Watching horses you're afraid to go near?" he asked in a soft, deep voice. Yet it hit her the same as if he'd yelled the words at her.

She stopped walking, rooted to the spot by his accusation. She trained her eyes on the trees in the distance. "I'm not afraid of horses."

"I know fear." He stepped around her to confront her once more. "And I see fear in your eyes every time a horse nears you."

"You don't understand," she muttered, looking up into his face.

"I think I understand more than most."

She wanted to believe him. Perhaps he did know fear. But how could that be? He was too arrogant to allow anything to bother him. He was a large man, thick with muscles and with hands accustomed to work. What could he possibly fear? She bit her lip and studied him for a moment. There was certainly more to fear in the world than horses. He had faced the dread of confronting his enemies only a few nights ago. Did it have something to do with Thornwood or his disappointment of two years ago? She opened her mouth to ask him. "Andy…"

"Come, give me your hand," he cut in as he opened his palm to her.

"Why?" She choked out the word, looking from his face to his hand before her eyes drifted back to his face. She was afraid of what she would see there, what he was planning.

"Trust me."

The warmth of his tone soaked into her bones, making her breathing turn shallow. She watched him for a moment, the steadiness of his stance, his eyes… Could she trust him? She lifted her hand.

He curled his fingers around her palm and gave her a slight nod before turning to stand behind her. His arm cradled hers as his chest brushed against her back. With one slow, deliberate movement, he lifted her hand into the air toward Shadow's muzzle.

When she realized what he was doing, she tried to pull back, bumping into the wall of his broad chest. She couldn't breathe. Twisting, she tried to plead with him not to make her do this, but he held her steady.

"Shh…easy… You can do it." He dropped the reins and laid his other hand on her shoulder, rubbing away the tension he must have sensed there.

She turned back around as he guided her a step forward. He lifted her hand once more. She was about to tell him she couldn't when Shadow lifted his head and she felt the horse's warm breath beneath her palm. She jumped, dropping the stick in her other hand and grabbing a fistful of Andy's coattail instead. He held her, never shifting, while she pressed her hand to Shadow's muzzle.

Her heart pounded. She hadn't been in this place since that dreadful day over a year ago. Alone, she wouldn't be able to withstand the uncertainty of being this close to a horse, this close to her old life. But Andy's strength seemed to surround her. She could feel the heat of his body against her back as his heart beat in a steady rhythm against her, through her. His hand had drifted to her neck at some point in the past few minutes, and he trailed his rough fingers up and down the top of her spine. Her breaths were ragged, and she wasn't certain whose touch was causing that.

"See? You're safe. I'm right here."

"Um-hmm," she chirped in a voice far too high to be natural.

He settled his hand back on her shoulder and gave her upper arm a brief squeeze. "I knew you could do it."

Katie turned far enough to look up at him. "I didn't." She smiled at him, amazed by his belief in her.

He stilled for a moment, looking into her upturned face as if seeing her for the first time. Then his eyes crinkled at the corners and a grin crossed his face.

In that small second of time, he seemed carefree and young. The burdens of life weren't weighing him down, and it was only the two of them in existence. Was this what happiness looked like? Was the same lighthearted gleam reflected back in her eyes? She wasn't expecting Andy to bring anything but hardship to her life, yet here they were grinning at one another.

"Now that you're this far, you'll be back on a horse in no time."

She pulled back, her smile faltering. "No," she stated, stepping out of his embrace and backing away from him and the horse. "My injury…I can't do that." She picked up her walking stick as if it proved her words.

"An hour ago you didn't trust yourself to get near a horse, much less touch one."

"I trust myself—it's the horses I find difficult in that regard." She'd never spoken of her worries to anyone. What was he doing to her? She couldn't think.

"I don't think so." He took a step closer to her, leaving Shadow to continue chewing on grass as he closed the gap between them. "I see the way you look at Shadow. You see to his care every day, and he's healing because of you. You wouldn't go to such lengths for an animal you didn't trust."

She swallowed and glanced away, looking to the grove of trees just to his right. "Perhaps I only want you gone from the estate as quickly as possible."

"Do you?" His deep voice rumbled from right in front of her, causing her eyes to snap back to his.

She couldn't speak; her face grew warm.

He grasped one of her hands in his as he searched her face. "Katie…"

Whatever he'd been about to say was lost to the sound of laughter coming from the small grove of trees on the opposite side of the stone wall.

They turned to see Sue stumbling into view as she dusted off her skirts, her husband trailing behind her. Steelings shook his coat into place and closed the gap in pursuit of his wife. The couple didn't appear to notice they were no longer alone, as Steelings reached out and grabbed Sue's waist, pulling her back to him. Katie shot a sideways glance at Andy, shrugging in silent question.

Unfortunately, judging by the concerned look on his face, he wasn't sure of the social protocol in such a situation. Should they speak to the visiting friends or sneak away, hopefully unseen? The dilemma held him frozen in place.

As they stood in plain sight of the couple now locked in a heated embrace, Andy mouthed words Katie should have understood and tugged on her hand.

"What?" she whispered with a shake of her head.

He sighed and tried again, pointing first to Shadow's Light and then to her with a whisper so quiet it was drowned out by the breeze.

She grinned and whispered a quiet, "I should what?"

He leaned close to whisper again, his voice rumbling out in a deep rhythm against her ear. She thought he said, "We should make Shadow's Light anthem have their piracy."

"Shadow's Light has an anthem?" Scotland must be a dull place indeed if he had time to write a song for a horse. And why would he want to sing it now? It made no sense.

He choked back laughter, placing his fist against his mouth and glancing away.

"We should get Shadow's Light…"

She nodded in understanding of every syllable he was whispering, which he clearly found amusing, since he shook with repressed laughter, unable to complete his whispered statement.

"Perhaps we should say hello," she breathed close to his ear.

"No," he whispered, still trying not to laugh, tugging on her hand to lead her to where Shadow's Light had wandered to eat grass. However, before they could take more than a few steps in that direction, the horse snorted and pawed the ground. Katie's eyes flashed to the clearing across the low stone wall as Andy froze in mid-stride, causing her to step on his foot.

"Apologies," she muttered under her breath. But she didn't look to see if he was upset or in pain. She couldn't look away from the couple practically ripping one another's clothes off in broad daylight.

Was this the way gentlemen behaved behind closed doors? She should look away. She blinked and looked back to Andy. Would he do those same things in private? Most likely he had already done so quite a few times. He'd touched her already. Even now, her hand was wrapped within his grasp.

What would his mouth feel like pressed to her breast? She'd witnessed animals in the wild, but this was different. There seemed to be feelings involved—passion, desire. She swallowed and shook the thought from her head. "I do believe we've missed the window of polite hellos being acceptable," she whispered.

"Do you think so?" his voice rasped out beside her. "Let's go."

"Where are we going?" she asked as he pulled her across the field.

"Away from unfortunate social encounters."

"That doesn't leave many places in my experience."

He let slip a bark of laughter.

All movement stopped on both sides of the low stone wall. Katie watched as Sue gathered her dress around her and Steelings tried to shield her from view with his body. Katie finally looked back to Andy, but the damage had already been done.

He met her gaze, amusement over their situation still lingering around his eyes, and murmured, "Perhaps we should run."

"Andy, my knee. I can't run."

He paused for a moment in apparent consideration before scooping her up in his arms and taking off toward Shadow's Light. She giggled as she tightened her grip around his neck. Her fingers brushed against his hair, soft and warm from the afternoon sun. The smile lingering on her face faded as she breathed in the scent of his shaving soap.

What *would* it feel like to have him kiss her? As much as he complained about her, he couldn't be interested in such a thing, could he? Surely not. But there had been moments when he'd held her close and looked at her with hope shining in his eyes. She dared a glance to his lips, trying to imagine what a kiss would be like.

"You're staring at me."

"I was just…thinking," she said against the lapel of his coat.

It was either obvious what she was thinking or he was busy with his own thoughts because he didn't push her for information. When they were well away from their previous location, he slowed his pace. Glancing down at her, he mused, "Even a simple walk with you is an adventure, Katie."

"It was quite...interesting." Her mind was still on the couple in the field.

"You shouldn't have witnessed such a private moment. I hope it hasn't scandalized you to a harmful degree."

"Sue seemed to enjoy her time with her husband," she mused. "Is that what it's like? The desire, I mean."

"I'm not sure that I should answer that question." He was still walking, his eyes focused forward as he spoke.

"Please."

He stopped. Letting her drop lightly to the ground, he stepped away. "It's not my place to talk to you about...that."

"Then who will?" Once she'd said the words, the reality of her question began to sink through her body. There wasn't anyone in her life other than Andy. And it wasn't as if her pet squirrel was any help in this regard.

He glanced away and ran a hand across the back of his neck. "Not here. Grooms could be watching us."

Her heart was pounding as she asked, "Are you going to dine with me tonight?"

He nodded and offered a quick, "Until then." Turning away, he strode toward the stables without a backward glance.

❧

Katie paced the floor of her cottage once more. It meant nothing. She knew it meant nothing to him, yet she paced. Walks together, dinners together, carriage rides together...she was simply a way for Andy to pass the time while here.

She should keep her distance from him, but there

didn't seem to be much point to that effort. He would seek her out as he had thus far. And then he would leave. No one would know of their time together. Once he was gone, she would be alone again in her cottage. But at least she would have the memory of him, the memory of his arms wrapped around her, the memory of his hand wrapped around hers, and the knowledge he would share with her tonight.

At the knock on the door, she forced herself to stop pacing. Spying her walking stick where she'd left it by the door, she dove for it and scurried back to the middle of the room. She leaned on the stick as she called out, "Come in."

"My apologies for causing you to wait for your dinner," Andy offered as he stepped inside. "I was told I needed to acquire some patience if I wanted to wear my own shirt this evening. Your servants certainly speak their minds."

Her stomach grumbled in response to the delicious smells coming from the basket in his hands. "As should we all," she muttered, wondering what they would be eating. "Without honesty, what do we have?"

"A well-run household?" He arched a brow as he set the basket on the table.

She joined him at the table, sitting in her usual seat across from him. "My father is rather unorthodox in the running of his house."

"Hmmm," he replied as he unpacked their dinner. It was the same pursed-lipped noise he always made when he had a contrary view of things.

She was still learning who he was, but that much she understood. "You don't agree," she supplied.

He paused to tap his fingers on the table in thought before meeting her gaze with a grin. "We should eat."

"He's always had a different outlook on things, since he wasn't raised expecting the title." She shrugged, picking at the plate of fruits with her fingers. "Father spends most of his time over at his mines anyway—he always has."

"He has mines? Where? What is there to mine in this region?"

"Jet." She lifted the small black stone from about her neck for him to see. "The mines are at Roseberry Topping. It's the hilltop you can see from the back gardens."

"How unusual," he mused, taking a bite of food.

"Is it? You have a business on your land."

He scoffed at the absurdity of her comparison. "Yes, but that's horses."

"Which explains everything." She popped a bite of apple into her mouth.

"Of course it does. Wine?"

"Yes, please." She watched as he filled one of the glasses he'd brought with him from the house. His hands were worn from his work with horses, yet he held the bottle with years of ingrained grace. What a contradiction he was. She smiled until she noticed he was watching her. Casting her eyes down to her plate, she searched for words to fill the silence. "I believe I'm still shaken from being so close to Shadow this afternoon."

"Is that truly what has you shaken?"

She couldn't lie, not about this. As monumental as it had been to touch a horse again, that wasn't what was making her nerves jangle now. The corner of her mouth twitched up in an effort to smile. "Perhaps not."

He stretched across the table to grasp her fingers within his as he stared into her eyes. "For now, let's eat." Releasing her hand, he settled back in his chair.

She nodded, the knot in her stomach unclenching a fraction. "It was nice to go beyond the pathways and the drive this week. I'd forgotten how much I missed the fields, being away from everything."

"You live alone in a cottage." He tore off a piece of bread, pausing to look at her before he ate it.

She shrugged. "It's the difference of night and day."

His eyes flared with the heat of the sun. "Because I was there with you?"

"No, because it was daylight. I spend my nights away from everything in my cottage."

His face softened as he laughed, the corners of his eyes crinkling as he did so. "Except when I disturb your precious solitude."

"Except then." She smiled before adding, "I don't mind...not overmuch anyway."

"At least I haven't yet worn out my welcome."

"Not yet," she returned as she lifted a piece of meat to her lips. "And you bring food, which makes any interruption forgivable." Not to mention what she would learn after they ate, she thought with the heat of a blush flooding her cheeks.

"Did you simply starve out here in the woods before I forced my way in your door?"

"No. Cook has a basket of cold meat, bread, and such sent down every afternoon. And I have a small garden."

"That patch of weeds by the door?" he asked with one brow arching high on his forehead.

"It's a lovely garden."

"It looks as if the woods overtook it a year ago. That wouldn't provide enough food for a rabbit to survive on."

She drew back in disagreement. "I grew tomatoes and cucumber this year."

His eyes narrowed on her.

"Very well. Perhaps it was only one cucumber, but I don't starve."

He smirked as he spun his glass in a slow circle on the table. When he looked up at her, she couldn't quite read the emotion in his eyes. "You may not starve, but you don't live well either, Katie."

Her brows drew together in confusion. "Of course I do. I keep busy…"

"I've kept busy most of my life, and this is where it has brought me."

Her chest tightened. "If you don't want to be here…"

"I don't know where I want to be." He stood, clearly needing something to do to settle his agitation. He took his plate to the wash basin below the window before turning back to her as he rested a hip beside it. He folded his arms across his chest and shifted his gaze back to her. "I worked every day to hold my stables, my life together only to have it fall apart. At the time I wanted to be there. I believe I did, at any rate."

His brows drew together as he shook his head. "The past two years have been spent filling my hours, watching days slip past. I didn't want to be there, but neither did I wish to leave." He shrugged. "And now I'm here…"

She swallowed and looked down at the empty plate before her. "Shadow is healing nicely. So you'll soon be gone."

"So I will."

She looked up as the silence drew on. There was a question lingering in his gaze. Why did his nearing departure hang so heavily in the air between them? Perhaps he was wondering the same. Pulling her gaze from him, she said, "We should most likely clean up this mess before that day arrives." She stood and began to gather the last of the food from the table.

"Indeed." He straightened from his casual stance and came to assist her.

"Andy, when you do finally leave here, what waits for you at home?" she asked as she carried her plate to the wash basin.

"Aside from a neighbor a bit too interested in my stables? I'm not sure. Everyday life, I suppose."

"But there's no other...I mean, no...lady waiting for you there?" She bit her lip and waited for his answer.

"No. The last lady I considered for that role is now the Duchess of Thornwood."

Katie tried to busy herself with sorting plates, but there were only two to move about to keep from looking at him. "She's lovely. Tall, blond, with fashionable clothing and a proper demeanor. That's the sort of lady you want."

"I think we've already established that I don't know what I want. Not anymore," he said from behind her.

Her head snapped around. "Truly?" She watched him for a moment. When it became clear that he wouldn't answer, she tossed out, "I do. Know what I want, that is."

"Do you?"

"Well, yes. I'm going to live out my days here."
She indicated her cottage.

"Alone?"

"I have Mr. Rumples to keep me company." She
smiled at her pet squirrel sleeping in the corner by
the fireplace.

"And fine company he is." Andrew braced his
hands on the back of the chair she'd vacated a few
minutes prior and sighed wearily. "But do you ever
wonder if there's more?"

"I'm certain of it. An entire army of them pelts me
with nuts whenever I walk up the path to the house."

"Not squirrels." He chuckled. "More…more life
to be lived than what is here. Even when I return
home…" He paused to push a lock of blond hair from
his face. "I'm not sure I desire that life anymore. Is
this…" He waved a hand at his surroundings. "Is this
truly what you want?"

"I don't mind things here. It's safe." She dried her
hands on a towel and looked at him from across the
small kitchen.

"Safe from what?"

She wadded up the towel and tossed it onto the worktable before she answered. "People, difficulty, looks."

"You've experienced them, too, then—the looks
that could melt flesh?" He grimaced.

"As if I'd sprouted an extra head." She exhaled and
sank back against the worktable behind her. "I don't
belong where I should. I never have. Earl's daughter
or not, I have no place among the *ton*."

"I'm not sure I do, either. Not anymore. Or

perhaps I do, but I don't wish for it as I once did. I didn't think Scotland changed me, but now I find I'm different. Here with you? Everything has changed." He moved to the fireplace, stoking the fire with more force than was necessary.

She rounded the table to join him. "You could choose not to return. Life in a remote cottage isn't all bad."

He straightened, turning back to her with a look that left her warmer than the fire could account for. "I can see where it would have its advantages."

She opened her mouth to speak, but no words came to her lips.

There was some unspoken question hidden in his eyes. "Unfortunately, my place is at my estate. And you have Mr. Rumples to keep you company."

"Unfortunately," she repeated, wishing she could step away from him, but unable to move away from his gaze. Finally, she cleared her throat and looked away. "You'll have plenty to keep you busy upon your return since you've been away so long."

"At first, that is true. There was a threat to my stables." He shrugged. "I'm unsure of the severity of it all. It could be enough to keep me busy, or it could be a gross over-reaction on the part of my mother."

"Is she likely to imagine the interest in your stables?" Katie asked, stepping closer to the fire with her hands outstretched. They were already quite warm, but it gave her something to do. The last thing she wanted just now was to embarrass herself like she had the other night in the carriage.

He leaned his forearm against the mantel, looking

into the flames as he spoke. "It's a neighboring lord. He's always been a bit mad. But when I left home, things were settled, quiet. We've never seen eye to eye on things, but we hadn't come to blows, either. I don't know what happened to change the circumstances. But recently I received a letter urging me to come home and suggesting some sort of nefarious dealings were afoot. That was where I was going when Shadow fell. I'm sure all is fine. However, until I lay my eyes on my home, I won't wholly believe it."

"Understandable." She glanced up at him and twisted her fingers together so she wouldn't accidentally touch him. "Do you know what the neighbor did to cause such an issue?"

"I only heard a report that two of my horses are missing. The neighbor and two other men were spotted in the area. There's no proof of wrongdoing, but he appears guilty."

"That's awful."

He pushed off from the mantel but kept one hand resting there. "I'm sure everything is in capable hands, but my mother disagrees."

"She believes there will be another horse theft?"

"Or perhaps worse. She's never agreed with my man of business on any matter and thinks only I can repair things now. I shouldn't have left her in charge." His jaw clenched as he stared into the flames. "She doesn't belong in the horse-breeding business. I should have known she'd make a muck of things. She's a lady, after all."

"As am I."

"Yes, but you're different."

"I am. I've heard that statement quite a lot over the years." Her throat tightened as she looked away.

He straightened, taking a step toward her. "I meant no offense, Katie."

She turned, looking back toward him. "Didn't you?"

"Most ladies care only for things with sparkles and frills," he said with disdain. "They fill a home with useless furnishings and fill a gentleman's life with the strife of paying for their whimsy. The point is that I should never have left such a fanciful person in charge of the estate. And here I am, too far away to be of any use."

"You're useful to me." She flushed. Had she truly said that? Her heart pounded in her chest. And what had she meant by it? She wasn't even sure.

He took a step forward, standing too close, yet neither moved away. "I'm of use to you?"

"I meant with the stables and the horses…and our walks together." He'd assisted her in overcoming the fear of being near horses only today. She wouldn't ride again, but because of him, she could return to the stables now. Their walks together…her mind returned to the scene she'd witnessed this afternoon. He'd also said he would help her by explaining desire to her, but she couldn't bring herself to say the words. With him so close, she was having trouble stringing sentences together, much less questions regarding intimate matters. She could feel heat rising up her neck.

"That was nothing."

"It was something to me." She needed to stop talking. This line of conversation was getting more and more embarrassing by the second. She'd spent her life rolling her eyes at simpering girls, and now she was acting like one of them.

"A lady who finds being near horses and the organization of tack endearing," he mused. "You *are* different, Katie." He reached up and lifted the long braid from her shoulder, allowing it to trail over his fingers before falling back against her body. His gaze lingered on her neck for a moment, heating her skin even more and causing her heart to race. When his eyes finally met hers, there was an intensity hidden in their golden depths.

Taking a small step back, she forced words to her lips. "You're going to leave here soon…"

His gaze softened as he closed the gap between them. "Katie, I can't pretend to know what will happen tomorrow, but I'm here now."

"Andy…" She couldn't think clearly with him so close.

"I know we need to discuss things, but there's something I must do just now."

Something he must do… He was leaving? "But it's night. What do you possibly have to do?"

"This," he whispered. He raised his hands to frame her face, pressing his mouth to hers. The touch of his lips was soft and demanding. Her eyes fluttered closed as the world seemed to hang there, suspended in their kiss. His hands held her in a light grasp, but she wasn't going anywhere. Rising to her toes, she pressed into the kiss, wanting more.

But then he pulled back. That was it? She knew there was more. She'd seen Steelings attempt to rip his wife's clothing off. That couldn't be all Andy wanted when she wanted so much more. She hung there with her eyes closed, waiting for him to continue. She didn't know what she needed, only that it was to be found here, with him.

She finally cracked her eyes open and blinked up at him. He'd broken the contact with her lips, but his hands were still on her. He was still there, watching her. She took a ragged breath. The greedy look in his heavy-lidded eyes said he did want more, much more. He was hungry for it.

In that moment she didn't care about anything other than not wanting this to be the end. Rising to her toes again, she closed the gap between their bodies. Her breasts pressed against the wool of his coat as she lingered before him, his lips just out of reach.

With an animal-like sound, his lips descended on hers with a fierce need she felt echoing within her own body. One of his hands circled to the back of her neck, pulling her closer, while the other delved into her hair. He kissed her once more, his tongue parting her lips until she opened to him. He pushed past her teeth, tasting her. Unsure of what to do, she copied his movements, tasting him, melting into him.

She needed to hold on to something to keep her world from tipping sideways. Slipping her arms around his waist, she splayed her fingers across his back. A moment later he ripped his mouth from hers with a guttural sound. Her eyes fluttered open as his lips drifted across her cheek. His rough skin grated against hers as he trailed kisses down the column of her neck. Her head fell back in response as her hands found their way to his broad shoulders.

He pulled her loose shirt down over one shoulder, exposing more of her skin as his mouth moved to the base of her neck. She grasped at his shoulders as her pulse beat against his lips, drawing a small whimper from her throat.

In the next second he was moving across the floor with her as she clung to him in a desperate bid to stay upright. His mouth traced the line of her neck as his body pressed against hers. She heard a chair topple to the floor just before her hip bumped into the table. Hopping up onto its surface, she pulled at his coat until it fell at his feet.

She wanted to be closer to him, to feel the heat of his skin beneath her fingers. She moved her hands over the solid muscle of his chest, cursing the layer of fabric between them. His fingers dug into her hair as he captured the lobe of her ear between his teeth. Sliding her hands around to his back, she grabbed at the bottom of his shirt until she could feel his hot skin beneath her fingers.

"Andy," she murmured as his mouth returned to hers. She didn't know what she was going to say— she only knew that he possessed whatever it was she wanted. She slid her hands along his spine, pulling him closer to her body. She was brazen, wanton, and she didn't care. She'd been called worse. She opened to him, her tongue tangling with his in a desperate fight for some exhilarating goal just out of reach.

He tilted her back a fraction, one hand sliding down to her hip to hold her there while he continued their kiss. She wound her legs around his waist, hooking her ankles around him to steady herself.

The motion brought their bodies closer. Her eyes flew open as something hard pressed into her body. Pulling back from their kiss in shock at what it must be, she almost stopped him...almost. But before she could think further about it, he growled and bit her lip, tugging her back into the kiss. She dug her fingers into his cravat in an attempt to unknot it. He was wearing too many layers of clothing. She didn't know what she was doing, but she knew that much for certain.

"Leave it," he muttered against her lips as he pressed the length of his body against hers.

She wrapped tighter around him, enjoying the way the hard planes of his body abraded her breasts and the insides of her thighs. She needed to touch him. Reaching for the knot of his cravat again, she looped her finger through the fabric.

But before she could go further he whispered, "Don't."

"Why not? I want..." She didn't understand what she wanted, but her body hummed with desire and her limbs were heavy with it. Desire—this was what she wanted to learn.

"I can't return to the house with part of my clothing missing," his voice rumbled into her ear as his lips moved down her neck.

"Who's around to notice?" she asked, arching into him as he leaned in to trace the peak of her breast with his tongue through her thin shirt.

He didn't answer her question, only teased her breast with his teeth through the fabric. Damn all this infernal fabric! He was driving her mad.

She wrapped a hand around his neck, slipping her fingers into his hair to hold him close. "Please." She whispered the word, not sure what she was asking for, but asking nonetheless.

He lifted his head to meet her gaze, searching for something there. "This wasn't supposed to happen."

"It wasn't?"

"No." His brows were drawn together in concern as he looked at her. He buried his fingers in her hair, unraveling the last of her braid in the process.

"Is it all right that I'm glad it did?" she asked as she lowered her legs from around his body. She couldn't quite meet his eyes as she sat before him like leftover dinner, but at least she'd been honest.

He tilted her chin up so that she could see he was grinning. "That is very much all right."

"Then don't stop." She knew she sounded desperate, but that was the way he'd left her.

He swallowed and glanced away with a mumbled oath she couldn't quite hear. "I can't take advantage of you in this manner, Katie. I won't." He dropped his hands to the table on either side of her hips and lowered his head with a rough sigh. "When I leave, I don't want to hurt you. And if we continue…"

He was stopping out of some sense of honor? This was her only chance to experience passion. Soon he would be gone and she would be alone again. This was her only opportunity, and he was worried about what would happen to her when he left?

He stood and pushed a fallen strand of hair from her face, his fingers grazing the rim of her ear as he tucked the hair back. "I suppose that was lesson one in desire."

She met his gaze. "That means there will be a lesson two."

"I have a feeling lesson three may well kill me, but yes." He chuckled as he placed a kiss on her cheek, the deep rumble of his voice making her arch into him.

"Why will it be difficult for you? It seems rather exciting to me."

"I suppose you will find that out in the end." He smiled as he pulled her shirt back onto her shoulders.

"I think I see now why ladies desire marriage," she mused as she scooted from the table. No sooner were the words out of her mouth than she regretted them. She glanced up at him with wide eyes. "Not that I want you to marry me now. That wasn't what I meant at all. I know you must leave the estate soon…"

"Shhh. I'm glad you enjoyed our evening together. I enjoyed it as well. We knew an hour ago that I would have to leave soon, and nothing has changed that fact."

But everything had changed with that kiss. And it wasn't only one kiss—he'd kissed her in a manner she'd never imagined. The way she felt in his arms… the way she'd acted…perhaps she had more in common with her light-skirt mother than she was aware of. But none of that mattered—all that mattered was here tonight. She'd hidden herself away for most of her life for a crime she didn't commit. It was her mother who abandoned the family, her mother who was dishonest—not her. Perhaps now it was time to live. She looked at Andy. In his arms she was strong enough to leave her cottage and face the world outside her door.

"When I do leave, I will settle this matter with Lord Hawkes straight away, and then I'll be free to…"

She cleared her throat and stared at him, trying to grasp the conversation. "Did you say Lord Hawkes?"

"Yes, he's the neighbor I was telling you about earlier."

The neighbor who was threatening his stables was her…uncle? How could this be? Her father was there on her uncle's estate at this moment on an extended visit, assisting with some business. His business had been with Andy's horses? Her father was obsessed with his mines. He didn't care one whit for horses, other than using them for hauling supplies to and from the jet mines. She looked up into Andy's face, trying to understand.

"Yes, but enough about him. There is nothing I can do to resolve things tonight, and I need to get back to the house before the servants begin to talk."

She needed to tell him her relation to Lord Hawkes. Perhaps she could reassure him of her uncle's nature. Although she'd never been fond of the man, if she was honest. But was telling Andy the correct course of action? He could use the knowledge of her family's past against her uncle somehow or harm her father. But Andy wouldn't do that. He wouldn't hurt her. And perhaps it would put his mind at ease. Or would it make him leave tonight? She couldn't stand by and not say anything, though. That wouldn't be right. She opened her mouth, still searching for the right words. "Andy…"

"I'll see you tomorrow." He leaned in and kissed her one last time, and when she opened her eyes, he was halfway out the door. She stood in silence watching him leave, knowing she would have to face this new turn tomorrow. Perhaps then she would know what to do.

Ten

ANDREW ASSISTED KATIE FROM THE OPEN CARRIAGE, handing her down onto the drive at Thornwood Manor. "I truly don't see the necessity of this gathering. Our dinner here was but a few days ago."

"They're only being neighborly, Andy," she returned as she slung a long traveling case of some sort over her shoulder.

What was she bringing to an afternoon tea anyway? With Katie, it could truly be anything. He was only thankful it wasn't in the shape of bagpipes. "Allow me," he offered, reaching for the leather case.

"No need. It's only something I promised to show Sue." She readjusted the parcel on her shoulder, clearly not wanting him to touch it. He shrugged, knowing he would discover the contents of the case soon enough.

"As for our hosts, they most likely believe we are sitting about Ormesby all day being weary of one another's company for entertainment."

"Is the state of being weary a form of entertainment?"

"Well, it's not a very good one, is it?"

"I enjoyed last night's entertainment far more than *weariness*," he whispered in her ear as she passed him.

A blush crept up her neck. Her lips were parted to reply when the dowager duchess called out, "You've arrived!"

Katie turned away to greet the older woman, planting her walking stick beside each step as if it was more of an extension of today's ensemble than a crutch. Andrew's eyes narrowed on the sway of her hips within the cream-colored day dress she wore today. There wasn't a trace of a limp. The memory of her legs wrapped around his body flooded his mind with questions of her honesty. He would have to discuss the "injury" with her later—for now, he needed his wits to deal with Thornwood.

"So glad you could come, dear." The dowager duchess pulled Katie along ahead of him into a side garden. "On the last warm day of autumn, one mustn't remain inside."

Katie looked at the woman at her side, and Andrew could see the edge of her brows drawn together in confusion. "How do you know it will be the last warm day of the year?"

"Oh, at my age, you simply know. Come along," she tossed over her shoulder to Andrew as she wound around a sundial and veered onto another path leading to the rear of the house. "My daughter-in-law and I have soundly beaten Lord and Lady Steelings in whist, and I fear we are all in need of refreshments."

"His Grace couldn't come?" Katie asked.

"No, he was detained by some business." It would have been a believable excuse if the woman's eyes hadn't darted over her shoulder to Andrew and lingered on him for one second too long.

He couldn't blame Thornwood for not wanting to attend tea in the garden with him. Not only did it seem like an activity intended for a group of ladies bent on gossip, but the gathering would also be dreadfully uncomfortable if they spent it in one another's company. The dinner had proven that much. He couldn't be sociable with Thornwood. Too much had come between them already.

They followed the dowager duchess through a small gate into a rose garden. The flowers were well past their prime for the year, but the garden was maintained to perfection. However, Andrew wasn't looking at the scenery as much as he should as they walked. He was watching the movement of Katie's hips in her dress and the swish of the fabric against the gravel pathway. Her hair was trapped in a loose braid, but the end was pinned at the base of her neck. Why had she chosen to dress today in honor of the outing? He wasn't complaining—she was beautiful. But it was curious.

His eyes drifted over her form, hidden by the cream-colored fabric, yet somehow more exposed than it had been in her breeches and shirt. Unlike in the silk concoction she'd worn to dinner, she seemed at ease in this ensemble. Apparently noticing he was looking at her, she glanced back and caught his eye for a moment.

They rounded the house with the dowager duchess regaling them with the tale of her win in whist. Perhaps this afternoon wouldn't be the nightmarish scene he'd envisioned when Katie had shown him the invitation this morning. Thornwood was absent; Andrew was with Katie… The only thing he was dreading now was facing Steelings and his wife after catching them in that field.

He shook the image from his head with a shudder and followed the ladies onto a large stone terrace at the rear of the house. The Thornwood residence was arranged to overlook the vast landscape with only the main house, the wings, and the edge of what must be the stables visible from this location. He itched to go look around Thornwood's stables in search of faults, but resisted the desire.

Tables were arranged to take advantage of the view from the terrace. And though this view belonged to Thornwood, and therefore Andrew would never admit it aloud, it was quite awe-inspiring. The land seemed to roll on forever in patches of green and gold. Hills erupted into stone-topped peaks, then tapered off once more. He understood for the first time what Katie meant when she spoke of troubles being far away, kept back by the distance of the moors.

He turned with a sigh and found himself face to face with Steelings.

"About the other day…" Steelings led in.

Andrew waved away whatever his friend had been about to say. "Can we agree never to speak of it?"

"That would be the wise course of action," Steelings replied with a nod. He lowered his voice and added, "Your secret is safe with me."

"My secret?" Andrew drew back, careful to keep his voice low. "You were the one caught in an indecent position."

"You and Lady Katie Moore," Steelings whispered with a raised brow and a grin.

"We were simply on a walk. Nothing more." There had been plenty more last night, but no one knew of that. He ran a finger under his cravat to loosen the knot that threatened to choke him.

"Right you are." He clapped Andrew on the back with an accompanying wink and a chuckle.

Andrew was about to defend Katie's honor when Steelings' wife joined them. "I hate to interrupt your discussion of what is certainly something terribly masculine, but tea is being served."

"Are there more of those cakes?" Steelings' eyes widened as he peered over his wife's head to the table at her back. "The ones with the layers and the cream?"

"I believe so." Sue sighed and smoothed her skirts across her hips. "If we continue our stay much longer, you'll have to pour me into my own carriage for the ride to London."

Steelings frowned down at his wife. "Would that be because you don't fit within a carriage with me or because I don't fit within a carriage with you?"

"Both." Sue laughed and turned to Andrew, apparently all awkwardness of yesterday either forgotten or forgiven as she announced, "The sweets at Thornwood are second only to those found in a French bakery."

"I won't tell the cook you said so, dear, or she'll be unbearable to deal with," the dowager duchess cut in as she waved them toward the table.

Andrew relaxed a fraction as they sat down to tea. There was an ease to their conversation that he'd never before experienced within the *ton*. Laughter as well as disagreements seemed to be permitted here over tea and biscuits. And subjects were not confined to the weather, fashion, and horses. He took a sip of tea, allowing the chatter to flow around him, chipping away at his dislike for Thornwood's home. Perhaps Katie was right—maybe this place was misunderstood.

"I should have the painting complete in a few days," Sue said around a bite of cake.

"Thornwood will be so pleased," Lily said over the rim of her teacup.

"It's a perfect gift for him," her mother-in-law added. "I'm happy you thought of it, Lily dear."

"I wasn't aware you painted professionally," Andrew mused, giving Sue a polite smile.

Lily grinned over at her friend, her face shining with pride as she said, "She did so in secret for quite a few years, you know."

"Yes, and I bought every painting. I suppose I can share *one* with the likes of Thornwood." Steelings laughed. "But only one."

Andrew smiled, suppressing the pang of guilt he now felt, knowing he'd thrown Sue over because of her work. It was for the best, though. The affection between her and her husband wouldn't have been possible with him. His gaze drifted to Katie. Her pale eyes were bright as she watched him over the rim of her teacup.

"Sue," Lily whispered to her friend to gain her attention, "don't sound any alarm bells, but are those the men we saw stealing from the Mitchells?"

"They're here? Where?" Sue asked in a hushed tone. Everyone else seemed too busy chatting to notice—everyone except Andrew.

"Outside the stables."

Andrew glanced across the lawn to the stables. There in the gravel before the entrance to the structure were two men crouched low at the wheel of Katie's carriage. What were they doing? He squinted into the sun and was already pushing back from the table to stand when one man lifted his head. The large highwayman.

Andrew gripped the edge of the table as his mind careened through events, attempting to catch up and make sense of the situation. Could it be coincidence that these same men kept appearing everywhere he went? Perhaps when he'd disappeared over the hedgerow at Ormesby Place they hadn't gone far, waiting for him. Or they could live close by and he was being overly paranoid. But either way, they seemed to be tampering with the wheel of Katie's carriage.

"What do you know of those men?" he asked Lily.

"Only that we caught them stealing a chicken," Sue interjected.

Lily nodded in agreement before adding, "Didn't they claim to be searching for some relation…"

"Stealing a chicken?" the dowager duchess called out across the table, drowning out all other conversation. "Who was stealing a chicken?" Her Grace twisted in her chair in search of the chicken thieves. "Why did I not hear of this?"

"Mother," Lily said as she laid a hand on the older woman's arm. "Do be calm, if you don't mind too terribly. There are strange men by the stables and they could be armed."

"By the stables?" Steelings asked as he rose slightly from his chair on the pretense of getting another piece of cake.

"Beside the carriage at the edge of the drive," Lily stated, her eyes focused on the biscuit sitting on her plate.

"Don't all look at once!" Sue exclaimed as the entire table turned to stare at the edge of the drive just visible beyond the house. "Oh, the lot of you would be rotten spies."

"Unlike you, of course," Steelings replied with a grin. "I'm sure chattiness is a quality they look for in espionage."

Everyone but Sue was busy craning their necks to see across the open grassy area to the edge of the drive. That man had been armed when Andrew saw him before. Someone could get hurt.

Andrew cleared his throat to gain their attention. "Ladies, you should go inside."

"While you go interrogate the men meddling with my carriage?" Katie asked.

"Yes."

"And what if you need assistance?"

"I prefer to repay my life debts one at a time," Andrew replied, earning him a narrow-eyed glare. "And Steelings will accompany me, won't you, Steelings?"

"Indeed. And this time they will not get away so easily."

"This time… You've seen these men before?" Andrew asked, but Steelings didn't answer because his eyes were trained on the men across the lawn.

Andrew turned at the sharp intake of breath across

the table. Katie's back was turned as she watched the men at the carriage.

"I saw it, too," Lily stated.

Andrew was about to ask what they'd seen when a glint of metal caught the sun. He couldn't make it out at this distance, but the table where they were gathered was well within range of a pistol. Chances could not be taken. "Ladies, you need to go inside now," he demanded.

The dowager duchess, Lily, and Sue stood to leave, but Katie dove to the ground.

"What are you doing? You need to get to safety."

"I am safe," Katie replied as she opened the case she'd brought with her.

"What do you…"

The rest of his sentence was silenced by a ground-shaking *Boom!* Time seemed to stretch out before him.

He gripped the table, watching Katie as she staggered backward and landed in one of the chairs. The smoking blunderbuss hung loose in her hands. He opened his jaw and rubbed his ears, trying to restore order to his head. Glancing over to where Steelings was standing, he saw his friend feeling his chest for damage done. Everything was silent except for the high-pitched ringing.

The table linens blew in the slight breeze, and the men in the distance scampered to their feet, but Katie didn't move. Andrew would ask her if she was hurt, if not for the whining in his ears.

Rounding the table, he shook a dazed Katie by the shoulder. But the moment he saw a smug smile creep across her face, he took off running. She was fine for now. And if he could catch up with the men, he could get answers.

"Would you like some company?" Steelings called out from just behind him a minute later.

At least he could hear now. If he could see where the men ran to, he might finally understand all of this madness. He glanced at Steelings, running alongside him toward the stables. "Did you see where they went?"

"Into that grove of trees. Did you see what they were doing to your lady's carriage?"

"No," Andrew ground out. They veered to the right of the stables and headed for the cluster of trees. "But I have an idea what they're after."

"What is that?"

"Me."

Steelings made an inarticulate sound of understanding as he kept pace beside him. "Are these men the reason your lady came to tea with a firearm?"

"No." He stopped to glare at Steelings.

"Are you planning to argue the fact that she's your lady or that she brought a blunderbuss to tea to protect you?" Steelings asked with a grin.

"Both!"

"Interesting."

"No, it isn't the least bit interesting." The last thing he needed was for talk of this day to spread.

Steelings threw his hands up in surrender. "Very well. I won't speak of it again. Much like the incident in the field, it will never be mentioned."

"Steelings?"

"Yes?"

"You're mentioning it now."

"Perhaps we should continue our search for the men," Steelings suggested with a nod toward the woods, but the men were gone.

Andrew scanned the spaces between the tree trunks, searching for a glimpse of dark clothing, but it was no use. They'd had quite the head start in making their escape. "They'll come back. If they are indeed looking for me, as I suspect, they won't go far."

As they rounded the corner of the stables, he saw Katie and the other ladies now gathered by the carriage. "They escaped," he called out to them.

"I don't care for the idea of ruffians trespassing on our lands," Lily said with a shiver.

"Perhaps they'd planned to steal the horses, much like that chicken we caught them with," Sue added.

Steelings moved to his wife's side, leaning an elbow on the side of the carriage as he said, "If that was what they wanted, why not take one from the stables, not harnessed to a rig?"

"It is odd. The question does remain, why linger in the drive?" Andrew asked.

Just then, a loud crack split the air around them and Steelings staggered backward as the carriage collapsed from under his arm. His long limbs flailed through the air as he tried to grasp something solid. Sue reached for her husband, steadying him as the carriage crashed to the ground beneath him. Wood splintered around them as the back axle severed into two pieces and what was once the wheel now lay smashed at their feet.

Steelings looked up at Andrew with a wry grin as

he mused, "I'm guessing that was supposed to happen on your drive back to Ormesby Place."

Andrew knelt to investigate the extent of the damage. That's when he saw it, the small piece of parchment about to catch the wind and blow away. The men must have dropped it when the gun went off. He reached for it, but Katie got it first. He saw her eyes flash when she twitched it open.

"May I see it?" he asked.

There was a moment of hesitation. But a second later, she handed it to him. His hand tightened as he studied the note. All he needed to know was at the top of the parchment—Lord Hawkes' seal. The remainder of the note was covered with mud and soiled beyond his ability to read, but the seal was intact. Glancing up at Katie, he saw the concern in her eyes. She was aware of the connection.

Only one question nagged at him: how did she know Hawkes' family seal at a single glance?

❧

The following morning, Andrew leaned against the fence rail as he oversaw repairs. Three of the grooms-men worked to rebuild the fence where a tree had fallen into the pasture. The tree had settled back into the earth some time ago, with only ragged logs lying in the grass now, but the gap in the fencing had already allowed one horse to escape, according to one of the grooms.

He sighed over the sad state of things. Everything had fallen into such disrepair, and they had done noth-ing. He couldn't fathom their thinking on the matter. Of course, he couldn't fathom his own thinking this morning, either. Here he was repairing a fence while the two men who had been hunting him for over a week were still on the loose. And he still didn't quite understand Katie's recognition of Hawkes' seal. It was yet another riddle to be solved and the pile was already getting rather tall. He pushed the hair from his face and crossed his arms.

After everything had settled yesterday afternoon, he'd spent the early evening discussing the issue with Steelings and Thornwood. They'd convinced him to lie low for a few more days before taking the southern road home. He couldn't argue with their logic, and it did give him a few more days in Katie's company, even if he had missed dinner with her last night. At the same time, it grated to know that danger lurked just out of his reach, threatening his life and that of his family, and he could do nothing to prevent it.

When would they come for him? Would they move on and wait for him farther south? Or had he just sealed his mother's fate with his decision to stay? He grimaced and pushed from the fence to pace, finding a small amount of comfort in the weight of the weapon strapped to his side. If they came near him today, he would be the one holding the gun.

He'd only taken one step when a wagon rolled out into the field. Katie was perched beside the driver. Today she was back in breeches and her hair was bound in her usual braid over one shoulder. The dress yesterday must have been for the benefit of the duchess. His chest tightened at the knowledge that she'd cared enough to listen to him.

He smiled up at her as the wagon neared. No matter the danger that sought him out, he would not squander this day with worry over the unknown. Today Katie was here with him, riddles or answers, she was here. He reached for her before the driver could hand her down, his hands lingering on her waist a second too long, but he didn't give a care who saw it.

"Good morning," Katie offered in greeting, the pink of her cheeks growing.

"Yes, it is." He smiled. *And it will only get better.* "I was wondering when you would find me."

"It wasn't difficult." She reached into the wagon and got her walking stick before turning back toward him. "You can hear the hammers all over the estate. I didn't know we had a break in our fence line."

"Soon you won't." Turning back to the driver waiting by the wagon, Andrew signaled him to leave.

"Won't I need that to return to the drive?" she asked as the man regained his seat and pulled the wagon around to leave.

"I hope not," he muttered to himself as he extended his arm to her. "Come. I have a surprise for you."

"What is it?" She hesitated to take his arm as she narrowed her eyes on him.

"It's a *surprise*." He nudged her with his elbow until she took his arm.

"Is it big?"

"It's a surprise," he repeated, leading her away from the repairs.

"Oh, it's small, isn't it?"

He laughed. "It's a surprise."

"Tell me the location at least," she pleaded as she planted the walking stick at her side every few steps.

"You're impossible. You know that, don't you?"

"Yes." She smiled up at him.

"I found a lone tree in a far field and arranged for us to have a picnic."

She stilled. "I know that place. Isn't it a bit unsafe to venture so far with those men looking for you?"

"Thornwood loaned me a pistol." He pulled back his coat to show her the piece where it nestled against his waist.

"I suppose as long as one of us is armed," she teased. "How will we get there?"

He turned and looked at her. "You can ride."

"No, I can't." Her words rushed out as she shook her head.

"Yes, you can, Katie." He laid his hands on her shoulders and forced her to look at him. He could feel her tremble beneath his grasp. He wished he could offer her additional comfort, but there were three grooms within sight of them. "Come. It's time."

"I really shouldn't with my injury." She blinked up at him as her eyes filled with unshed tears. "The doctors said…"

"Katie, I think we both know the truth."

"Clearly not, since I have no idea what you're referring to," she stated, pulling away from him a fraction, yet not leaving, either. Her breathing was ragged. He watched her shoulders rise and fall for a second.

Perhaps this had been a bad idea, but there was no turning back from it now. "When I kissed you the other night, you wrapped your legs around my body."

"I…recall." Her eyes darted to his and then away again.

"When you weren't thinking of your injury, you used your legs."

"Oh…I…" She studied the grass between her feet as she twisted the walking stick in her grasp.

"I'm glad you did," he added, taking a step closer to her.

"Even so," she mumbled, "I can't ride a horse, Andy. Not anymore."

"You can ride with me. I'll keep you safe, Katie." He gave one of her hands a quick squeeze. "I know how important horses were to you, how important they still are. Trust me."

He mounted the horse he'd ridden from the stables and leaned down to pull her up with him. The sounds of hammering stopped. "Katie." He nodded in encouragement as he extended his arms.

She glanced back to the grooms where they paused in their work to watch her. Escaped strands of her hair blew across her face as she bent to lay her walking stick on the ground at her feet. Turning back to Andrew, she gave him a slight nod and stepped into his grasp.

As he settled her before him, he could feel the thrum of her nerves and stiffness of her body. The horse must have sensed it too, because the mare began to toss its head around. "Shhh, easy," he murmured, unsure which female he was speaking to.

Katie was shaking as she pressed her body close to his. He brushed a kiss against her hair under the guise of gathering the reins. Holding his breath that this would work, he flicked the reins.

As he urged the horse forward, Katie whimpered and shrank into his arms. Adjusting the reins in one hand, he pulled her close with the other. She gripped the arm wrapped around her waist with both hands and held on tight.

"You're all right. We aren't going to go fast. I've got you. I'm here." He kept a constant stream of calming words flowing near her ear.

A few minutes later, she began to relax into his hold. He'd done it. He'd gotten her on horseback, albeit with assistance, but on horseback nonetheless. He'd planned this little outing while he lay awake last night trying not to think of the men looking for him, knowing if he could only get to this point, all would be fine. Yet, the more she relaxed her spine and melted into him, the more panicked he became.

What was he doing? He would be leaving in only a few days, and here he was with a lady wrapped in his arms.

For the first time in his life, his actions held no logic. He had no plan, no agenda, and no idea where things were headed with her. All he knew was the scent of wildflowers on her hair, the warmth of her skin as she rested the side of her forehead against his neck, and the smile in her eyes when she glanced up at him.

When they reached the large lone tree on the crest of the hill, he eased the mare to a stop. Swinging to the ground, he moved to lower Katie from the horse. Her face held a range of emotions he couldn't label. Because words couldn't possibly say what he wanted to tell her, he pulled her forward and wrapped his arms around her.

She buried her face in his chest, her hands hanging limp at her sides. Something was wrong. He heard her sniff a second later. He'd made her cry? He was only trying to help her. His shirt grew wet beneath her face, and he moved his hands over her back.

Raising one hand to her hair, he stroked her fiery locks. "Don't cry, Katie. You did it."

"I know," she mumbled against his chest. "That's why I'm crying."

"It's over. I knew you would be able to ride again." Even though she still shook from head to toe, he was proud of her. She'd overcome her fear and sat atop a horse again. He smiled and kissed her hair.

"Only with you," she replied, lifting her head to look him in the eye.

"You'll be back to tearing across fields soon enough."

"No." She wiped away the last of her tears. "I'm not strong enough to ride alone."

"We'll see. Come, let's enjoy the day."

She nodded as he took her hand and led her to the base of the large tree on the hilltop. The leaves were a deep shade of red against the blue sky, the color of a fine wine or Katie's hair in candlelight.

"I used to come here as a child." She smiled up at the long branches twisting into the plume of foliage overhead. "I'd forgotten the beauty of this place."

"I stumbled across it while riding a few days ago and I keep returning." From this hill, the view rolled off into the distance around a single stone-topped peak. He turned back to Katie, pleased to share this day with her. He wasn't certain how much more time he would have here on her estate. Soon the road would be safe for travel. Thornwood had offered him a horse for his journey again last night. He grimaced and reached up to curl his hand around the lowest branch of the tree. Today he was here. Today was all that mattered.

"The border of our lands lies just over there along that stone wall," Katie was saying. "As soon as I was able to ride, I would come here. I remember telling Father I was checking the borders."

"You were out here alone? Rather far for a child, isn't it?" he asked, squinting into the distance to see the low stone wall to which she was referring.

He saw her shrug out of the corner of his eye as she muttered, "I survived."

"I shouldn't be surprised. You live alone in the woods now."

"Surely you did something of an independent nature when you were young." She took a few steps forward, kicking at the clumps of yellowing grass.

He'd always been one to stand alone, but his ventures weren't explorations to find pretty views. He was too busy for such things. He shrugged as he said, "I began riding horses when I was quite young...and started on my path in horse breeding when I was ten years of age."

"Always working, aren't you?"

He exhaled a ragged breath. "Sometimes we aren't given a choice in the matter."

"Well, today you have a choice." Her pale green eyes sparkled with mischief as she said, "I've just spied the length of rope I hung from this tree years ago."

"You climb trees as well?"

"Of course. Come on." She laced her fingers with his and led him to the other side of the tree trunk.

Looking up at the old rope looped over a high limb, he ran a hand over the back of his neck. "If this has been here for some years, I don't know how stable it would be to…"

She grabbed the rope and lifted herself off the ground with a smile. "I would wager you've never swung from a tree."

"You would be correct." He chuckled as he gave her a push, watching her swing in a wide arc before returning to his arms.

She looked down at him as she clung to the rope, standing on one of the worn knots at the end. "Today you will."

He gave her another push, watching as the long braid in her hair whipped out behind her. "Must I?" he asked, as his hands settled back on her waist.

"Andy, if I can ride a horse today, you can swing from a tree branch."

"Very well." Grabbing the rope above her head with one hand, he pulled her back toward the tree trunk to hold on to one of the branches. He secured the lowest knot of the rope between his feet and with a grin in her direction, let go of the tree.

Together they flew into the air as he slipped one arm around her waist. With a laugh, she arched her back, soaring them higher into the cloudless autumn sky. How much of life had he missed as a result of always being focused on his work? It all seemed so terribly pointless while he was swinging through the air with her. He'd had to work to secure his home, but he'd never stopped. He'd never taken the time until he met Katie.

His heart was light for the first time, perhaps ever. As they slowed and began to spin together, the loose pieces of her hair flew around him. He was free—free to choose to swing from a tree for the afternoon rather than mend fences or train horses. He was free to live.

The rope shifted within his grasp a fraction. Glancing up, he saw the rope fray at the same time he heard the *Crack!*

They were falling before he could jump down. Tightening his grip on Katie, he saw the wide-eyed look of panic on her face for a second before they were tumbling to the ground together, landing with a thud.

He removed the length of rope from between them as he rolled Katie to the grass at his side. "Are you hurt?"

She laughed and sat up, dusting grass from her shirt. "I'm fine. I should ask you, since you broke my fall."

"I believe I'll live," he chuckled, looking up at the tree.

"At least I haven't killed you."

"Quite the opposite." He sat forward, bracing an elbow on his knee.

He suddenly wished that he could always be there to break her fall. He knew that wasn't possible, but he wished it all the same. His eyes fell to her legs, covered in cream-colored breeches now hopelessly stained with grass. "Katie, what happened?" He nodded to the leg she claimed was injured. "I know it must be difficult to discuss, but…"

"I fell from my horse." She shrugged.

"That much I know. How long ago?"

"Only last spring, but so much has happened since

that it feels like a lifetime. I never thought I could be hurt. I belonged with the horses." She tossed a wry smile in his direction before continuing, "That's what everyone always said, anyway."

"But then you were hurt."

"Yes. On my morning ride. I was near the mines for a change of scenery. Well...in truth I saw my brother, Trevor, leave the side garden with Roselyn. She had been acting a bit off the day before and I was curious what was happening. I saw them leave for their walk together and followed them."

"Trevor. Isn't he the brother who passed away not long ago?"

"That day," she confirmed.

"That day? Was your riding accident involved?"

"In a way. I wasn't the only one to follow Roselyn and Trevor that morning. I saw my brother, Ethan, follow them as well. There was a scuffle between my brothers. I was some distance away, but I saw them come to blows while Roselyn watched. They wound up at the mouth of the mines on Roseberry Topping. I circled around the hillside, where a patch of woods hid me from view. That's when I heard Roselyn scream. I knew something was wrong."

She closed her eyes against the memory. "I urged my horse forward, jumping walls and hedges...in the next moment I was on the ground. I watched the sun set that night, alone. That's the last I remember. I woke a week later with my head bandaged and my leg in a splint. Trevor was gone. Roselyn had fled the scandal. Ethan had gone in search of answers. And I could no longer walk properly."

"One of your brothers was there when the other fell to his death?"

"It was terrible. Roselyn blamed Ethan for some time afterward, I understand. But the man responsible eventually paid for his crime. And Ethan and Roselyn are married now. Her betrothal to Trevor wasn't to be. They're happy together. I'm pleased at that outcome, at least."

"You don't seem pleased."

"I am, though. Truly. And I fill my days in everyone's absence. I have my projects to keep me busy."

"Indeed you do. Does your leg still hurt you, or has it mended?"

Her breathing turned shallow as she stared down at her hands in her lap. "I use a walking stick."

"Katie," he warned. He knew she didn't need the crutch, but not to what extent. He needed to know, to understand. "You didn't answer my question."

She swallowed as she lifted her eyes to his. "My knee catches if I overexert myself. It always aches a bit by the end of the day."

He nodded, relief that she wasn't in horrible agony every day washing through him. "And it's this knee?" he asked, laying a hand on the side of her leg.

"Yes."

He ran his hand up her calf, lifting her knee from the grass. His fingers drifted across the surface as he felt for damage. "You tore a tendon."

"How did you know?"

He shrugged and continued to rub gentle circles down the outside of her knee with his thumbs. "Does that hurt?"

"No."

"You know, if you were a horse, I would have had you put down," he teased.

"I'm aware."

He looked up, meeting her gaze above her freckled cheeks. His smile slipped from his face as he watched her. He needed to say the words that had tormented him every night for the past week. He didn't know why it was so important to do so, only that it was entirely necessary, and it must be done now. "I was wrong to consider such injuries beyond repair. My apologies."

Her lips curled up into a smug grin as she tossed her hair back and let out a loud, "Ha!"

So much for heartfelt remorse. His eyes narrowed on her as he tossed out, "Yes, perhaps there's something here worth saving... One never knows."

"Do you think so?" she mocked.

He nodded, a sly grin creeping across his face. "Perhaps."

"You all-knowing, arrogant pain in the..."

His lips covered hers before she could finish insulting him. He wanted to taste the sunshine held within each tiny fleck of color across her nose and cheeks. He wanted her wrapped around him with wild hair flowing free in the breeze. He pushed her to her back and moved over her in one fluid motion. His hand, still cradling her injured knee, slid up the outside of her thigh. She kissed him back, opening to him as he plundered her mouth.

Wrapping her arms around his back, she pulled at the fabric of his shirt. A moment later, he felt her fingers trail across his bare skin. She traced the line of his spine up to his shoulder blades, pulling his shirt up as she moved. The touch of her fingers seared his skin until he pulled back from her to free himself of his shirt. The slight chill of the autumn afternoon met his skin, but he didn't care.

He heard her breath catch as he tossed his shirt aside. His gaze returned to hers, hoping the desire he felt would be reflected there. Yet her expression was unreadable as her eyes slid down his neck to his chest, then fell to his stomach. His heart pounded as he struggled to control his ragged breaths.

"I didn't intend on any of this happening, Katie." He brushed the hair back from her face as he lay propped on his forearm above her. She still didn't meet his gaze. He held his breath and said the words he knew he must say. "If you want to stop…"

Her gaze snapped to his. Her lips parted to speak, but she said nothing, only shook her head. They stayed there, frozen in a moment of uncertainty that seemed to stretch to the end of time. Then she lifted her hand and laid it on his chest. It was a featherlight touch, but the force of it could have led him as if pulled by chains. She slid her hand up to his neck and tugged him back into their kiss.

Her lips seemed to seek the answers to the questions she couldn't speak. He met her mouth with a driving need of his own, tangling his tongue with hers in a quest for more. Her fingers curled into the hair at the back of his neck as he took her mouth. But he wanted more. He wanted to touch her, to feel her curving body beneath his palms. Without further thought, he rolled to the side, taking her with him and settling her across his waist, above the gun at his hip.

She gasped at the sudden movement, taking a second to gain her bearings.

He kept his hands on her hips, afraid he was moving too quickly for her. His breath was ragged as he forced himself to remain still beneath her. His hands, however, refused to be ruled by logic as they slowly drifted up her sides and back down again.

The wind blew through her hair, whipping it across her face, caressing everywhere he wished to kiss her. Her skin was flushed where her shirt was open at the neck. He couldn't wait any longer. He needed her, more of her.

She leaned forward on her knees to continue their kiss, her breasts pressing to his chest as she moved closer. Her body wrapped around his and he groaned. Perhaps this had been a bad idea. After all, he couldn't very well finish things with her here in the dirt—she deserved better. And she wasn't his, not in truth. However, he needed to see what she kept secret within that loose shirt. He would go that far but no farther.

He began raising her shirt over her belly, then slipping it over her breasts.

When he broke their kiss to pull it over her head, she smiled and asked, "Is this lesson two?"

Those blasted lessons. Why had he ever agreed to such a thing? But in the next second she was sitting on his stomach, bared to him. His mouth went dry. He tried to answer her, but his lips refused to cooperate. He lifted his hands to her sides, skimming them over her narrow waist to cup her breasts with his palms. He was about to flip her to her back to continue what he'd begun when her eyes darted up and grew wide at some sight above.

"What is it?" He tried to glance around, but she was already dropping down to lie on top of him. His hands landed on her hips where they still straddled him. "If you're trying to look innocent, this is the wrong way to go about it."

"The men from Thornwood Manor," she whispered into his ear.

He eased her onto the grass beside him, rolling to his stomach to have a better view. The two were following the wall that bordered the property. Thornwood and Steelings had been right about one thing: the men weren't giving up easily. Andrew looked around for their horse, hoping the men wouldn't see such a large clue to his and Katie's presence. He sighed, seeing the horse had wandered away to some shade on the opposite side of the field, unnoticed by the men.

"What should we do?"

"I don't suppose continuing what we started is an option," he groaned.

"Not with men who wish to harm you wandering by."

"When did you become so practical?" he teased, raking his eyes over her half-naked body.

"When did you become so careless?"

"Perhaps it's the company I've been keeping." He trailed his fingers down her spine to settle on her hip.

"Stop that. We're in danger, aren't we?"

"Only if they see us." He glanced around at the tall grass surrounding them before shifting his gaze back to the men. They were moving farther away now.

"What's in that direction?" he asked Katie.

"The road to town. But it's too far a distance on foot."

"They must have set up camp nearby," he muttered as he watched them grow smaller in the distance.

"Andy, how long have these men been after you?"

"Since I decided to return home."

"What do you think they want? They're hunting through the countryside for you. What happens when they find you?" she asked, the color draining from her face.

"They won't catch me, Katie." He tucked a lock of hair behind her ear as he looked into her eyes.

She sat up when the men were gone, reaching for her shirt. Confusion and concern warred in her eyes when she looked back to him. She opened her mouth to speak, but no words came out. She must be scared for him. "Andy," she finally began, but then stopped there.

He wasn't sure how to alleviate her worry. No one had ever worried over him before. With a sigh, he reached for his shirt. "About that picnic..."

Eleven

Dear Andrew,
You are needed at home with an urgency I cannot put into words…

"I SHOULDN'T SAY SUCH A THING," LADY AMBERSTALL complained.

"You will write the words as you see them written before you." He pointed to the parchment lying on the desk with the point of the letter opener.

"Why do you want me to say such things?"

"I thought I made myself clear on the subject." Hawkes shook his head with a casual wave of the letter opener. "Upon Lord Amberstall's return, he will go to the hidden lake on your property where I will give him a warm welcome to his home." Finally, he would have his hands on Amber Hollow lands. He'd waited long enough for his men to deliver Amberstall. It was time to deal with matters his way. And what he would gain would surely provide enough wealth to save his own estate—it had to.

"What exactly is your plan involving my son? I will not allow you to harm him."

He grimaced and walked to the window behind Lady Amberstall's chair. He'd considered taking control of Amber Hollow while the lord was away, but it had the potential to be a messy affair. He didn't need anyone arriving in time to stop his progress. No, Amberstall would arrive at just the intended time. And then he would die. "I will do as I see fit," he murmured.

"If I pen this note, I will have your word on it. You will not hurt my son."

"You will write the note and I will not hurt you."

...Our lands are not safe. I am not safe. Return immediately, please.

"Please?" He scoffed, looking over her shoulder. "I didn't tell you to write that."

"My son will surely be suspicious if I don't exercise manners in my correspondence to him." Her chin rose in indignation. There was something hidden in her eyes, but he couldn't decipher it. "You could use some help with your manners as well, my lord."

Manners? She was his captive. Did she not grasp that fact? "I will allow you to live another day, and you will say 'thank you.' How do you like those manners?"

"Not very well, if I can be honest. You've kept me in your home for over two hours and have yet to offer me tea. It simply isn't done, Lord Hawkes."

"It isn't done?"

"No, my lord. It most certainly is not." Her lips were pursed in condemnation in the same manner one of his governesses used to effect on a daily basis.

He had hated that governess. How did anyone

tolerate this woman's endless opinions? "You will copy the last of the letter I provided…now." He leveled a glare at her and turned to leave the room.

"Where are you going? You can't leave me here. I'm a guest in your home."

Perhaps this hadn't been a well-conceived plot after all. He paused with his hand on the doorknob. Turning back to her, he offered her a smile, "Did you think you were a guest here? My lady, you are a hostage. Do enjoy your stay. I'll send for tea."

He was always late for their dinners together, so she had time. Katie sank back into the warm water of the bath. The scent of lavender swirled around her on the steamy air. It was a lovely scent. She smiled over at the small vial of oil she'd received in the post from Roselyn. It wasn't a scent Katie would have selected, but that was what made it special—even if it did make her miss her friend terribly. Her hair already hung damp down her back where it had begun to curl from the heat of the fire.

Closing her eyes, she leaned back, enjoying the gentle slap of the water against her skin. Her fingers were wrinkled like the dried fruits Mrs. Happstings would send her in the winter months. She wasn't sure how long she'd been in the water, only that her knee had ceased aching and she had no desire to change that fact. Rolling about half-clothed in the grass this afternoon had its benefits, but she was certainly enjoying being clean now.

Just then there was a knock at the door. Katie

jumped, splashing water out of the tub. "Blast and the devil!" she exclaimed, taking in three facts at the same time: she was naked, there was now water all over her floor, and the towels were still sitting across the room on the table.

The door cracked open. "Katie? Is everything all right?" Andy's voice filled the small cottage.

"Um…yes." She sank lower into the water and twisted to peek over the rim of the tub.

"I thought I heard…" He stepped inside and stilled, seeing her bathing before the fire. "I should just… I'll…"

"It must be later than I thought," she offered in explanation as she attempted to sink lower into the water.

He held the basket of food in his hand but made no move to set it down, as if he'd forgotten he was holding it. "I'm a few minutes early. I could come back later…or dine alone tonight, since you're…busy."

"Don't leave." She could feel the heat of a blush spread across her cheeks at her words.

He looked conflicted as he stood rooted to the floor, and when he finally spoke, his voice sounded rougher than usual. "Don't tempt me."

"I'll get out," she suggested. "We can have our dinner once I'm dressed."

"Not likely," he muttered.

"You aren't hungry?"

He smiled. "You haven't any idea what you're doing, do you?"

"I was bathing until you arrived," she said with a tight grip on the edge of the tub. "If you could just hand me the towels from the table…"

He ran a hand through his hair. "I can't believe I'm considering such a terrible idea." he muttered. He crossed the room and retrieved the towels, bringing them to the thick rug where the tub sat. "I'll be damned for this."

"For assisting a lady in need?" She raised a brow.

"Ha! In need of what, is the question." His eyes traveled the length of her body, before he blinked and tore his gaze away, focusing on the towel he gripped with white knuckles. He handed it to her while looking pointedly into the flames.

"Dinner," she replied as she stepped from the tub.

"Indeed." He hesitated a moment. Then with a labored breath, he spun on his heel and moved across the room to set the basket on the table with a speed that suggested this side of the small cottage might burn him.

Katie glanced down to ensure she was covered. Her shoulders were exposed down to the swell of her breasts but mostly covered by her hair, leaving only her legs exposed below the soft fabric. She scurried to the cabinet in the corner and pulled on the robe Mrs. Happstings had insisted she own to ward off the chill of the wilderness.

She'd tried to explain to the woman that there was no difference in climate between the house and her cottage, but the housekeeper hadn't listened. She smiled down at the pale blue fabric, thankful she had it now, though not for the reasons Mrs. Happstings had anticipated.

Andy still had his back to her where he stood at the table. As she joined him, he handed the plate in his hand to her. "This is for you."

She'd never seen one plate piled so high with food. Fruit threatened to fall from the sides as most of a meat pie took up the center of the plate. "I don't know that I'm that hungry."

"What? Oh. Right." He glanced at her with a tension visible in his face that she wished she could ease somehow. But a second later his eyes were trained on the plate of food once more.

She wasn't precisely relaxed at the moment, either. Somehow, however, he seemed more uncomfortable than she did.

"Did you remember to bring a fork?"

He chuckled, some of the tension leaving his face. He looked up at her with a sigh, apparently giving in to their unconventional situation. "Thankfully, tonight we won't have to share."

She searched for a neutral subject to discuss so neither of their minds would return to the scene he'd walked into only minutes ago. She took a bite of food. "Shadow," she blurted out before she could even swallow.

"What about him?"

"He's healing nicely," she rushed to explain. "A few days ago, he wouldn't have been able to walk as he can now."

"Because of you."

She smiled. "You bred a strong horse."

"Someone wise once told me strength couldn't always be found in muscles," he returned with a grin.

She looked up into his face, hanging on his smile for a moment. When she'd met him, she hadn't known this warm, kind man existed beneath his arrogant exterior. Now, she wished she could wake to that smile every morning and fall asleep dreaming of it every night. When had this happened? She watched as he took a sip of wine and offered her a glass. "Andy, I want to know more."

"About horses?"

"Not horses." She could feel the heat of a blush creeping up her neck. "The next lesson."

He shifted in his chair. "I shouldn't be the one to teach you. It isn't my place to do so."

"But will you?"

"Damn it all, Katie, you shouldn't ask things like this of me. I've already gone too far." He slumped back in his chair with a defeated sigh.

"Because you'll leave here soon?" The words almost caught in her throat.

"Yes, I must leave soon. I have a few days at best. And what will become of you when I go? You aren't experienced in these things, Katie. You don't know what you're asking for."

She was beginning to shiver, whether from sitting so far from the fire in only a thin robe or Andy's words, she wasn't entirely sure. She wrapped her arms across her chest as she said, "I can take care of myself. I always have."

"I know that."

"Then why?"

He was silent for a moment, concern drawing his brows into a deep vee. "Because I want to." His chest rose and fell with labored breaths. "…Perhaps too much. Katie, I want to show you all of those things. I want you."

"Isn't that a favorable condition, since you're here with me?"

"Not for a gentleman with any honor. Not for me."

"Oh. I see." But she didn't see. All she knew was that he would leave in a few days and she would be alone again. She would live out her days here in this cottage, which she'd thought she wanted not two days ago. But now...

She shook her head. Now, this cottage, even with all of her hobbies piled high in the corners, seemed empty without Andy. But he was here tonight. If he would only fill her memories so that she could seal this evening up like a jam jar to pull out in the cold winter months ahead, she might survive until spring.

"Katie, don't look at me in such a manner."

"Why not?" She blinked at him, unaware that she was looking at him in any particular fashion. "It doesn't matter anyway. I want to enjoy this night, and all you can think of is your honor? I thought you..." Her words broke off as he stood and rounded the table.

"I want to enjoy this night together as well—more than you know." He traced the edge of her robe with his hands, pulling the garment off her shoulders.

"I thought you were an honorable gentleman," she said with a nervous smile, drawing the edges of the robe up to somewhat cover herself, although not well.

"I was mistaken." His eyes grew a shade darker as she watched him. "Katie, you're beautiful. Even with the breeches you insist on wearing..." He broke off. His hands slid down her upper arms, warming her skin as he moved.

She couldn't quite breathe. "You changed your mind? This is lesson three in marital relations?"

"No," he said before lowering his head to hers on a sigh. "Perhaps." His low voice rumbled over her scalp, sending shivers down her spine. "I don't know what this is… Unexpected, to be sure. Let's not examine it, for I think we'll both find it madness by tomorrow."

She trailed a hand around his body, pulling him a fraction closer. "I won't."

"Something tells me neither will I—which is madness in itself." He took a small step back and wrapped her hands within his. "Katie, I can't make you any promises. I don't know where this might go. I know that I care for you. I know that I don't want our time together to end. But with so much uncertainty…"

"Shhh." She rose to her toes and pressed a kiss to his lips. "Let's not think about that right now."

He released her hands to wind his arms around her waist, pulling her closer. His callused fingers dragged against her spine through the robe, making her arch into him in a silent plea for more. The robe trailed behind her on the floor, exposing more and more of her skin with every movement. Her bare breasts now rubbed against the linen of his shirt with every shaky breath. Looking deep into her eyes, he nodded and kissed her again. His lips slashed across hers, drawing a small sound of need from her throat. Together they stumbled toward her bed. She fumbled desperately with his shirt, wanting to see him as he now saw her, to touch him as he touched her.

He finally tore his shirt over his head and tossed it to the floor. She trailed her fingers down his broad chest to his stomach, enjoying the twitch of his muscles beneath her touch. But when her hands dipped to the waistband of his breeches, he lifted her from the floor with a growl and tossed her onto the bed.

She landed on the soft quilt, laughing up at him. It surprised her that she felt no fear or embarrassment, exposed to him as she was. He accepted her, told her he cared for her. She was strong, free, and for the first time in her life, truly happy.

With one knee on the bed, he leaned over her, kissing her until she was left dazed. She wound her arms around him, pulling on him in her desire to be closer. Closer to what, she didn't know. When he broke their kiss, she heard her own sound of complaint before she could stop it.

He grinned at her before kissing a path down her neck. Her head fell back as his tongue caressed the base of her throat, trapping her wild pulse with his mouth.

Gripping his shoulders, she dug her fingernails into his skin with a ragged breath. He shifted over her, his hands drifting over her skin as if memorizing her by touch. His palm skated around the outside of her breast while his thumb rubbed the peak, making her squirm.

He met her gaze with a dark look in his eyes, the curve of his mouth promising untold mischief. She tried to breathe. His hands were hot on her skin. What would come next? Where would he touch? Where would he...

His lips trailed across the curve of her breast. She arched into him as he took the hardened peak into his mouth. Moving her hands into his hair, she held him close as he brought a moan to her lips with the flick of his tongue.

He moved lower still, pressing kisses down her belly. His hands drifted over her waist to her hips. But when he moved one hand to the top of her thigh, his brows drew together and he paused.

"Don't stop, please don't stop," she begged, not caring how it sounded. In this moment, her life seemed to depend on him continuing.

"It isn't right. I shouldn't."

"Please." Her breathless whisper hung in the air between them.

His eyes met hers in the dim candlelight as he moved his hand to the apex of her thighs. The heat of his palm melted something deep within her as he held his hand there, searching her face. She shifted beneath him, as if reaching for something just beyond her grasp.

"This is what you want," he stated.

"I want you." Her thighs parted. She didn't know what she was doing. Her body seemed to be under his control, and all she knew was that every part of her was screaming for him not to stop.

He stood, his eyes never leaving hers. She was about to protest when he kicked off his boots and unfastened the placket of his breeches, letting them fall to the floor. He had a muscular build with a broad chest that tapered down to… Her mouth went dry as she tried to think of words, but there were none. He was magnificent. She licked her lips and forced her eyes to travel back to his face.

He moved to join her on the bed. Lounging beside her, he traced the line of her shoulder with his fingers. The air around them felt fragile, as if the entire world could shatter at any moment. And then in the next moment it did, falling down in tiny pieces as his lips returned to hers with an urgency she matched.

She wound her hands over his shoulders to delve into his hair as his hand skimmed down her side. He deepened their kiss, his hand moving back to the apex of her thighs, stroking her body until she arched into his touch. Grinning against her lips, he moved over her. His mouth trailed down her body, kissing everywhere his hands had touched earlier as he dipped one finger into her depths. She grabbed his shoulders and tried to sit up at the invasion, but fell back to the quilt again with a twitch of his fingers.

What was he doing to her? She would ask, but the words wouldn't form on her lips as he rubbed his thumb over the very core of her. His kisses moved steadily lower, luring her into some sort of dark trap of need. She grasped fistfuls of the quilt at her sides as his mouth settled where his fingers had been a second ago. With every flick of his tongue, she felt herself coming apart, breaking into tiny shards only he could put back together again.

He moved his fingers into her again, pulling her over the edge into darkness with his mouth. She dug her heels into the quilt as she reached for his blond head, needing the connection with him more than the air she was struggling to breathe.

She grasped his hair as she cried out, "Andy!" into the night. The tension of the moment was ripping her apart piece by piece with whatever he was doing to her. Everything seemed to press in on her with a force and pace she couldn't overcome until suddenly she fell over the edge into a wondrous state of bliss. He placed one last kiss between her thighs, giving her chills at his touch as he pulled his hands free of her. When he lifted his head to look at her, she could see the hunger she'd felt only a moment ago reflected in his eyes.

"Andy," she began, unsure what to ask, only that she wanted to do for him what he had for her. Instead, she slid her fingers down his body as he moved closer to her. Watching his face for a reaction, she curled her fingers around the length of him. There was a second of labored breath as a dark look crossed his face before he laid his hand on her arm, stilling her movements.

"Don't."

"Why not?"

"My judgment isn't at its best at the moment."

"Then trust me. I want this."

"If I wasn't damned before, surely I will be now," he said as he lowered his body back over hers. He trailed his lips down her neck, his breathing harsh against her skin.

Drifting her hands down his back, she grabbed his hips and tried to pull him closer. His hard body pressed close to hers, yet not close enough. He groaned and his teeth grazed her shoulder as his hands delved into her hair. She could feel him poised at her entrance, but still he held back. She trembled with anticipation. She needed him. Why was he waiting?

"You know I would never hurt you." His voice came out in a deep, raspy whisper near her ear.

"Yes," she said somewhere between a plea for more and an acknowledgment of his words.

"You trust me," he confirmed as he slid a hand down her body to tilt her hips toward him.

She gave him a quick nod of agreement. Of course she trusted him. And she wanted him, pain or no pain.

There was a dark, tortured look about his eyes that she wanted to ease and devour at the same time. What was happening to her? "Don't stop now, please..." Her voice trailed off as he thrust into her, stretching her, filling her until she felt she might rip apart. He paused, looking at her with concern, buried deep inside her but not daring to move.

She waited, hoping for more, yet fearing it at the same time. Her heart pounded as his body pressed close to hers. He was watching her. The moment between them could be measured in shallow breaths until she gave him a tiny nod.

The worry in his eyes eased as he withdrew, only to push into her once more. This time there was no pain. This time her body relaxed into the motion. He increased his pace, thrusting into her as she struggled to hold on to the world around her. She arched her hips and met his desire for more with her own need.

She wound her arms around him, clinging to him as she stretched for some unknown place. All she knew was the weight of his body on hers, the heat of his skin beneath her palms, and the tension in her body as she reached for more.

As he drove into her, her very existence came crashing in on her, building into a fury of need for something just beyond her grasp. When she thought she might not survive it, she cried out.

He practically growled in response and drove into her once more as she pulled him over the edge with her. She shattered into tiny pieces of her former self, and they collapsed onto the bed together.

They lay there, still joined for a moment in a heap of intertwined limbs and gasping breaths before he rolled from her, taking her with him and settling her across his chest. Neither spoke for a minute as he held her close, stroking her hair.

"Thank you," she whispered against his chest.

"Katie? In case you were wondering, I'm glad I trusted you. Tonight was…incredible. You are incredible." He stroked his fingers over her hair and down her back in slow, mindless movements.

After all the nights she'd been content to be alone, she found tonight was different. "Stay with me," she murmured.

"There will be talk if I do." He kissed her temple and smoothed her hair away from her face.

"There will always be talk." People had been discussing her for years, and they wouldn't stop now. Would they even notice? They already avoided her as if she were a wild animal.

"I won't leave." He rubbed his hand over her lower back in a gentle caress. "Not yet."

"Not yet," she repeated, clinging to the words. It should be enough. She'd shared nine days with him. It was a moment, a blink of the eye, but it should sustain her. Only she knew it wouldn't. Nine days or a thousand would never be enough. She inhaled the scent of him, tried to memorize the tangle of their legs together, how his body felt pressed to hers. She looked up to meet his gaze, resting her cheek on his chest.

He ran his hand through her hair. "I'm not going anywhere, Katie. I'm here."

If only she could believe him.

Twelve

ANDREW SHOOK HIS COAT INTO PLACE, ANXIOUS TO BE outside on such a perfect autumn day. He gave the mirror a nod of approval and turned for the door. The grin covering his face since last night hadn't budged. And, he had to admit, it wasn't the promise of nice weather outside that had him rushing this morning—it was the promise of Katie.

Even though he'd only been away from her bed a few hours, it felt like days had passed. The way her hair had tumbled around him, her soft skin against his, the seductive lilt of her voice, her laughter…he wanted more. But once he had more, would he want more after that? Could he ever have enough to walk away from her? He stopped mid-stride.

If he did walk away from her, it would be with the knowledge that she would be left alone in her cottage—forever.

He found he couldn't bear the thought. He grimaced. She belonged with him. He glanced out his window overlooking the garden. Just beyond that tree line lay the path to Katie's cottage. He could almost see the smoke from her chimney puffing into the air. Blinking the image away, he stared at the grove of trees. Soon everything they'd shared would be gone like chimney smoke on the wind. He couldn't stay here much longer, whether Shadow was healed or not. With the countryside being combed for his existence, he could only stay another few days for his trail to go cold before he would have to move.

Yet the thought of leaving made him slightly ill. He was dreading his return to his own life, that much he knew. But there was something more on his mind— something with wild flames for hair and a dusting of freckles across her nose. He cared for her. But did caring for someone usually involve this degree of anxiety? He jerked at the knock on his door. He would have to think about this conundrum at a later time.

He moved to answer the door. It must be Mrs. Happstings with his laundered shirt. He shrugged, glancing down at his all-black ensemble. He was starting to become accustomed to it. When he returned to town he would have to add more black to his wardrobe. Throwing open the door, however, he was surprised to see the butler standing in the hall holding a letter in his hand. "This arrived for you in the morning post, my lord."

Andrew nodded his thanks and took the letter, waiting for the butler to turn and leave before he tore it open. Who knew he was here? His mother, of course, but surely she wouldn't write to him. She knew of his delay. She must understand. He had an injured horse. That couldn't be rushed. His heart pounded in his chest. Had things become more urgent? He turned the note over and, indeed, saw the familiar hand of his mother there. Opening it, he scanned for information.

...Our lands are not safe. I am not safe. Return immediately, please.

"Please?" He muttered the word to himself. It was the "please" that gave him reason to pause. She never said "please." That could only mean... He frowned as he traced the looping letters of the word with his finger. The men who were after his head were still in the area, so Hawkes himself must be threatening her safety. "Unless there are more men than the two..."

Andrew read the note two more times. He had to help her. Mother had only said "please" on one other occasion, and that had been upon the death of his father. Things must be dire indeed. He'd told himself that as long as the men were searching the woods for him here, his home was safe. Of course, that had been an easy lie to tell himself, since it kept him here with Katie a bit longer. And now his family was in danger. He couldn't fail—not again.

Katie would understand his rush, but this couldn't be good-bye. He would think of some reason to see her again. Shadow's Light—he would have to come back for his horse. He would simply return home, patch things there, and return to retrieve Shadow... and see Katie one last time.

He tossed the note aside and left his room, pounding down the stairs to the downtrodden beat of his heart.

He sped out the door and was entering the stables

before his mind could catch up with his actions. "Have you seen Lady Katie this morning?" he asked one of the grooms.

The groom paused in brushing down the horse to look at Andrew. "I saw her go in the house not a half hour ago. You didn't see her?"

"In the house?" he repeated. "Why would she be there?"

"Lord Ormesby returned at first light this morning. She's with him…in the house."

"Lord…her father is here?" His heart skipped a beat before slamming into his chest as the world crushed in on him. It was over. He had to leave. Her father was home. It was all ending so quickly. He blinked and refocused on the groom who was still speaking to him.

"Yes, you must've just missed them."

"Very good." He couldn't listen to any more. He needed to collect his thoughts. He swallowed and moved past the groom to go to Shadow's stall. The events of last night threatened to choke him, much like Katie's father would do soon. Perhaps the timing was fortuitous. This morning he'd planned on spending tonight much like last night, and the night after that… He swore and lifted the latch. How quickly things change.

Stepping inside, he stood for a moment staring at Shadow. It was as if he understood Andrew's panic, as he stomped and shifted to the side in agitation. "I know, ol' boy. I know."

Shadow's leg looked better. He could most likely make the journey south, but Andrew would take the mount Thornwood had offered in case he needed to make a quick escape from those men on the road. "You can't gallop just yet, I don't believe," he muttered.

Shadow huffed and tossed his head.

"I know you think you can. But you need to stay here for now. If you don't stay…" *I will have no excuse to return.*

He almost wished to not have the offer of a horse from the Thornwood stables, to have Shadow still badly injured. He wanted to be forced to stay, if only a bit longer. But even staying here, there wouldn't be any more dinners in the cottage, no more unchaperoned outings. And he was needed at home. It was over. He would make one last trip to gather Shadow and say a proper farewell.

Unless… He could be honorable. He could offer for her.

His heart pounded against his chest. Marriage. Marriage to Katie, and all he had to do was confess his crimes. She could come with him to Amber Hollow. He wouldn't have to leave her. Perhaps they could be together again as they were last night once they reached an inn. But the promise of marriage wouldn't buy him that liberty. He would have to wait for the banns and such, but she would be his. He grinned and gave Shadow a pat on the shoulder. "Perhaps all will work out after all, ol' boy. We shall see."

❧

Katie took small steps into the main hall of her old home. Stopping before the library door, she shot a glance up the staircase before turning the knob to go inside. Andy would still be upstairs at this hour. She needed to see her father and inform him that they had a guest before Andrew made an appearance and her father got the wrong idea of things.

She shook her head to force the blush from her cheeks. Her father would be correct if he did suspect something of happening with their guest during his absence, but that didn't need to be mentioned. She didn't want Andy to be forced into marriage. He didn't deserve to be trapped in that way. No. She would let him leave. Shadow was growing stronger. It must be done.

And if she shooed Andy away from here fast enough, he would never know the horrible truth of her family. Her connection to his tormentor would fall away, because she would no longer have a place in his life. For all of these reasons, it was the correct course of action. She took a breath to settle her nerves.

It was odd that the place she'd feared returning to for so long wasn't as frightening as letting Andy leave. She sent a wry smile up the stairs and stepped into the library, shutting the door at her back. Her father was standing over his desk, sifting through the papers and correspondence piled there in his absence.

"Have some food brought in for me, won't you, Celersworth? I can see I have quite a bit of work ahead of me today."

"I'll see what I can do," Katie offered with a smile.

Her father spun around, his round, brown eyes growing wider. "Katherine. You're…"

"In the library? That I am." She held her hands out to the sides to show that she was also standing on her own, but he didn't seem to notice.

"I'm surprised to see you here." He took a step forward but stopped himself from crossing the room to her. He laid a hand on the back of an armchair before shifting to stuff his hands in his pockets.

"How was your trip?" Katie chirped the question with a quick glance over her shoulder to ensure the library door was closed. She needed to jump ahead through these pleasantries, but she couldn't jump too quickly or her father might be suspicious. He was already shocked that she was here. She took a few more steps, moving farther into the room.

Andy would be coming downstairs soon—she couldn't take all morning with this. She wiped her sweaty palms on her breeches and tried to focus on conversing with her father.

He sank into his favorite chair by the fire, running a weary hand through what was left of his dark hair. "Must we discuss it?"

"That bad? Surely it was nice to see family." She moved to the chair nearest where he sat. It was odd—she hadn't been inside the house since Trevor passed away, but it didn't seem such a haunted structure now.

"Ha! Your uncle didn't seem too pleased to see me."

"Why not?" While she was here, perhaps she could get some answers for Andy. Why would her uncle want his stables, and what did that have to do with her father—a mine owner? She sat forward in her chair a fraction. "It was *business* advice he desired, was it not? That's what you said was the purpose of your trip, anyway." There was a note of accusation in her voice, so she added, "I can't think of anyone more qualified on that subject matter than you."

"I want nothing to do with his shady business dealings," her father grumbled as he poured himself a drink from the decanter on the table beside him.

"What do you mean?"

"He's mad. He has his mind set on some neighboring lands. He's convinced he could make a small fortune, under the right circumstances." He shrugged and took a drink from the glass.

Andy was right. Her uncle was after his stables. But why? "Does he need a small fortune?"

"It would seem so. Poor investments," he added for explanation.

"And what of the circumstances?"

He rubbed his eyes before resting his elbow back on the arm of the chair. "That's the disgraceful part of the whole rotten business. Upon further discussion, we decided I should return home while he handles things there. It was for the best, really. I needed to see to things here." He smiled, closing the topic of conversation.

"Things here are fine. Never better," she rushed to say.

"Nothing of interest has happened while I was away?"

She swallowed, dropping her gaze to the rug, unable to look him in the eye. "No." The word was spoken before she could stop herself. Something inside her wouldn't allow her to bring up their guest.

Perhaps she could convince Andy to stay tonight in her cottage and leave tomorrow. No one would know of it—including her father. She could have one last night with him. But she knew it would never be enough. She sighed. If tonight was all she could have of Andy, she would treasure it.

"Really? Nothing happened while I was away? You know my sight has not left me yet."

Her heart was pounding as she lifted her eyes to meet his. "What did you see?"

"Katherine," he admonished. "Do you truly believe I can be away for a month and not notice that certain things happened while I was away?"

She'd hoped that would be the case, yes. So much for keeping Andy a secret. Her brows drew together in concern. "I…suppose we need to discuss a few things, then."

"Indeed we do. You know you can't keep secrets from me. I *am* your father."

She nodded, knowing she must tell him of Andy's stay on their property, but hoping she could make it seem more innocent than it had been in truth. "It began almost two weeks ago. I should have written to let you know of it, but everything was happening so fast. And I didn't know how to tell you."

"You needn't worry on that score. It pleases me to see you happy. You should know that."

"I do know that," she lied. If her father's wishes included her happiness, her life up to this point would have been quite different. She shook off the thought to focus on the conversation. "I just didn't think you would support…"

"I'm quite proud of you," he offered with a smile.

"Proud." She searched his face, trying to understand.

"There's no need for modesty, Katherine."

"Isn't there?"

"You got our stables back in working order. I saw the repairs to the roof when I arrived. This means you've been there—within the stables. And now you're here." He paused to take a sip of his drink. "I knew you would regain your senses one day and come back to the family."

"Father, I didn't…"

"It brings joy to my heart, truly it does."

She couldn't find the words to tell him all that happened while he was away. But, in a sense, he was correct. She couldn't deny that she was sitting inside Ormesby Place or that she now went to the stables every day. She'd changed, and it was because of Andy. She smiled as she studied her hands. Glancing up, she noticed her father was watching her with a curious gleam in his eyes.

She should be honest with him, but with honesty would come either Andy's departure or a forced marriage—and she didn't want either. It couldn't be over, not yet. She needed more time, more of him. And the only way to have even another moment was to stay silent. Her heart sank at the thought of tonight being their last night together, their last dinner in her cottage. Her vision blurred for a second, but she blinked away the emotion.

"Is something the matter?" her father asked, his eyes narrowing.

"No, nothing." She pasted on a smile and stood. "I should let you rest."

"We'll talk later."

She nodded and moved toward the door. She needed to find Andy and tell him of her father's return. At least then she could be honest with one of the men in her life.

❧

Andrew heard someone nearing Shadow's Light's stall as he set aside the pitchfork. He held his breath that it wasn't Lord Ormesby come to murder him for his liberties with the man's daughter. But with a quick glance around the corner, he sighed in relief. "There you are, beautiful." He grabbed Katie's hand and pulled her into the stall.

"Shhh, someone will hear you." Her eyes were wide with worry as she turned to back out of the stall.

"When did you become concerned with what people hear?" he asked, tugging her back to him.

"I don't know, but I blame you for it entirely." She was teasing him, but some underlying worry was causing a crease between her brows.

His grin faded as he watched her. If he asked her to be his wife, what would she say? She could very well refuse him, and then this would be his last moment with her. He took a steadying breath and led in, "I have something I need to tell you."

She cleared her throat. "As do I. I've been at the house this morning."

"I heard as much."

"Oh." She bit her lip. "So you know about my father's return?"

He nodded, wanting to move on to his topic of conversation. After all, it would greatly affect the discussion of her father, depending on her answer. "Katie, I received word from my home today."

"You're leaving." She looked away from him and bit one of her fingernails. "I suppose this really is it. I was hoping you could stay one more night with me, hidden away in my cottage."

"I can't," he replied, as saddened by that fact as she was.

"Well…it was a pleasant interlude, while it lasted." She lowered her hand and turned back to him. She attempted to smile, but it didn't reach her eyes, which were filling with tears.

He reached out and grabbed her hands, holding them within his own as he pulled her closer to him. Looking into her eyes he said, "Come with me."

"What?"

He tried to concentrate on the words he spoke as the thoughts flooded through his mind. "Your father returned home on the same day I must leave… I could talk to him, I could…"

"No! Don't talk to him." Her shoulders went rigid with fright.

He tilted his head, looking into her eyes as he attempted to comprehend her reaction. "You do understand what I'm saying, don't you?" His grip tightened on her hands.

She pulled her hands from his and took a step backward. "That you wish to speak with my father, which is impossible."

"That I'm asking for your hand in marriage."

"Oh." She stood looking at him for a moment, her face expressionless. "But if you talk to him…" She broke off, closing her eyes against some horrible fate. "You can't talk to my father, Andy."

"Katie, will you be my wife?" he tried again. He needed an answer before his heart imploded.

She said nothing, only stared at him with the crease between her brows growing deeper with her concern.

He finally broke the silence between them, his voice thick as he said, "I…seem to have greatly misjudged our situation. My apologies."

He took a step to move past her toward the door when he heard her say, "I do want to marry you."

He paused, almost afraid he'd imagined her voice. Turning back, he asked, "You do?"

"Yes, let's go now," she replied. Her words were rushed in her excitement. "There's no need to talk to my father. You can speak with him later—after we're wed."

"I'm not going to kidnap you, Katie. It wouldn't be proper."

"Blast being proper."

He moved closer to her, laying his hands on her shoulders. "I don't want to wait for the banns either, but we must."

"It's not that…"

"You don't think your father will approve of the match?" What sort of tyrant must her father be to frighten her so? Andrew was a lord. She could do worse.

"I'm sure he'll approve… I only…"

"I know you're nervous, Katie. But I was there with you to overcome your fear of horses, I was there with you last night, and I won't abandon you now. There is nothing your father can say to make me leave your side."

"Nothing?" Her eyes were shining with unshed tears. "Do you mean that?"

"Of course. Be strong, my Katie."

She smiled as she wrapped her arms around his waist.

"Is that a yes?" His heart was pounding as he looked down into her upturned face.

"As long as you don't leave me."

"I promise."

Thirteen

KATIE STEPPED INTO THE HOUSE AT ORMESBY PLACE for the second time today. This time she had Andy at her side, yet she was more rattled with nerves than before. She glanced up at him. He'd promised not to leave her side. He was a man of his word—honorable to a fault. So she had no need to worry, but that didn't calm her anxiety. There was no way to keep the truth from him now. Who her family was, their ties to the threats to his property, the threats to him. The question was: would he forgive her for not telling him?

"Katie, if you grasp my fingers any tighter, I'll lose all blood flow," he murmured in her ear.

"Oh, sorry." She gave him a sheepish smile and loosened her grip.

"Just let me speak to your father. You don't have to say anything. I'll see if he is willing to allow you to come with me, provided you bring a maid along for the journey. If not, I'll come back for you in a few weeks. All will be fine. We're going to be together forever."

"Andy…what would you do if you discovered something distasteful about my family?"

"Every family has something distasteful lurking behind the closed doors of the ancestral estate. You have nothing to be concerned over."

"Just know that I..."

Her father stepped into the main hall, drawing her attention. She watched as his eyes fell to their joined hands. "Is this the house guest I heard we had from Mrs. Happstings? I found it curious you didn't mention him earlier, Katherine. Now, I suppose I see why."

"Father, this is Andrew Clifton, Lord Amberstall. Lord Amberstall, my father, Lord Ormesby."

"Lord Amberstall," her father repeated with a shocked expression.

"I appreciate your hospitality, Lord Ormesby. As I'm sure you heard, my horse and I had an accident along the border of your estate. Your daughter was kind enough to assist me."

"I can see that."

Katie's hand began to sweat within Andy's grasp, but he made no move to release it. "Father, perhaps we should go into the parlor."

"Yes, there are things I would like to discuss with you, my lord," Andy added.

"Indeed."

They walked in silence into the parlor.

"Lord Ormesby, this isn't a discussion I expected to have, and yet I have not come to it lightly. I've been here only a short time..." He paused, glancing to Katie with a warm smile.

"Is your primary estate in southern England, Lord Amberstall?" her father interrupted.

"Yes," Andy answered, taken aback by his interruption.

"And you were traveling there when your horse was injured." He raised a brow, even though he hadn't asked a question. He already knew the answer.

"I managed to walk away from the incident, but yes, that is how I became detained here. Your daughter was kind enough to allow me to stay while she saw to my horse."

Her father rubbed his eyes. "You have been here in my home for a fortnight?"

"Almost, my lord. Ten days, I believe. Your estate is quite nice. I assisted with a few..."

"Your estate is Amber Hollow, is it not?"

"Father, don't!"

"Yes, it is." Andy shot a curious glance at her before turning back to her father. "Do you know my family?"

"In a manner of speaking," her father said, his round eyes narrowing.

Andy smiled as he said, "My mother makes the rounds in London. I suppose you've met her on occasion."

"No, I've not had the pleasure."

Katie's heart pounded in her ears. Why couldn't they have simply run away together like she suggested? She'd been so close to happiness, only to stand here and watch her father destroy it with his words. Helpless to stop the conversation, she waited...and hoped.

"Oh, well, a familiarity with my family and estate should make this a welcome conversation at any rate."

"That's debatable."

"Father, please hear him out."

"He has a right to know, Katherine."

"A right to know what?" Andrew turned to her, his brows drawn together in concern.

She opened her mouth to speak, but no words came out. He had promised he would stand by her side. Would he? She struggled for air as she looked up at him.

"Katie, what do I have a right to know?" Andy asked.

"She's Lord Hawkes' niece, of course."

"Father!" How could he blurt out a thing like that? The truth was bad enough without his painful delivery of it.

"My apologies, Daughter. But did you think you could hide that fact forever? I could be mistaken, but I believe he was about to ask for your hand in marriage. It's always best to be honest in these situations, Katherine. After all, I've been Hawkes' guest for the past month. I know of Amberstall's troubles there. It would be wrong to act as if I'm unaware."

Andy pulled back from her a fraction. "Is that true?"

Katie could only stare at him as accusation filled his eyes, her future happiness falling to the parlor floor and shattering like a piece of unwanted china.

❧

"Why didn't you tell me?" Andrew untangled his fingers from hers and turned to face her.

"I wanted to tell you."

"You do as you please with everything else in your life. If you wanted me to know of this, you would have told me."

"I didn't think you would understand."

"Understand what? That you've been protecting my enemies from me since we met?"

"That's not true."

He pushed the hair from his face and shifted away from her. "I don't know what's true anymore, Katie."

Her betrayal ripped at his heart. Everything he'd believed was nothing more than a ruse to hurt him.

Ormesby cleared his throat. "Perhaps I should leave you two to discuss things."

When no one answered, the older man left the room. Katie hadn't denied anything her father had said. Andrew couldn't get beyond the hurt of it. He cared for her, and she had used him.

"You probably knew the moment I stated my name," he spat the words at her as he began to pace the floor.

"No, I didn't know the nature of the business my father was assisting him with." She drew her arms up to wrap around herself as she looked at him with wide-eyed panic.

"When I told you of the trouble on my estate, you must have known then. Katie, why didn't you speak to me?"

"I was going to, but…"

"But what? You lied to me."

"I didn't want you to leave," she admitted.

"Didn't want me to, or couldn't allow me to?"

"I don't know what you're talking about."

"Did you think you'd do your family a service by keeping me here, waiting for your father's return?" It was rather convenient that she'd strung him along until the day her father came back.

"No." She shook her head.

"That's why you refused to sell me a horse," he muttered in realization. "How could I be so blind?"

"That has nothing to do with…"

"And when Shadow began to heal, you had to invent some other reason to keep me on the estate. So you seduced me."

"No, I didn't. I only ever…"

"When I arrived last night and you were bathing… that was planned." He ran a hand through his hair. "I'm such a fool."

"No, you're not. I didn't plan for that to happen."

"You've been waiting for your father to return home. Why? So he can do the job of those henchmen and deliver me to Hawkes?"

She shook her head as a tear rolled down her cheek. "I would never…"

"You've plotted against me from the beginning. And to think, I believed you—the naïve miss, tortured and shoved to the side by the world," he mocked as his eyes narrowed on her.

"Andy, I would never hurt you like that."

"You already have." He stepped away from her. He watched as tears spilled down her cheeks. How long had she practiced before a mirror to be able to produce convincing tears? Lies. It was all lies.

"I overlooked your wild hair, your odd interests, your unconventional pets, your freckles, your manner of dress, your complete lack of propriety…even a blasted limp you invented, but you've pushed me too far, Katie. You are made of flaws, and I dismissed all of them to be with you! I thought I had changed and grown to overlook your faults and stand at your side. And now, this. I won't be made to look the fool again."

An hour ago he'd proposed marriage to her. How had he not seen the signs of her betrayal? Well, this time he would not slink away to lick his wounds. This time he would return to his estate and confront his enemy. And Lady Katie Moore could damn well find someone else to toy with, because Andrew wouldn't be around for her amusement any longer.

He turned and stormed out the door, leaving his clothing, saddlebags, trust in women, and his dignity to be stuffed away in a drawer at Ormesby Place and never heard of again.

❧

Katie followed him into the main hall, only to see the front door slam shut. She blinked, jolted as much by the sound as the finality of it. She took a few steps toward the door, waiting for it to open again, or perhaps for it to dissolve like sugar in a glass of lemonade so that she could watch him walk away, just as everyone else had done in her life.

She touched the door. The painted wood was cool beneath her fingers. Would he regret leaving and return? She wanted the door to open, but she wasn't going to be the one to turn the handle—she couldn't. Her vision blurred as another round of tears filled her eyes. Resting her forehead on the smooth wood, she pleaded, *Come back. Please, come back.*

Why hadn't she told him about her family a week ago when she discovered the connection?

She pushed off from the door with a small sob and moved to the bottom step of the main staircase. When she was eleven, Katie had waited there for two days for her mother to return, so it was only fitting that she go there now. Pulling her legs up to her chest, she shrank into the corner with her eyes still on the door.

He hadn't meant it. He couldn't have meant

it—except maybe he had. *You are made of flaws, and I dismissed all of them to be with you!*

Andy's words echoed in her mind, only unlike echoes, the sound did not grow dimmer with time. The words were still as loud as they had been ten minutes ago when he said them in the parlor. She hadn't imagined the connection between them—he asked her to be his wife, after all. Only last night, she'd trusted him enough to lie with him. She'd let him... She sniffed and pulled her legs tighter to her body. If she was flawed before, she'd certainly allowed him to complete her destruction last night. And now here she was, back where she began—broken and alone.

⁓

Her father cracked open the door of her cottage. "I knocked. I wasn't sure if you could hear me."

"I heard you," she mumbled, not bothering to lift her head from the comfort of her bed where she faced the wall.

"The staff is worried about you. I know I don't usually visit you here..." He moved into the cottage and closed the door. "But you can't hide here forever, locked away from the world."

He'd kept her locked away from the world most of her life, and now that she wanted time alone to drown in her sorrows, he had issue with it? She huffed into her pillow. "I'm not locked away. You came right inside."

"You know that's not what I mean, Katherine. You can't continue living this way."

Anger surged through her veins at his callous words. He couldn't be serious. She rolled to her other side so that she could see him. "Now you want to make improvements to my life? Only yesterday you sought to destroy it."

"You are the one who lied, Katherine. Not I."

"A fact you were all too pleased to put on display before a gentleman seeking my hand in marriage." Her chest tightened as she fought for air. He'd always been distant and uninvolved. To think, she'd been sad about that fact in the past. Now she wished nothing more than for him to leave her alone—forever.

His chest puffed out and his jaw tightened at the accusation in her voice. "I am not the one at fault in this situation."

She sat up. "This was all your fault!" she screamed.

"Katherine, you led a gentleman to believe you were someone you are not. And I care enough about your welfare to demand honesty. If you begin a relationship with lies, no good can come of it. Look to your mother as an example of that."

"This wasn't about you or Mama. This was about me. This was *my* chance at happiness." Would Andrew have loved her? Perhaps eventually. Now she would never know.

"Katherine, I was only doing what I believed to be right. This world is full of difficult decisions and…"

"Katie," she stated, breaking off his speech.

"What was that?"

"Katie. My name is Katie. Katherine was my mother. She deceived you, not me. You've painted us with the same brush for far too long." She stood, her hair hanging in a tangled mess around her face. "I am Katie. I didn't leave you nine years ago. You left me." She took a step forward, kicking a chair aside with her toe.

"I wasn't welcome in your home from the time Mama ran away, simply because I was female, because I looked like her. So, I came here. I've tried to have a life within these cottage walls, Papa, but it's time for me to leave—to have a life of my own. And then you see fit to destroy my chances at that?" She shook her head as her eyes bored into him.

"I'm not perfect, I admit that freely. And I know it wasn't easy for you after your mother left. I never knew why you wanted to move here. I thought you needed time to heal…"

"I needed to be loved. That's all I've ever wanted."

He sighed and sank into a chair at the small table. "Katie, we will find a husband for you. But you must believe me, what happened was for the best. Secrets and families at odds with one another are not the basis for a happy marriage. I know you can't see that now, but perhaps one day you will understand. And I don't think he will fare well against your uncle anyway. I don't want my daughter involved in such dealings. Another gentleman is out there…"

"I don't want another husband. I loved *him*." She said the words into the still air of the cottage, knowing she spoke the truth. "I love him still."

He said nothing, only nodded. A moment later he stood to leave, digging into his pocket as he did so. "Amberstall left this on the desk in the blue suite along with a few personal items. I didn't think it my place to read it. But perhaps you would like it…to remember him by." He held up a folded piece of parchment and laid it on the table.

"Katie, there will be contentment in your future. I know it doesn't seem that way today…"

"That's the problem, Father. I don't want contentment anymore—it's not the same as happiness."

"And you will find it one day, but not with Amberstall. I won't allow it."

"You've already made your opinion known on that subject."

"And if I need to make things more final than I already have, I will. Don't test me on this."

He left without another word. She stood there for a heartbeat before racing to the table to pick up the piece of correspondence Andy had left behind. Moving back to her bed, she sat down and curled her legs under her as she ran a finger across the folded edges of the parchment—the only piece of him that remained.

❧

Andrew rode into the yard of the small inn and dismounted. He gave the horse a pat on the shoulder, refusing to feel guilt over the theft of the horse from the Ormesby stables. The last thing he'd wanted was to face Thornwood today, and Shadow wasn't strong enough, not for the kind of riding Andrew was going to do.

"Staying for the night, my lord?" a boy asked as he gathered the reins from him.

"Perhaps. Give him a ration of oats and let him rest in the rear of your stables, but keep him saddled for now and out of sight. I may need to leave quickly." He handed the young groom a coin and moved toward the door.

He could hear the rumble of voices and laughter

before he reached the inn. This must be the chosen venue in the area for catching up with neighbors. Candles lit the diamond-shaped panes of glass in the windows and illuminated the silhouettes of the patrons inside. Normally, this would be a place he might enjoy, but not this evening. He'd been a fool to lose so much time pining over a lady who dealt in deceit, and even more a fool for wasting another day cooling his heels before a campfire in the woods, wondering if he should return to her. "Idiot," he mumbled to himself.

Now, he could feel someone on his trail, but who? The men searching for him had been rather clumsy in their pursuit thus far. It could be the same men, but he didn't believe so. Whoever followed his path now was more cautious, watchful.

This was how this little adventure began, and he didn't particularly want a repeat of any event from the past two weeks. His mind circled through the nights he spent with Katie in her cottage, their walks together, her smile… He rubbed his eyes, focusing on his surroundings as he opened the door.

The thick smell of lager and smoke greeted him as he entered the inn. Moving to a shadowed corner of the establishment, he signaled for a drink. As much as he disliked the idea of pausing in his journey a second longer than necessary, he needed to wait out whoever was trailing him or risk being killed in the dark of night on the road. Not to mention that the drink was much needed in his current frame of mind.

How had he failed to see the truth behind her lying eyes? Had he learned nothing in his life? But, then again, he'd never been bested by a woman before.

He'd followed her about like a lost dog, all the while thinking he was assisting her, that she needed him. The worst part was that he still wanted her. What was wrong with him that he desired such a flawed female who clearly never felt the same for him? His chest tightened and he gritted his teeth against the emotion coursing through his veins. It was over. He had to move on, and the first step in that journey was to lose whoever was trailing him.

A tankard of lager was placed before him, and he drained half of it in an attempt to clear his muddled mind. Pushing the hair away from his face so he could see properly, he leaned back in his chair, watching the door. He didn't have long to wait. Only a few minutes later, the door swung open and a man stepped inside. He removed his hat and trudged to the bar at the other end of the open room.

Andrew should have guessed it. Katie's father was in league with Hawkes. She'd probably sent the man after his head with her blessing. Andrew drained the last of his drink and set the large glass back down on the table with a loud *clunk!*

"Whiskey," Ormesby said as he leaned on the bar top.

"What brings you this far south tonight?" The barkeep poured a measure of dark liquid into a small glass. "I thought you'd gone back to Ormesby for a bit."

"My stay there was brief," he grumbled. "I'm headed south again."

"Back on the road, eh?"

"So it would seem." Ormesby reached into his pocket and laid something on the bar, pushing it toward the barkeep. "Henry, in all honesty, I'm look-ing for someone."

"There were two men Thornwood found sneaking about the countryside. Been quite the talk, you know, even this far away. They've managed to give His Grace the slip thus far, but he's not one to give up easily."

"I don't like the sound of two men stalking about the countryside, but I'm sure Thornwood will handle things properly." Ormesby took a sip of his whiskey, setting the glass back down in front of him. "I was actually going to ask about a gentleman who might have stopped here. Traveling alone on horseback, a young gentleman."

"Not that I can remember."

Andrew had never been so thankful for the borrowed black clothing than he was right now. He'd always thought the ensemble made him look more like a pirate than a gentleman, and apparently the barkeep agreed.

Ormesby slid more money across to the man as he said, "Keep a lookout for me, then?"

"What do you want with this gentleman?" The older man's eyes narrowed on Ormesby. "If you don't mind me asking."

"There are some business matters we need to see to," Ormesby replied.

Andrew almost snorted into the dregs of his lager. He was sure the man did have some business to attend to with him—mostly concerning Andrew's untimely demise. Ormesby would be hard pressed to find him, however, if he was ahead of Andrew on the road. He signaled for another drink. It appeared he would be staying the night here after all.

Fourteen

KATIE PULLED THE COAT CLOSER AROUND HER SHOULDERS to keep the chilly autumn wind at bay. She'd spent the evening alone in her cottage after her father left. At the end of it, she'd come to two conclusions. One, she would always love Andy, even though she would never see him again. And two, she couldn't live here any longer.

Therefore, today she would begin the rest of her life. Her first stop would be Thornwood Manor, where she would ask Lord Steelings if she could go with him and his wife to Scotland. She didn't know where she would go from there, but she certainly couldn't stay at Ormesby Place any longer.

She stepped into the stables with her chin held high, even though she knew her eyes were red from crying and she was even paler than usual. Spying one of the grooms sorting the tack supplies, she stepped farther into the building. "I need to use the carriage today. Could you have it brought around?"

Turning from his work, he dusted his hands off as he said, "I'm sorry, Lady Katie, but it's not here.

And we only have the one now, since the other still needs repairs."

"Where is it?"

His eyes narrowed in confusion. "Your father took it last night."

"Did he need something in town?" At night? It didn't seem likely. Something was off.

"Didn't he tell you? He went back south. I heard him tell the driver they were returning to his brother-in-law's estate."

"Returning..." The words died on her lips. There was only one reason her father would want to go back there—Andy. She should go on with her plans. She could get to Thornwood somehow without the use of the carriage—the old wagon they used for hauling materials about the property, perhaps. She offered the groom her thanks and moved past him.

She shouldn't care what happened to Andy. Her father would go back to her uncle's estate and assist in his tormenting in some fashion. She would go on to Scotland for a time and then consider her options. Her father wouldn't hurt Andy—surely he wouldn't. And why should it matter to her even if her father did do some damage to him? Any future between them was over.

You love him. That's why.

She was standing outside Shadow's Light's stall before she realized where she was going. Looking up, she saw movement. "He didn't take you?" She opened the door and stepped inside. "I didn't know you were still here."

Shadow huffed and shifted his weight.

"I know how you feel." She closed the door behind her and turned back to Shadow. "He left me behind as well, you know."

She laid a hand on Shadow's cheek and felt him press back into her palm with a toss of his head.

"I suppose we're alike in that...both healing from injuries, both cast off." Her hand fell away from the horse. "Do you think he ever cared for me? He said he did... Perhaps... I don't want to know the answer to that question."

She leaned back against the wall as she watched Shadow. "Do you want to know the sad part about all of this? I miss him." She gave the horse a wry smile and shook her head. "I know I shouldn't. The things he said... Yes, I'm aware he's done the same to you. Waving a pistol about and talking of putting you down... I don't think he meant it."

She pushed off from the wall with her heel and took a step toward Shadow. "He was only upset because you were hurt. He said things he shouldn't because he cares for you so much. You were injured and he didn't know what to do. So you see, he was only angry because he loves you and thought he would have to say good-bye."

Shadow nudged her with his head.

"Don't argue," she reprimanded as she ran her hand over Shadow's mane. "Blast it all, now I'm having conversations with you, too."

He nudged her again.

"What is it? Andy *was* only angry because he loves you and thought he would have to..." Was the same true of her?

Had he only said those things because he was hurt by the secret she'd kept? If that was true, then Andy did care about her. She frowned as she laid her forehead against Shadow's muzzle. Did it matter if he cared for her? After all that happened?

"Blast it all. I can't let Father hurt him." She had to go help him, even if she left afterward. She reached into the pocket of her jacket and curled her fingers around the note Andy had left behind. Whether the stubborn man wished it or not, she had to go to his aid.

"Shadow, are you feeling up to a ride?"

The horse tossed his head, clearly anxious to leave.

She ran her hand over his back. The question was whether she was feeling up to a ride. She took a shaky breath and turned, reaching for the saddle hanging in the corner.

❦

"Brother, what are you doing back?" Hawkes asked as he descended the last few stairs to the main floor of his home. Charles had made it quite clear when he left that he wouldn't be back anytime soon.

"We need to speak." Charles shot a dark look at the butler before adding, "In private."

"Very well. Let's go to the drawing room."

"You scarcely use that room. Why not the parlor?"

"It's being *used* at the moment." He grinned at the closed parlor door. He wasn't sure how much longer he would need Lady Amberstall, but until such time as she proved unnecessary, she wasn't going anywhere.

"If you have a guest, I can wait for you to conclude your business."

"That won't be necessary. She is an extended guest."

"Oh." Charles shook his head but didn't ask any further questions as they made their way to the drawing room.

"If you've returned for another attempt at changing my mind, you're too late. You were too late when we spoke before." Hawkes hoped Charles had returned with a change of heart. After all, he was the one with the knowledge of explosives.

"I have new information that changes things a bit," Charles said as they entered the drawing room.

"Information about Amberstall?" Hawkes raised a brow as he shut the door so they might speak in privacy.

Charles nodded. "When I arrived home, I found him on my estate."

Seconds ticked by in silence as Hawkes searched his brother-in-law's face, attempting to understand his words. "Those bloody bastards!" he finally exclaimed as he moved across the room to the liquor decanters on the table in the corner. "Rastings and Smarth have been wandering the area for nearly a fortnight, and you find him in a day! Worthless, dirty…"

"Katherine, um…Katie, that is, brought him to me."

He turned back to Charles with a smile. "I always have been fond of that girl. Did you leave him locked away at a nearby inn?"

Charles shifted uncomfortably on his feet and glanced away, running a hand over the back of his neck.

"You did bring Amberstall to me, did you not?" Hawkes asked, taking a step toward the center of the room.

"I did not. He left my home rather quickly, and

I had difficulties tracking him." There was more to this story. Hawkes could tell by the disgruntled set of Charles's shoulders.

"But he is returning to Amber Hollow," Hawkes suggested.

"That is my understanding."

"Just as well." Hawkes turned back to the decanters to pour them drinks in celebration of their pending wealth. His plan was coming together and just in time. He smiled down at the glasses as he filled them. If he released Lady Amberstall today, her son would see the bruises. And if he was lucky—which he certainly was today—Amberstall would be enraged enough to fall right into his trap. "I have enough time and warning, with your assistance, to do away with Amberstall and use his lands for my purposes."

"That's where we have a problem," Charles said.

"I don't see how. Things are finally falling into place." Hawkes crossed the room and handed the drink to his brother-in-law. He would use the man's own mother to lure Amberstall to his doom—it was brilliant, really. As long as she didn't alert the authorities, and he would see to it that she would never do that. He grinned. He could be very persuasive.

"You can't kill Amberstall."

"Not this again. Charles, you can't bring me information to help my cause and tell me I'm not to use it. I need this. You know I need this."

His brother-in-law took a sip of his drink and leveled a glare at Hawkes as he lowered the glass. "There has to be another way."

"I cannot turn back now," Hawkes stated with a

shake of his head. "It's far too late to have squeamish misgivings."

"That isn't the issue here." Charles rubbed at his eyes.

"Then what is?" Hawkes couldn't wait to hear the pious reasoning of a man who had profitable mines on his property and wanted for nothing.

"Katie," he said, setting aside his drink and crossing his arms over his chest.

"What of her?" This had nothing to do with his niece, not *that* niece at any rate. The niece he was counting on was to be wed to Amberstall's distant cousin and heir soon, and she would allow him anything he wished. All he must do was remind her of what she had to lose, what he knew, and she would hand over access to Amber Hollow in an instant.

"It seems that during Amberstall's stay at Ormesby, my daughter became rather fond of the man." He pursed his lips in distaste at the idea of Katie involved with the young lord.

"Brilliant! This should simplify things. He was left alone with your daughter for a time, yet refused to follow the honorable course of action, so we were left no choice but to duel—and he lost. It explains it all."

"But he did try to do the honorable thing," Charles muttered to the ceiling as he moved to sit in one of the chairs.

"Try," Hawkes repeated.

"I stopped him and told him of our family connection to you."

"You are on my side after all, Brother." He crossed

the room to sit opposite Charles. "I'm pleased to hear of it."

"Katie wasn't," Charles muttered with a shake of his head. "I don't know that she'll forgive me. She says she loves him."

"Does she?" His eyes narrowed in thought as he took a sip of his drink.

"I believe so."

"And he is equally fond of Katie, I presume?"

"It would seem. So, you see why you can't go ahead with this plan of yours. Think of your niece."

"Yes, Katie. This does change my strategy a bit. Love is a thing of wonder. It makes people do most anything." Hawkes grinned and drained the last of the liquor in his glass. His day was improving by the second.

❧

"Mother?" Andrew stepped into the main hall at Amber Hollow, breathing in the familiar smell of furniture polish and dinner being prepared in the kitchen. "Are you at home? Mother?"

He shut the door behind him and took a step further inside. The last time he'd stood here was over two years ago. Nothing had changed, yet the silence was unnerving. He didn't remember the house being this quiet on any occasion. He hadn't expected a fanfare to be played or anyone to yell hurrah, but there wasn't even a maid bustling about. Nothing.

He stood there for a moment, scanning the hall for signs of life. Moving to the base of the stairs, he called out again. "Is anyone home?"

The butler stuck his head around a corner at the

sound of Andrew's voice. "My lord! We'd given up hope of your arrival."

"Is Mother about?"

"She's being seen to in her bedchamber. She'll be very pleased you've returned, very pleased indeed."

"Seen to," he repeated. "Is she ill?"

"No, but she's had quite the time. I'm sure she'll tell you of it."

"I have no doubt on that score." What dramatic malady did she have now? He was already regretting his return home. He would believe the entire plot against his family was of her invention to convince him to ride south, if not for the henchmen and Ormesby's involvement.

He trudged up the stairs after the butler, noting the new tapestry on the wall and the new vase on the landing. He shook his head. She would never change. It was odd that her spending habits didn't bother him now as they once had, even after what they had done to his father all those years ago.

By the time he reached her door, he realized he was almost looking forward to seeing her. What was wrong with him? Taking a breath to steady his nerves, he entered his mother's bedchamber.

"Andrew, you're here! Oh thank heavens!"

"Mother," he whispered as his eyes widened on her. She sat propped on pillows in the bed with one eye blackened and a bruise covering one side of her jaw. He crossed the room in an instant. "What happened?"

"Why don't you leave us, Jackson, Maryanne?" Lady Amberstall nodded toward their butler and one of the maids with a hint of a smile.

"Who did this to you?" Andrew asked, not wanting to wait for the room to be cleared of servants.

"You don't know how relieved I am that you didn't listen to the warning in that dreadful letter." She wiped a tear from her cheek. "I've been beside myself with worry. Oh, Andrew…"

"Mother, who hurt you? Surely Lord Hawkes didn't beat you."

Her nod sent heat to his blood as anger seared through him. He turned for the door in an instant. Lord Hawkes would regret his actions within the hour. How foolish he'd been not to believe her, not to rush back on a stolen horse a week ago. He clenched his jaw, his hands already balling into fists at his sides. He shouldn't have been away so long. He shouldn't have lingered with Katie. He shouldn't have…

"Andrew," she said in a soft voice.

He turned back to see she was indicating a chair with the wave of her hand. She was bruised about the wrist, too. Had Hawkes bound her hands? And if so, why was she free now?

"I have to go see Hawkes, Mother. This will not stand." His voice shook with his anger.

"I know that, but first we must talk."

"Talk? He hurt you! I can't sit about chatting when there is work to be done to fix this mess for good."

"Andrew, there is time. Come and sit." She nodded again toward the chair at her side. "There is much to tell you."

༄

Katie threw her leg over Shadow's back and slid to the ground. "I think we managed that quite nicely. No one fell. We're still whole and unharmed." She gave the horse a pat on the cheek as she tried to still her shaking legs. She'd made it. Well, she'd made it to the inn on the road south out of Great Ayton, but it was an accomplishment nonetheless.

She glanced around in search of a groom to see to Shadow while she stepped inside in search of her father or Andy. They would both be long gone by now, but perhaps she could discover when they'd passed by.

Not seeing anyone, she shrugged and wrapped Shadow's reins around a post. "I'll be gone but a few minutes," she told the horse.

She almost waited for his response, but shook her head and moved toward the door. She stepped inside and blinked into the cloud of smoke filling the room. Was this what men left the comfort of home for—smoke and drink? She took a step forward, trying to act as if she belonged there.

"Good evening," she offered the table of local men staring at her near the door. "Good evening," she said again to another table she passed. Only a few nodded in response. The rest simply stared. She kept walking, aware of the room full of eyes following her every move.

"Good evening." She smiled at the barkeep. "I'll have…" she paused to glance around the tavern to see what everyone else was drinking. All she saw were tankards of some sort of ale. "The drink you're well known for, it would seem."

The man's brows drew together in concern, most

likely for her sanity. A moment later he filled a large glass and set it down in front of her.

Someone walked up beside her and leaned against the bar at her side. She saw his arm raise to signal for a drink. As soon as he left again, she would discuss her issue with the man behind the bar. Only the man didn't leave once he had his drink. Instead he sank onto the stool beside hers.

She sighed, annoyed at having to be polite to some local man when she only wanted to ask if anyone had seen her father. "Good evening," she said without looking up.

"That's what I hear," he replied.

"Do you?" she asked, taking a curious sniff of the brew in her glass.

"You should know since you're the one who called it good. Personally, I'm more inclined to say cloudless."

She glanced up at the curious statement. "Thornwood!" she exclaimed, relieved to see a friendly face.

"Cloudless evening," he replied, lifting his glass to her.

"What are you doing here?"

"Drinking. And you appear to be sniffing. Fine way to spend a cloudless evening."

"I'm actually searching for my father." She lowered her voice and leaned closer to add, "And Lord Amberstall."

"Popular fellow," he mused, taking a swallow of his drink.

"You've seen him then?"

"No, you just aren't the only one looking for the poor chap."

"My father." Her eyes narrowed on him. Thornwood must know of his whereabouts. "What did he tell you?"

"I haven't seen Ormesby. I did see the two henchmen clearly out for Amberstall's blood, but I lost their trail a few days ago."

"Yes, I saw them as well." Katie looked back at her drink as the thought of what those men had interrupted under the tree that afternoon threatened to strangle her.

"I heard about the scene at tea." He chuckled into his lager as he took a drink. "So, you've moved on from shooting firearms to drinking in taverns. Tell me, will you leave nothing for the menfolk to claim as their own?"

He was jesting, but she couldn't bring herself to return his wit in her current state of mind. She sighed and offered him a wry smile. "I'm only here because I thought my father would have come this way."

"Perhaps I can help," Thornwood offered.

"I doubt that." She was in such a tangled mess that there wasn't a thing anyone could do. "I should go. My father isn't here and neither is Amberstall."

"Wait." He motioned for the barkeeper to come near. She saw the flash of a coin as he laid it on the wooden counter. "Have you seen Ormesby come through here?"

"Last night, Your Grace," the man replied as he polished a glass with a rag.

"Did he say where he was going?" Thornwood asked.

"Headed back south. He mentioned he was looking for someone. A lord, I believe."

"Andy," she breathed. "I have to go, Thornwood. I have a long journey ahead of me."

"A long journey where?" he asked, standing from his stool at the bar.

"To rescue Lord Amberstall." She turned and walked out the door.

The air was cool as the day turned to night, and she wrapped her arms around her body to keep warm. Walking toward the stables, she saw Shadow where she'd left him tethered to a post. "I hope you're strong enough for a long ride."

Shadow's Light tossed his head against the pull of the reins, clearly ready for the journey. But was she as prepared? She sighed and pulled her old riding coat tighter around her shoulders. She didn't even know where she was going, other than south. The last time she'd visited her uncle on his estate she'd been no more than six years of age.

"Lady Katie," Thornwood called out from the door as he stepped outside. "What do you mean by 'rescue Amberstall'?"

She turned to face him. How much should she tell? She nearly ignored him and rode away, but Thornwood had been almost a brother to her. And when she saw the concern in his eyes, she knew she had to tell him the truth. "I believe my father intends to do Amberstall harm."

"Why would you think such a thing? Unless you…" He cringed. "Is this an issue of Amberstall's honor?"

It was a moment before she comprehended what Thornwood was asking. "No. My father saw to it that honor was no longer a factor between us. Amberstall left. My father disappeared shortly after…and here we are." She couldn't waste time explaining things to the duke, not if she hoped to catch up to Andy and her father on the road. "I have to go."

"You truly think your father would hurt Amberstall?"

"I don't know anymore." She shook her head and tried to squeeze out the horrible idea that was now taking root in her mind. She exhaled and looked back at Thornwood. "But I do know neither my uncle nor the henchmen he sent would show Amberstall any mercy, and my father has spent a great deal of time in the company of my uncle of late."

"The men looking for Amberstall work for your uncle?"

She untied the reins. "I'm sorry, Thornwood, but I must leave now."

"I can see you're riding again, and I find it curious you no longer have a limp or need a crutch. So I'm sure you're prepared for battle, but do you know the roads south?"

She blushed and busied herself checking Shadow's saddle. "I'll find my way. I have to try."

"I'll lead you to Amber Hollow, if that's where you're going. I was already on my way to London to see to some business I have there."

Katie turned back to him, looking up into his sharp gray-blue eyes, so similar to his sister's, yet so different. "Why would you do that?"

"Because I owe Amberstall a debt." He shifted and mumbled an oath to himself before continuing, "I once made his life a bit difficult."

"A bit difficult? He fled the country because of you."

"I didn't know you were aware of that," Thornwood said.

"Of course I'm aware."

"I didn't have a choice at the time, just so you know. I loved Lily and he was competition for her hand. I was desperate." He stepped closer and lowered his voice to add, "A desperation I now see in you."

Her eyes filled with tears but she blinked them away. She was not going to start weeping all over again. It was over. There was nothing she could do about that, but that didn't mean she had to let Andy die. "Unfortunately, I believe that ship has sailed."

"Lady Katie, I happen to know a great deal about ships, and that ship has yet to leave the harbor."

She smiled and placed her foot in the stirrup, swinging up onto Shadow's back. She took a calming breath and wound the reins around her hand. He was wrong, but she had no time to argue with him over it. "I hope you're right," she said as she urged Shadow into motion.

Fifteen

Andrew shook his coat into place and took the steps to the lawn two at a time. He'd waited patiently for his mother to drift off to sleep that afternoon before he'd left her side. No one raised a hand to his family and lived to tell the tale. She could say what she liked about the events of the past months and Lord Hawkes' financial difficulties—he would not forgive the man any time soon.

Reaching to his back, he confirmed the blade was held safe there, ready for what was to come.

The sun cast long shadows across the grass as he made his way to the grove of trees. The hidden lake was the destination of the nature walk his great-grandfather had installed when he took over the estate from Great-Great-Uncle Henry. It was an odd place for Hawkes to lie in wait for him, although it was near the border of the vile man's lands and far enough away for screams not to be heard.

"He will be the one screaming," Andrew snarled, adjusting the knife strapped to his back beneath his coat. The note Hawkes had forced Andrew's mother to pen instructed Andrew to go directly to the dam at the hidden lake. Although he wasn't about to step into a trap set for him, he did want to know what was planned. Even with his mother's recounting of things on the estate, he had too many questions. But tonight he would get answers, and then he would get revenge for what the man had done to his family.

The woods flew past him in a blur of his own thoughts. He wound through the trees from memory, stepping over the low spot where water always gathered when it rained and around the tree he'd carved his name into as a child. This was his land. He'd lived his life here, as had his father and grandfather.

He shook his head. "Two years away," he mumbled. That was apparently all it took to have one of the neighbors pressing his nose into Andrew's business and injuring his mother in the process. Lord Hawkes would pay for his crimes.

Andrew stepped out into the clearing, taking a moment to make sure he was alone before moving forward. The sun was slipping deeper into the horizon, bathing the field in golden light. The gentle *swish, swish* of the tall grass against his boots was the only noise he heard. Perhaps his mother had been mistaken about the man's intentions, or maybe Hawkes had changed his plans.

The lake was just around the bend now, past the large boulders where Andrew often sat for a few minutes when out for a ride. He still couldn't make sense of any of this plot against him. Why here? Wasn't the man after Andrew's stables? Why not meet there? The fact that there was any plot at all was a bit shocking in itself. After all, his lands were entailed and would pass to his second cousin if something happened to him.

But Andrew had never considered that outcome an option. One day this land would go to his own son, although that would mean marrying. At any rate, when Andrew passed from this world, his lands would go to someone of his bloodline, and Hawkes certainly was not that lucky chap.

Andrew reached the boulders and decided to wait there. In a few minutes' time the sun would fully set and he could advance under the cover of night. If Hawkes was waiting for him, Andrew didn't want to make his arrival an announced affair. He sank to the ground and leaned his head against the boulder at his back.

Staring off into the growing darkness, he tried to unravel the plot against him, yet his mind kept swerving back to the one place he'd told himself it couldn't go—to Katie. For someone so naïve, she'd certainly fooled him. She'd known all along about his plight, her family's involvement…

Everything had been a lie. He ran a hand over his weary eyes, trying to rub her image from his mind. He was home now, away from her lies, her seduction. Perhaps if he remained busy, her memory would fade. But, even as he thought it, he knew it wasn't true. The fact remained that simply filling the hours didn't equal happiness in life, and it never would. He loved her. No matter how she'd hurt him with her deception, he loved her still. So he would do what work he needed to do on his estate, busy or not. He would go on with his life. And he would look back on this and be glad for it, because through all of this he'd met Katie.

He noticed that the moon was on the rise now. He gathered his wits and stood from behind the boulder. It was time to move. He walked in silence through the clearing, keeping to the hillside where exposed rock glowed silver in the pale evening light. As he neared the lake, he cut through the woods, slowing his pace to step over branches without anyone hearing. When he reached the tree line where the grass grew down to the edge of the water, he stopped.

Men milled about the dam. Andrew squinted through the tree branches to see, but he could only make out silhouettes above the moonlit lake. He sank down beside a tree trunk. What were they doing? He could see the ripples on the water from the wind, shining in the silver light of the night, but where the men stood was completely shadowed by the patches of trees on either side of the stone-walled dam.

Someone lumbered from the woods and stepped out onto the grass-covered dam dotted with boulders. Andrew cursed the large rocks his grandfather had placed about the dam for fishing perches. The boulders were casting odd shadows and making it impossible to see what was happening.

"We brought in the extra line like you asked us to, m'lord," someone called out.

Perhaps this wasn't such a poor place to observe the situation, as their voices carried across the water. Andrew leaned against the tree trunk.

"And where are the rest of the supplies? Line doesn't do much good alone."

"Right you are, m'lord. I'll see to it straightaway."

Andrew pushed aside a fallen tree branch so he

could see more clearly. What did they mean by line? If they were going to use it to bind his hands, they could bloody well think again.

"They're worthless, Charles. One simply cannot find decent help these days."

"It's not too late to give up this scheme of yours, you know." That was Ormesby. The man's voice was still in Andrew's head from their confrontation inside Katie's home days ago.

"Of course it's too late. Now hand me that line Smarth left lying in the mud." That voice with the hardened edge to it must be Hawkes.

"It just seems to me…"

"We've been through this," Hawkes snapped. "I know you don't agree, Brother, but you gave me your word months ago that you would help me with this portion of the job."

"I did. But at the time you spoke as if Amber Hollow would be yours when we attempted this."

"And this is when you choose to argue details with me?"

"Let's just be done with this so I can return to my own work, not to mention my daughter who I left heartbroken and alone."

"Katie," Andrew breathed, the leaves of the trees rustling around him in response. Ormesby had said she was heartbroken, but that couldn't be. Andrew was the one who had been betrayed. And here was the evidence of her betrayal—men walking about his property, plotting some nefarious deed. If only he knew what they had in store.

He shifted and strained to see what they were doing.

They'd now brought in lanterns—for as much good as the light did him. The three lanterns sitting in the grass on the top of the dam cast only a small amount of light and made everything else darker by comparison. In the first circle of light stood Hawkes and Ormesby, chatting like they were ladies at tea. Andrew ground his teeth and shifted his eyes to the right. A man was kneeling on the ground working on something...

Andrew whispered an oath. He shouldn't have waited for nightfall. He needed to get closer if he was going to get any information at all.

"Did you locate the supplies?" Hawkes asked another man who joined them—one of the henchmen.

"Everything's loaded and on the way."

"It should be here already," Hawkes argued.

"There's time, Hawkes. You can't rush these things. Speed will get you killed in this game."

What was Ormesby talking about? Andrew crouched low and looked for a closer location. He would have to circle back away from the lake and come up on the high side of the terrain. Conscious of every stick to crack underfoot and every rustle of leaves he passed, he slowly made his way up the hill and, ironically, toward the border of Hawkes' land. Making a wide sweep of the lake, he eyed the water below and the men moving around it.

First, he slipped behind a large tree, then crouched low behind a bush. Every step brought him closer to his enemies and closer to the answers he sought. For the second time, he was thankful for the all-black ensemble he still wore from his journey home.

He was near enough now to hear someone

hammering, and he could almost see. His eyes scanned the edge of the forest, seeing a fallen tree trunk. If he could only reach it, he would have a nice view of whatever they were working on.

He listened for a minute before making his move, his fists clenching with anger that these men were on his land. Amber Hollow had been entrusted to generations of his family, and he wasn't going to be the one to fail—not this time.

"You'll want to run that line across the ground," Ormesby's gruff voice rumbled across the lake. "And fasten it there. No, not like that. Do you want to kill us all?"

Andrew raised a brow and almost grinned. Better them than him. But how were their lives in peril in the first place? He had to get closer. Taking a few deep breaths, he tore from his hiding place and ran for the fallen tree at the edge of the water. He dove onto the ground and lay there, waiting. *Still, be still.* If they'd seen the movement, he hoped they thought him an animal. A moment later, when he was sure no one was still watching, he lifted his head. His eyes narrowed on the sight before him. Were those explosives? His heart pounded as he looked again at the water's edge.

Explosives lined the dam, *his* dam on *his* lands. An animal-like growl escaped his throat. What possible purpose could they have for blowing up the dam on his lake? His mind flew to the valley below the dam, the way the land curved before leveling at the drive leading to his home. "The stables," he whispered.

If the dam were to fail, the stables would be flooded. His horses, his life's work, would be swept away with the current. But if that was what they indeed had planned, why had they lured him here to stumble across it? He was missing some key piece of information, and he knew it.

He was lifting his head to take another look when someone grabbed the back of his coat. Andrew tried to twist out of the man's grasp, landing an elbow in his ribs. He turned to take a proper swing at the villain when he felt the knife at his back being pulled from the scabbard.

"Looks like this time you get to be the one with a knife to your throat," the man murmured just loud enough for Andrew to hear.

"Do you think so?" Andrew sneered as he stepped to the side just as the man moved forward with the knife. Catching the man's wrist, Andrew bent the man's arm behind his back and took back his blade. "Did you know I've been taming and shoeing horses since I could walk?" he asked in a hushed tone, not wanting to raise any more alarms than he already had.

"Can't say that I did."

"I bet you know other things, though, don't you? Like Hawkes' plans this evening."

"Sworn to secrecy, I am," the man muttered as Andrew lifted the knife to his throat.

"Tell me the plans," he whispered. Andrew didn't allow for any interpretation of his words as he pressed the blade to the man's throat.

"He's rigging up the dam with explosives."

"Why?"

"I don't know," the man stated in a small voice as he shrank from the blade, but Andrew knew it was a lie.

"Why?" he repeated with an urgent whisper.

"He wants you dead, m'lord. An' he wants the lake."

"It's not his. None of this is his," Andrew grated in his ear. "This land has been in my family for over a century, and I built those stables with my own hands."

"I only know what I hear, m'lord."

There was a rustle of leaves behind him. Before Andrew could turn, something crashed into his head. All he knew was blinding pain as he fell to the ground.

෴

Katie drew Shadow to a stop in the drive at Amber Hollow. It was dusk, no time to call on a lady she'd never met. Turning to Thornwood, she asked, "Are you quite sure this is a good idea? It seems a waste of valuable time to me, and we already lost half an hour for you to send that note to Lily."

"I had to inform her of my whereabouts. She thought I was going to London for two days and would be home by Saturday, which I've explained three times already."

"Yes, but this stop isn't necessary," she complained with another glance up at the house.

Thornwood sighed and looked over at her. "We need more information before we can form a plan."

"Yes, but the note said…"

"That note could be news of a week ago, if not more," he cut in, drawing his horse up beside hers.

"I suppose." She looked up at the stately manor looming above her. Andy hadn't had many happy things to say about his mother. She glanced down at her breeches, dirty from the ride. Pulling her coat tighter around her, she nodded. She didn't have much choice in this matter—she would have to face his mother. It didn't matter what the woman thought of her anyway. Katie had no future with him. She was here to save Andy's life. And as soon as that was done, she would leave.

Throwing her leg over the horse, she slid to the ground. She gave Shadow a pat on the cheek. "Do you remember this place? You're home now."

Shadow's Light huffed into the evening air and tossed his mane. At least he was pleased about being here.

Thornwood dismounted from his gray beside her and gave her a nod of encouragement. "Let's go inside."

"We could have gone to my uncle's home directly, tried to reason with him," she pleaded.

Thornwood raised one eyebrow at her in response.

"Oh, fine." She lifted her hand and rapped on the door. Blast him, he was right. It would do no good to go to her uncle's estate, and if they needed to be sneaky about this rescue, they would lose the element of surprise. Thornwood had explained war strategy to her at length on the ride south, but she didn't have to be pleased about the next step now.

When the door opened, Katie was caught between curiosity about Andy's home and the desire to run and dive into a bush before being seen. Fortunately, Thornwood shoved her forward into the hall to end her inner battle on the subject.

"Your Grace…" The man's eyes grew wide as he looked at Thornwood. "Is Lord Amberstall expecting you this evening? I was unaware of any such plan."

"No. I am here to aid Lady Katie Moore, Lord Ormesby's daughter."

"Oh?" The older man turned to Katie.

Katie swallowed her nervousness and gave the butler a polite smile. "Is Andy...I mean, is Lord Amberstall at home?"

"Perhaps we should begin with the lady of the house?" Thornwood supplied with a meaningful glance in Katie's direction.

It was true that the last time she'd seen Andy he'd insulted her and stormed away, slamming doors. Perhaps he didn't wish to see her. She bit at her fingernail. "Yes, that would be the thing to do," she grumbled. She wanted to see him. He'd left the estate two days before her—he must be here somewhere. She glanced around the hall, half expecting to catch a glimpse of him. She told herself it was to see that he was safe, but in truth she just wanted to look at him once more.

"Her ladyship is resting upstairs," the butler intoned. "If you would like to wait in the parlor..."

"Oh, we don't want to wake her. We will simply call on Lord Amberstall," Katie replied a little too quickly.

Thornwood shook his head and covered his chuckle with a cough.

"Pardon me, my lady," the butler said. "But I didn't say she was sleeping, only resting."

"Is there a difference?" Katie asked.

"One involves hot chocolate and a large selection of books," the butler replied.

"We will wait here," Thornwood offered, shooting Katie a raised brow.

Once the butler was gone, she turned to Thornwood. "What was that about?"

"What?"

"We need to find Amberstall, not stand about here all evening while his mother wipes clean her hot chocolate mustache and deems it time to see us."

"Calm yourself. The best chance of discovering the truth behind all of this is to discuss it with the only one who has been here for months…" Thornwood nodded toward the door in greeting before finishing, "Lady Amberstall. Good God! What's happened to you?"

"Thornwood." She assessed him with her good eye, as the other was bandaged. "I thought it would be a dark day indeed when you would be at my doorstep again."

"And you were correct," Thornwood quipped with a glance at the window. "By the look of you, I believe it may be true in the more metaphorical sense as well."

"I'd rather not discuss it." She touched the bandage over her eye, revealing a bruised wrist in the process.

Katie's chest tightened. It was her fault this had happened. If she'd simply allowed Andy to take one of her horses, he could have helped his mother. But perhaps she was jumping to conclusions. The woman could have tripped on a rug or some such—but some part of Katie knew that wasn't true. "Did Lord Hawkes do this to you?"

Lady Amberstall's gaze jumped to Katie, her lips pursing as she took in Katie's dusty shirt and wind-blown hair. "How did you come to know of our family's business?"

Katie wound her fingers together to keep from biting her nails. Where to begin? "Your son told me of…the dispute."

The woman stepped closer to Katie, studying her

from head to toe. "You must be the lady who helped Amberstall with his horse."

Katie glanced down at her clothing, knowing she was dressed as a groom, but she'd always thought Andy thought more of her than that.

"He wrote and told me about you. I was hoping I would get to meet you. Although I thought I would have to wait until the season when your family would come to town."

"He wrote about me?" Katie shifted on her feet, her throat closing around the words.

"Certainly. And I can see why." Lady Amberstall tried to smile, but the bruising on her face wouldn't allow it.

Katie's heart was hammering in her chest. This woman had almost been her family a few days ago, before Katie's father had ruined things for her. Now, here she stood in Andy's home, talking to his mother, and yet he couldn't be farther from her reach. But she refused to dwell on what almost was and would never be—that wasn't why she was here. She took a breath and glanced to Thornwood. "We rode quite a long distance to get here…"

"And you ride." Lady Amberstall clasped her hands together. "I'll ring for tea and we can get acquainted."

"I fear there isn't time for formalities," Thornwood cut in.

"There is always time for tea."

"We're here because Lady Katie is concerned for Amberstall's life. We followed her father, Lord Ormesby, south. We have reason to believe he is in league with Hawkes."

Lady Amberstall gasped. "Why would he help such a man?"

"Because they are family."

"Lord Hawkes is my uncle," Katie added in a small voice. She swallowed and looked away, not able to meet the woman's eyes.

After a moment of silence in the room, Andy's mother said, "We certainly don't choose our relatives, now do we?"

Katie looked up with a slight smile as she pulled the letter from her pocket. "Amberstall left this behind at my home. I shouldn't have read it but..."

"That vile letter! He said he didn't take heed of it." Andy's mother's shoulders rose and fell with angry breaths.

"I believe he did," Katie said.

"Where is he?" Lady Amberstall turned and moved to the door, calling out into the hall, "Andrew?"

"Am I to understand that letter wasn't factual?" Thornwood asked.

"That letter was part of Hawkes' plot." Lady Amberstall held up her bruised wrist in explanation. "I was lucky to escape with my life. Five days he held me there. When he released me this morning, I ran on foot through the woods to make sure I wasn't followed, that he hadn't changed his mind. The man's mad. I should have told someone, the authorities perhaps, but Hawkes warned me against it." She paused, apparently overcome with emotion from her trials. "Amberstall arrived shortly after I reached the house. He saw what you see now. I told him not to alert the authorities, but that we must do something about that vile man."

The butler stepped into the doorway. "My lady, we are unable to find his lordship."

Katie looked down at the letter in her hand, knowing where he'd gone.

Thornwood was already taking steps toward the door. "Have word sent to the stables to release the horses into one of the fields for the night, and have them guarded. Amberstall believes Hawkes' interest lies in the stables. Until this is settled, that building isn't safe."

"Yes, Your Grace," the butler stated with a concerned glance at Andy's mother.

"I will go to the hidden lake to investigate." Thornwood assured them. "I'm sure that is where Amberstall has gone."

"He wouldn't," Lady Amberstall whispered to herself.

"Go in search of someone's blood for what they did to you? Yes, I believe he would indeed."

Katie looked from Andy's mother to Thornwood and back again. "I'm coming with you."

"No, you are not."

"I can't stay here and wait while my father assists my uncle in ending Andy's life." She shook her head, trying to rid her mind of the image.

"She is correct. She must go with you, Thornwood."

"Did that blow to your head addle your mind? It could be dangerous."

"Do you really think you can stop a lady in love?" Andy's mother asked.

"In…" Katie turned to the older woman, unsure what to say in return.

"Go. There will be time for us to chat later."

Thornwood ran a hand through his already disheveled hair. "Very well. Now, Lady Amberstall, exactly how hidden is the hidden lake?"

Sixteen

Why was there blood in his mouth? And who had tied him to his bed?

Andrew licked his lips and cracked one eye open. His head was throbbing too much to see with any clarity, but he knew one thing for certain—he was not in his bed.

He tried again to open his eyes, and this time was more successful than the last. He couldn't move from where he was sprawled in the grass except to confirm that his feet were in fact bound together, as were his hands. Pushing with his feet, he moved himself enough to reach the boulder that sat nearest one end of the dam. With a swing of his bound arms, he managed to sit up against the rock.

He was surrounded by explosives, all of it rigged to blow the dam to dust—and him along with it.

"*Psst.*"

Had he imagined that noise? With the throbbing in his head, it was distinctly possible. But then he heard it again.

"*Psst!* Amberstall!"

Turning toward the woods at the edge of the dam, he saw Thornwood hiding behind a tree on the near bank. "What are you doing here?" Andrew whispered in return.

"Rescuing you."

"Then rescue me, already. These bastards are about to set this contraption off."

"We have to wait for your guard to move away," Thornwood uttered from his hiding place.

"Oh, good. You're not alone. Did you bring Steelings with you?"

"No, Lady Katie."

"Why would you bring her here?" Andrew's urgent whisper caught in his throat as he turned to catch a glimpse of Katie. "Where is she?"

"I brought Thornwood with *me*," Katie whispered as she peered out from behind a bush. Her red hair caught the light from the lantern for a second before she ducked back behind the foliage.

Andrew shook his head. Katie was here. She'd come this far south to…rescue him? Was that what Thornwood had said? Her family members were the ones plotting against him, and she was here to rescue him? But that would mean… *That you blamed her when she wasn't involved.* He mumbled an oath. If that was true, what was she thinking, walking into such a dangerous situation? "Katie, you must leave at once. This is no place for a lady!"

"Stop yelling or you're going to…oh dear." Her head dropped back behind the bush again.

He lowered his head to the large rock for a second, almost not wanting to turn and look. Almost. He shifted to look toward the far bank where his captors were gathered.

The large guard was moving across the dam toward him, his fists already clenched for battle. "Keep quiet!"

"Rastings, is something the matter?" Hawkes asked.

"This one won't keep his trap shut."

"Won't he?" Hawkes stepped over the lines run to the explosives, taking careful steps as he neared. "Soon that won't be an issue."

"I was only complaining about the lack of hospitality at this little get-together of yours."

"He's lying. I heard him say something about a lady."

"Well, there are no ladies here. And no drinks either, while we're on the subject. You really should learn how to throw a party."

"The party hasn't even begun." Hawkes sneered down at Andrew. "The excitement will soon begin, and you will be at the center of it. I believe it will be quite the *crush*." He turned away, laughing.

As soon as Hawkes stepped away to speak with Ormesby on the far bank and Rastings returned to his work, Andrew turned back to the spot where he'd last seen Katie. He blinked into the darkness, willing his eyes to see more clearly. Where had she gone?

"We'll have you out in a minute," Thornwood whispered from the shadowed woods. "Then we can decide what to do about this mess."

"I hope we have a minute," Andrew mumbled.

Thornwood moved into view as he clung to the shadow of the rock, crouching low behind the boulder. "Give me your hands first."

Andrew extended his hands as far as he could

behind him, but it wasn't far enough for Thornwood to reach. He eyed his guard and scooted to the side.

Thornwood moved around the corner of the rock and lifted Andrew's wrists, trying to untangle the knot of rope in the dark.

The guard turned to take a closer look. If he took a few more steps, he would see Thornwood, and Andrew's chances at rescue would be blown to as many tiny pieces as Andrew soon would be. He held his breath as Thornwood tugged at the rope bindings.

"It's too tight and I don't have a knife," Thornwood whispered, pulling at the ropes.

There wasn't enough time. The guard was nearing. Then, he saw a flash of red as Katie stepped into the light on the opposite shore. He could read the determination in her eyes even at this distance.

"Katie, no!" he hissed, but it was too late.

"Pardon me, but I'm looking for my uncle and father."

All eyes turned to Katie, while Thornwood continued to work on the bindings at Andrew's wrists. "She may have just spared your life."

"Idiot. Why is she doing this?" Andrew whispered. "Work faster, Thornwood. I have to go help her." Rastings turned toward him for a moment, his eyes narrowing on Andrew in the dim light before he moved away again.

"If you don't know why she would risk her neck to save yours, you're the idiot."

Andrew frowned. "She wishes to make amends for lying to me about her family."

Thornwood exhaled an almost silent scoff before whispering, "If she's only here to make amends, do you think she would waltz so easily out onto a dam piled high with gunpowder without a thought for her own safety?"

"She cares enough for me to not want to see me die by her uncle's hand," Andrew returned low enough not to be heard.

"You know she rode here. All the way from her home on Shadow's Light, at a pace I had difficulty keeping."

"She rode?" Andrew smiled, overcome with pride in her.

Thornwood continued working on the ropes during their whispered conversation. "And she isn't feigning an injury any longer. I'm sure you noticed."

"She gave up on that ruse last week." Andrew turned and murmured, "You knew?"

Thornwood shrugged. "She forgot to limp when she was on your arm at dinner."

The ropes loosened enough on Andrew's wrists that he could shimmy his hands free.

"Keep your hands behind your back for now while I untie your feet. We don't want them to discover you've escaped until the right time."

"When is the right time?" Andrew breathed the question.

"I'm hoping it will present itself."

Andrew watched as the smaller of the two henchmen led Katie to her uncle.

"My darling niece. Just who I was hoping would join us this evening." He glanced to Rastings and commanded, "Seize her," at the same time he raised a pistol to Ormesby.

"Hawkes, no! She can't be involved in this!" Ormesby bellowed, his eyes on his daughter.

Rastings moved forward to grab Katie, holding her to his chest—his dirty, villainous chest. How dare he touch her? Andrew ground out an angry growl and lurched forward, only stopping when Thornwood grabbed his shoulder.

"Your feet are still bound. It's not yet time."

"Damn the time," Andrew murmured. "He's hurting her."

"She's strong. And that hold he has on her is quite simple to break. Let's wait a minute and see what unfolds before we strike."

"What are you planning, Uncle?" Katie wiggled against the large hands wrapped around her arms. "Tell this man to unhand me."

"I'm afraid I can't do that. You see, I may need you later, and this way I know exactly where you are."

Ormesby stood at gunpoint in the center of the dam, helpless to assist his daughter. "Hawkes, she's your niece!" he attempted, but he was ignored.

Katie kicked her foot behind her, hitting the henchman's shin with the heel of her boot. His grip on her seemed to tighten instead of loosening. Sending her elbow into his ribs, she gave several punches. "Let me go!" She twisted and finally unhinged his grasp on her.

Andrew almost cheered, but Thornwood whispered for him to stay silent, as if it were all part of some larger plan he'd orchestrated.

Stumbling away from the man, Katie was almost to the line of trees on the far side of the dam when he reached her once more. "Not so fast, m'lady."

Andrew muttered a curse as he watched. Her own family was set to hurt her. His eyes slid to Ormesby where he stood beside a crate of explosives with Hawkes still pointing a gun in his direction. The older man's gaze was on Katie with a look of pure horror. Andrew knew the feeling quite well. If Thornwood would ever free him from his bonds, he would murder Hawkes for what he was doing to Katie. What kind of family turned on one another in such a manner? "This is why she shouldn't be here."

Thornwood tugged at the knots in the rope around Andrew's feet as he hissed in his ear, "It was Lady Katie's idea to come assist you, and your mother agreed."

"My mother…" Andrew tried to turn toward Thornwood, but he was shoved back forward by Thornwood's elbow in his shoulder. He exhaled in aggravation. "You listened to her?"

"She was quite convincing." Thornwood shrugged as he pulled the last of the rope from Andrew's feet. "There, now we just need a plan to incapacitate Hawkes and the two henchmen, and then, of course, rid the dam of the explosives."

"Any ideas?" Andrew asked as he pulled his legs back around.

"Always."

❧

Katie's feet brushed the edge of the stone dam as she was hauled to its center. She glanced down as her captor swung her close to the ledge. The rock seemed to go on forever below her, fading into darkness. The lake must be deep to be held back by such a wall. The valley below would be flooded if her uncle succeeded in destroying this strip of land

and wall holding the water back. She had to do something to stop him.

Pushing the henchman's arms from her, she took a step toward her uncle. "You don't have to do this," she said in an attempt to reason with the man.

She stumbled forward as her captor shoved her in the back and caught herself on a crate of explosives a few paces from her uncle.

"Sit down, my dear niece," her uncle commanded, a grin twisting the corners of his mouth upward.

Since he was waving his pistol in her face, Katie did as he asked, sitting on the edge of the wooden box. She looked down at the wood beneath her hands. At any moment, it could explode. She glanced back to where Andy sat on the opposite end of the dam. Thornwood must still be working on Andy's bindings because he hadn't moved. She needed to give them more time. If she could keep her uncle talking and focused on her, perhaps Thornwood would have the time he needed to free Andy.

"No horse or stable is this valuable. You don't have to threaten the dam." She looked up at her uncle as she spoke. "This will not achieve the result you're seeking."

He laughed. "Do you really think my interest lies in the stables?"

Had she misunderstood the entire situation? Andy had told her that his stables and horses were the source of the friction with his neighbor. She shook her head in confusion. "Doesn't it?"

"Silly girl." Her uncle spat the words. "I only want what is below my feet. I've struggled for years while

Amberstall prances about on his horses." He waved his pistol in Andy's direction before turning it back on her father. "And then that charlatan, Lord Crosby, came along two years ago and took everything from me. Everything! And so I'm simply using his example and taking what is attainable and lies *so close* to where I eat and sleep."

"No matter your opinion of Amberstall, that gives you no right to his property," Katie replied.

"By this time tomorrow, a blessed union will occur. Lady Bertha Williams will be wed to the young Mister Pepering."

"Pepering? What does my second cousin have to do with this, Hawkes?" Andy called out.

"The question is: what does darling Katherine's cousin have to do with this?" He shot Katie a smile that turned her stomach before continuing. "And the answer, fortunately for me, is everything." He ripped a piece of aged parchment from his pocket, waving it in the air for everyone to see.

"I don't know if you can read in this light, but I certainly can't," Andy said. "Perhaps if you unbound my hands and gave me a lantern…"

Her uncle shot a look of pure hatred at Andy. "Not likely. Allow me to explain." He stepped around Katie with the pistol and the parchment held high in his hands. "This is a map of these lands—a map your family sought to suppress generations ago when they discovered the gold buried here, Amberstall."

"Gold?" Andy replied.

"Yes, a wealth of gold runs through this valley. Do you really think your great-uncle had this lake constructed for his fishing enjoyment?"

"Yes," Andy said. "That's precisely what I've always thought."

"You're as foolish as my niece." Her uncle sneered down at her. "This lake is here to conceal the great wealth of the Amberstall estate which will soon be mine." He tapped the parchment with his fingers, his eyes flashing like a wild animal's in the moonlight.

"I hate to disappoint you, Hawkes, but this area has always been a part of Amberstall lands."

"And so shall it remain," Hawkes replied with a grin, "but it won't belong to *you*."

"This property is entailed, Hawkes. Even if you manage to kill me tonight, you can't have Amber Hollow."

"No, I can't. My niece's new husband, Mr. Pepering, however…" He broke off to let loose a loud cackle that sent chills down Katie's spine. "He will be only too happy to take up the Amberstall name and lands. And his new wife owes me…let us call it…a large debt."

"You believe my cousin Bertha will allow you to mine on her land for gold?" Katie had only met Bertha once when she was very young, but she didn't seem the sort to give in to mad uncles even then.

"With what I know of her, she will allow me anything I desire. And I very much desire the gold that lies below this lake." He held up the parchment, waving it in the air. "And this map indicates precisely where it can be found."

"Can I see that?" Katie asked.

"Certainly not. You will simply give it to him." He indicated Andy with his pistol.

"I thought we were family, dear uncle."

"Don't spin your web of lies for me. I have it from your father that you're smitten."

Katie's mouth fell open as she struggled for words. Glancing to Andy, she saw he was looking at her, but it was too dark to interpret his expression.

"Give the document to me, then," her father said, moving closer to Katie as he spoke.

"I've already discussed this with you at length, Charles," her uncle grated.

"Discussed it, yes. However, this is the first time I've laid eyes on the map."

Her uncle paused in consideration.

"What? You think I will side with my daughter over you? She is but a girl, and we stand to make a fortune here."

Katie's eyes narrowed on her father, unsure if he was being truthful and putting a higher price on wealth than her life or not. He'd always chosen his work over her, but there was something in his eyes that made her wonder this time. She only hoped her uncle didn't notice that same hint of dishonesty.

"Careful," her uncle warned as he handed the parchment to her father.

Charles opened the document and knelt by the lantern to read it. A moment later he stood, took a step to the side, and placed the document in Katie's hand.

"What are you doing?" she whispered, looking up at her father.

"*What are you doing?*" her uncle screamed into the night as he dove forward toward Katie.

She lifted the map in her hands and sent her uncle a glare intended to melt flesh. "I'll shred this if you come a step closer." When he stopped, she glanced to her father. Why had he given the map to her after all he'd done to assist her uncle?

"You're the one in the middle of this, and I put you there," her father explained, his eyes darting between her and her uncle. "I've made some regrettable decisions, Katie. But I would like to look back on one thing I did this night and know it was honorable."

"You idiot!" her uncle bellowed. "What of your percentage of the gold? We need that map to find it, or we'll have to dig for months. I don't have months. I need funds now!"

Hawkes took a step toward Katie, and she began ripping the map. He stopped again, but it seemed to cost him his last remaining shred of humanity as he growled at her from a few paces away.

"My percentage isn't worth my daughter's happiness," her father said.

"Very well. Our business dealings are done. I only needed you to rig the dam anyway, which seems to be in order now." He raised the pistol and fired.

A loud crack filled the air. Katie sucked in a quick breath, holding it as she looked down to see if she'd been shot. Her hands shaking, she turned with wide eyes to see her father fall to the ground. "Father? *Father!*"

Ormesby released a loud bellow of anguish as he clutched his left arm.

She started toward her father, alarmed to see the fabric of his coat shredded and growing red on the outside of his arm. She needed to go to him, but with one glance toward her uncle, she knew she couldn't. Not now. "Father, are you all right?"

"Kill that bloody bastard," he groaned.

She lifted the lantern from the ground and brought it with her as she edged away. With her eyes on her uncle, she commanded, "Move him away from these explosives."

"Have you not noticed I'm the one holding the pistol?"

"And I am the one holding the map to the wealth you desire—a piece of paper. I also have a source of fire. It's not a good combination." She lifted the lantern in her hand in warning.

"Move Ormesby from the dam," her uncle shouted to his men in a half-crazed voice.

"Next, you can have them free Amberstall." She grinned, pleased to finally have the upper hand.

"That won't be necessary," Andy said.

Her gaze slid to the side where he was crossing the dam with Thornwood just behind him. That was when another shot was fired.

She turned back to her uncle, his pistol raised toward Andy and a cloud of smoke rising from the barrel.

Andrew ran forward, determined to pull Katie to safety as the shot was fired. He could hear the bullet meant for him sail past his ear, then the metallic *click* as Hawkes cocked the pistol again. Andrew's boots slid on the rubble as he lunged for Katie, pulling her down to safety and knocking the lantern from her hand in the process.

Her scream filled the air as the lantern fell, shattering among the lines for the explosives.

"Thornwood, see to Hawkes," Andrew shouted as he threw Katie over his shoulder and took off for the tree-lined shore at a run.

"Andy, no! The explosives…the lantern…" Katie tried to warn him, pounding on his back with her fists. But he already knew.

Laying her down in the grass, Andrew had already turned back to the dam when he called out to her, "Stay there."

He could see Thornwood ahead of him, fighting with Hawkes as the glow of lit fuses swarmed around them like bees. Thornwood ducked as Hawkes swung for his head, clearly out of ammunition and now set to bludgeon them with his weapon. Andrew neared, but not fast enough. Thornwood cracked his fist across the man's jaw, sending him staggering backward. Andrew needed to reach the fuses and stomp out the fire, or they would all be blown to pieces.

He glanced up from the light-covered dam at the sound of the deep bellow. Thornwood was standing alone looking down at the stone wall of the dam. Hawkes was gone. Andrew looked over the wall into the darkness, seeing nothing.

"I only meant to bust his lip. I didn't mean to…" Thornwood broke off with a shake of his head.

"He did this to himself, Thornwood."

"Amberstall?"

"Hmm?" Andrew replied, still staring into the dark crevasse at the bottom of the dam.

"We need to put the fuses out rather quickly."

"Indeed." But as Andrew turned to begin stomping out the fire all around him, he heard another scream pierce the night. His eyes flew to Katie, his heart already in his throat. She was scrambling backward toward the woods as the larger henchman crossed the dam to close in on her, the glint of Andrew's knife shining in his hand.

He watched as she got to her feet only to trip on a log and fall back to the ground. Time seemed to slow down as she kicked to free herself. The man with the knife was closing in on her, but if she was able to run, she might be able to lose him in the woods. As her eyes met Andrew's in the moonlight, he knew she couldn't get away in time. Her old injury would prevent an extended foot race. She may be able to walk, but she couldn't run. He was larger. He was faster, but there was nothing Andrew could do to stop what was happening. Katie was frozen on the ground in fear as the man neared the far edge of the dam.

"Katie!" Andrew called out, but he already knew he couldn't reach her before it was too late. He looked down at the explosives and the fuses burning bright all around him. Glancing back to where the man moved purposefully across the dam toward Katie, he mumbled an oath. It was the only option. Everything would be destroyed, but she would be safe—and that was all that mattered.

"It's a risk," Thornwood said at his side as he came to the same conclusion.

"Run," Andrew said, as he kicked the fuse burning bright near his foot toward the box of explosives. Turning away, he reached the shore just as the first explosion took place. The force threw them to the grass.

He scrambled to his feet. Looking through the smoke and ash, he saw the villain flung over the stone wall with the force of the blast. Was Katie safe? The smoke was thick and his eyes burned with it as he looked for any sign of her on the opposite bank. Finally, he saw her sitting in the grass in front of the fallen log, unharmed. It had worked.

He breathed for the first time all evening, or so it seemed. Dropping to his knees, he covered his face with his arm as another explosion blasted into the night sky. The wall cracked further under the weight of the water. In a great rush, the lake crashed through the breaking dam, flowing away from where they sat on the safety of the banks. The roar of the water ripping through his land filled his ears as he watched it wash away.

His horses, his stables were gone. He'd been entrusted with the safekeeping of this land when his father passed away—every tree was his responsibility. And he'd failed. All his work, a lifetime of toil, and for what? The greed of another man had taken it all. He grasped a fistful of dirt, crushing it beneath his fingers.

It was his fault. He'd caused the complete devastation of his family's land. With an angry jerk of his arm, he threw the dirt into the receding water, watching as a breeze caught it and blew it away—like everything else in his life.

A moment later, the same breeze cleared the smoke-filled air enough to see across the water. Katie sat on the opposite bank. Through the swirling haze of smoke, he watched her. She was alive. He'd destroyed everything, but he'd saved her.

Perhaps he hadn't failed after all. Perhaps for the

first time in his life, he'd chosen correctly. He'd chosen Katie.

When she looked back at him, the moonlight dancing off her skin, her gaze held a question. And it was one he didn't yet know how to answer.

He did know she was unlike any lady he'd ever encountered. If he made a list of her oddities, it would stretch across what had once been his lake. But in spite of that... He shook his head and watched through the smoke as she rose to her feet.

If he wished to keep her in his life, he would have to marry her. He hadn't given it much thought before when he'd asked her, but now...shouldn't he consider such things? He was a lord. He owed it to his title, didn't he? He couldn't have an unfit Lady Amberstall. And she did have awful manners.

She would race horses through public streets. He would be known by all of society as the lord who had the wife who didn't adhere to any rules.

But what would his life be like with a lady who was quiet, well-mannered, and not opposed to wearing dresses? He might have a contented life. But it wouldn't be a life with *Katie*. Perhaps the proper thing to do was to let her leave and never look back. The problem was that he was damned tired of being proper.

Seventeen

"YOU DESTROYED YOUR LAND," KATIE STATED, STARING at the hole in the earth where the dam had been only a minute ago.

"And my stables. This valley leads back to the front lawn where the stables sit…" Andy ran a hand through his hair. "…sat. The structure certainly isn't there any longer."

"Such devastation…" Katie muttered. She couldn't believe the amount of wreckage caused by one evening.

"I did what was necessary."

"But your stables are your life. And your lake, your estate?"

"Yes, that was unfortunate." Andy nodded as he looked out across the mud pit where the lake had been a few minutes ago. "I always liked this lake."

"This was my fault. My family did this. I…"

"Had nothing to do with the evil that happened here tonight," Andy cut in.

"Well, no, I didn't, but…" She broke off, her eyes narrowing on him. "You no longer believe I was involved?"

He shook his head. "I began to see reason sometime

after I was bludgeoned with a rock, but before you tried to set fire to your uncle's documents."

"I was only doing what I thought to be right."

"Is that why you rode for days to reach me and then risked your life to save mine?" He raised a brow in her direction. "It was the proper thing to do? You've never before cared so much about proper behavior."

"When I saw that my father left after you..." She looked away. "I had to come."

"You rode here, facing your fear of horses, to save me," Andy said, stepping to the side and catching her eye in the process.

Turning back to him, she countered, "You destroyed your property and your stables to save me."

"And I would make the same choice again. And again. And again."

"Why?"

Before he could answer, her father lumbered toward them with Thornwood. "Amberstall, you have my apologies and my gratitude for doing what I could not and saving my daughter."

"It was the proper thing to do." He tossed a grin at Katie.

"I'm going to escort Ormesby to the wagon parked on the other side of the hill and have him taken back to Amber Hollow," Thornwood said. "Hawkes and Rastings won't be needing a ride anymore and Hawkes' other man escaped on foot, so I thought we could put their transportation to good use." Thornwood nodded toward the man at his side as he added, "He'll need a doctor."

"Nonsense! I've had worse injuries than this over-seeing work at the mines."

Katie spun to look at him. "Father, you were shot with a pistol. You will see a doctor."

"Very well. Amberstall, I don't want to impose after everything else, but is there a doctor nearby?"

"I'll send for him to come immediately," Andy said.

"Very well," Ormesby replied. "I'm sure he'll have me bandaged and ready for travel by the morning."

"By the morning?" Katie repeated, her heart stopping as she looked at her father with wide eyes. They couldn't leave. Not yet.

"I insist you stay," Andy said, stepping forward.

"We will need to leave by early afternoon. I've been away from my estate for too long already. I'm sure you understand."

Andy nodded. "I do."

"I appreciate the hospitality. Katie, come along. You can ride back to the house with me in the wagon."

"Oh…I can walk, you know," she said with a glance at Andy.

"In the middle of the night across unfamiliar terrain with a gentleman?" her father scoffed.

"Is that ill-advised?" she asked.

"I'm no expert on the ways of ladies, but I'm fairly certain it's frowned upon to be alone with a gentleman in the woods at night."

"It's all right," Andy said with a thin smile. "We'll finish our conversation in the morning."

She nodded, unable to find the correct words to say. Tomorrow would be their last conversation. She would tell him good-bye and walk out of his life, just as he had walked out of hers. Tearing her gaze away from him, she turned to follow her father and Thornwood. She took one step, and then another. It wouldn't be so difficult tomorrow. She was walking away from him now, after all, and she was still alive.

As she stepped over the rubble where the edge of the dam had been earlier, she finally fell victim to temptation and glanced back. Andy stood on the bank of the drained lake. The moon was shining down on him, streams of pale silver falling over him where he stood in the center of the wreckage.

The look of devastation in his eyes caught at her heart. She wanted to smooth away the crease between his brows and hold him close. But he was not hers to console, not anymore. She needed to continue after Thornwood and her father, and she would—in a minute. Right now she just wanted to watch him, to let him know that even though she wasn't by his side, he wasn't alone.

That was when she noticed it. His look of devastation wasn't directed at his wrecked land; he was looking at her.

❧

It was surprising how such a simple thing as water could devastate when it existed in large amounts. Last night, the water had raged through Andrew's property, uprooting trees and clearing deep grooves in the land before finally slamming into the eastern wall of the stables. He squinted into the morning sun falling across the wreckage all around him. Only one corner of the building still stood, for as much good as it would do him. And all because of some old story and a false map. There was no gold. There had never been any gold. It was only a tale someone most likely told to entertain children.

Andrew kicked aside a piece of wood and stepped onto a pile of bricks that was once the southern wing of his stables. All he'd built in his life, all his work, and here he was back at the beginning. Yet the prospect of starting over didn't strike fear in his heart like it had not too long ago. One of his horses pranced around in the clearing he could now see without the building present. The horse was young and had yet to be trained, and yet he was perfect.

Andrew smiled as he crouched down to pick up a brick from the pile. Perhaps his business was splintered into a million pieces. Perhaps everything was wrong, everything was flawed. But his horses were alive, thanks to Thornwood's quick thinking, and the sun would continue to shine.

"It looks as if you have some damage here," Katie called out from the edge of the wreckage.

"It would seem so." He chuckled and tossed the brick back onto the pile.

"I know someone quite good with stable repairs," she said, climbing onto the heap where he stood.

"Do you indeed?"

"Yes. He's a bit annoying when it comes to proper behavior, even though I have it on good authority he eats with his fingers on occasion. But if you can overlook that, he does fine roof repairs."

"I fear this needs a bit more work than a leaky roof, since it no longer has one."

"The gentleman I speak of can accomplish it—if anyone can." The last bit was said so quietly, he almost didn't hear it.

"A gentleman?" he asked in mock surprise. "I don't need some fancy lord fussing about, calling out orders."

"He's not as fancy as he appears on the surface."

"No, I don't believe he is." He glanced across at the sun rising over the trees in the distance.

He'd stayed up most of the night rolling over the possible outcomes of this day in his mind. Should he ask for her hand in marriage again? After the things he'd said to her at her home, would she say yes if he did? Now the sun was up, and he still didn't know if he was on sure footing. But if this was to be their last time together, he would savor it.

"What will you do?"

"Rebuild it. What choice do I have?"

"You could choose not to rebuild it. Or rebuild it but use it to house lost cats or store old shoes?" She tapped her chin in thought. "Keep wheels of cheese?"

He held up a hand. "You've proven your point. No need to suggest I rebuild to use the structure to start a blanket-weaving business."

"I would never suggest something so silly." She smiled up at him.

He shook his head. "Once something is gone, you sometimes realize it was only a pile of bricks, nothing more." Turning toward her, he added, "But sometimes you realize it was much more."

"Is it only a pile of bricks, or is it more now?"

"The stable? Oddly enough, it's a pile of

bricks—that's all it ever was. But this…us?" He swore and looked away. He'd made a mess of things with her.

She glanced over her shoulder at the drive. "I have to leave in a few hours."

He exhaled a harsh breath. "I'm aware."

"I checked on my father before I came outside." She looked down at her feet as she rocked on the unstable surface. "His arm is well bandaged."

"Don't leave." He said the words before he could stop them.

"I agree. I don't think he should travel so soon, either."

"That isn't why I don't want you to leave," he admitted.

"Oh."

"Katie…do you ever wonder what would have happened if we'd met in London?" he asked as he moved a brick around with the toe of his boot.

She shrugged. "Perhaps we did. You walked past me to have a dance with some perfect miss. I was too busy staring out the window to notice."

"Am I so predictable?"

"Yes."

Perhaps she was right. He had spent his life being as predictable as the sun rising in the morning. But not today. Today was a new day. He bowed with a grin.

"What are you doing?"

"May I have this dance?"

"This is hardly a ballroom floor," she replied, kicking at the mud-packed bricks under her feet.

"I believe I may prefer it to polished wood." He held out his hand to her.

She rolled her eyes and took his hand as he swept her into a waltz across the water-ravaged land. It took a degree of concentration to avoid the tree limbs and other debris. He maneuvered around a section of stable wall left standing and under a piece of the roof leaning against a pile of wood that was once a horse's stall.

"If your staff sees us, they will think you lost your mind in Scotland."

"Most likely. But then life at Amber Hollow can be a bit tedious. It will give them something to discuss."

"Neighbors plotting against you. Explosions at the lake. The flooding and destruction of the stables... quite tedious. I don't see how you can stand it."

"Life is an adventure with you, Katie."

She smiled as he twirled her around a pile of tangled tree branches. In that moment, time didn't exist. She wasn't set to leave in a few short hours. There was nothing that needed to be said before the hourglass ran empty. There were only the two of them dancing together in the mud. Her eyes were bright with laughter as she clung to him, trying to keep from stumbling.

He moved his hand farther down her back as he forced his mind to document every second. The way her hair always escaped its braid to fall around her face, the feel of her pressed against his body. She might never forgive him completely for the things he'd said, for the way he'd treated her when he left, but he would always have the memory of this moment when they simply danced.

"Should I be humming a tune?" she asked.

"Who needs music? We have birds, the wind in

the trees…" He stopped talking to listen, but at the prolonged silence she started laughing. "Laughter? London is missing something by not dancing to the sound of laughter."

"I think I did dance to laughter once. Only it wasn't planned that way. I just forgot the steps and caused a collision on the floor."

"You're dancing perfectly now. We'll choose to believe it was the fault of your dance partner at the time," he offered with a wink.

"This is much easier than the last time I attempted it."

"I've always waltzed well."

"Interesting." She studied him for a second. "I was thinking it was the mud dance floor."

"Perhaps it is." He twirled her to a stop because eventually all dances, no matter how perfect, must end.

⤜⋅⤛

Katie moved away from Andy as she picked her way through the debris. She stepped around the large puddles until she reached the one remaining corner of Andy's stables. Pressing a hand to the bricks still cool from the wet night, she peered around the corner. What had the building looked like before it was washed away? She should have paid more attention yesterday when she rode past the structure. But there was no way she could have known what would unfold last night.

What remained of the building hung above her like a spire piercing the sky, holding fast to its former greatness. She cast a wry smile up at what had once been the corner of a hay loft. Reaching up, she grabbed the edge of the boards jutting from the tower above her. She lifted her feet and hung there for a moment.

"What are you doing? That could collapse."

"That's what I'm checking." She swung her feet and pulled against the wood but it didn't move. "Seems sturdy enough."

"Sturdy enough for what?"

"Going up to take a look."

"There's nothing to see. Nothing is left."

"Lord Amberstall," she said in her haughtiest voice, "I would like a tour of your stables, and if you don't oblige me, I will be forced to scale this wall alone."

He laughed. "Above, you will see the two sections of wall making the corner of the stables."

"Ah, what fine walls they are."

His hands wrapped around her waist, their warmth seeping in through the thin fabric of her shirt as he lifted her high enough for her to climb into the loft. "And straight ahead you will see—" He braced his boot against the edge of the wall and pulled himself up beside her. "You will see my estate."

The land slid off into the distance in a patchwork of fields held in by stone walls and dotted with trees. The leaves were changing color for the year. Soon they would fall to the ground, their moment in the glow of the sun at an end. But today, they reveled in one of their last days of life. She glanced at Andy.

Like those leaves, she would never be here again. This afternoon when her father was prepared for the journey, she would leave with him and continue on with her life. All she had with Andy was this moment.

She turned back to the view before them. "And to think, you once blocked this view with a building."

"I only added to the existing structure. Someone years ago must have chosen this location for the stables. Perhaps this was where they hid the gold that's clearly *not* under the lake." He looked down as if expecting to see gold shining up through the debris beneath their swinging feet. With a glance back at her, he smiled. "No gold."

"Did you need the imaginary gold?" She chuckled, gazing out across fields bright with the golden morning sun and lined with trees ablaze with yellow and orange. "I have all I need before me."

"As do I."

She leaned back, bracing her hands behind her. "It's beautiful, isn't it?"

He brushed the hair back from her face. "The most beautiful sight I've ever seen."

Her breath caught. She closed her eyes for a second, not wanting to know she'd mistaken his meaning.

He trailed his fingers down the line of her jaw and turned her head with a featherlight touch. "Look at me."

Taking a breath, she opened her eyes, the heat of his gaze holding her there. Did he truly think she was beautiful? What about all of her flaws? "I thought…" She couldn't finish. She couldn't make herself say the awful things she'd thought—not now.

"Do you know what makes you beautiful?"

"No." She watched as he studied her for a moment. She could feel the heat of a blush rising in her cheeks.

He lifted the long braid from her shoulder and slid it

over his palm. "When your hair catches the wind and looks like wildfire spreading across a field, it's a beautiful sight. When you're outraged at something I've said, and you wrinkle your nose, making all of your freckles dance about—it's beautiful. Your opinion that nothing is bad in the world, only misunderstood, is perhaps the most beautiful of all.

"The way your breeches cling to the curve of your hips..." He broke off with a grin, tracing one finger over the bridge of her nose and making her realize she was wrinkling it in outrage. "I find I now prefer breeches to dresses. The view they give is quite nice."

She swallowed, daring to ask the only question on her mind. "You don't think those are all flaws?"

He looked deep into her eyes and said, "Beautiful flaws. Beautiful, perfect flaws." His hand drifted to the back of her neck and pulled her a fraction closer.

She could feel the warmth of him around her. He was so close, yet he hadn't kissed her. Did he want to? Even now after everything that had happened? The moment seemed to stretch out as far as the view of the fields. Her breaths grew shallow as she looked into his eyes. "Andy," she whispered, pleading for something she didn't know how to express in words.

He seemed to collect himself at the sound of her voice and pulled back, his hand drifting down her arm.

That wasn't what she wanted at all. She sighed and looked forward again, not wanting him to see the frustration in her eyes.

But when his hand slid all the way to her wrist, he turned her palm over, tracing the silhouette of her fingers with his own as he spoke. "I used to dream of one day having the perfect life here, finding a wife befitting my rank and station, having children who would smile and march about in silence. I would build my business to be known across England as the best horse breeder the country possesses."

"And now?"

"I'm sitting in the ruins of my former life and I couldn't be more pleased." He ceased drawing lines up and down her fingers to slip her hand into his.

She swallowed and looked down at their joined hands. "Because you don't want to be the best horse breeder anymore?"

"Perhaps. Perhaps not. I don't have to decide that today. Success doesn't lie in a building or a single racehorse."

"Then why are you so pleased?" She forced the words out of her mouth and held her breath for his answer.

"Because I'm here with you. Even my worst day is made better by you."

She exhaled on a shallow breath and turned to meet his gaze. "I…don't know what to say."

"I'm hoping in a moment you'll say yes…" He cracked a wry smile as he added, "Again." Concern filled his eyes, drawing his brows together as his grip on her hand tightened a fraction. "Will you marry me?"

"Really? Even after all that's happened?"

"All that matters is what happened between us." He glanced down at their hands with a smile. "You can't control the actions of those around you. I once thought I could, thought I had to be strong…" He gave a little chuckle and shook his head. "I thought

I had to control it all and make everything perfect to hold on to contentment in my life."

She almost jerked away from him. Was that all he felt for her—contentment? Could she marry a man she loved, but who felt only fondness for her in return? He had said she was beautiful, and many marriages began with less. She swallowed her disappointment. Being at Andy's side would be a happier future than venturing to Scotland alone, wouldn't it? She would live out her days with a man who certainly cared for her; that would have to be enough. And perhaps one day love would grow, on his part anyway. She bit her lip as she tried to be rational about the situation.

"Is that what you have now—contentment?"

"There is no place I would rather be than here with you in what's left of the hayloft." His gaze heated her skin as he shifted closer to her. He hadn't answered her question, but she was having difficulty remembering why that mattered when she was here with him.

His lips met hers. She slid her hand over his chest where his heart pounded. The steadfast *bum bum, bum bum* against her palm matched the need she sensed in his kiss. He may not be hers completely yet, but his heart was beating for her now. He wanted her. Perhaps one day he would love her, but today he wanted her. And today, she decided to forget about what would happen one day and kissed him back.

His hands slipped around the back of her neck, tangling in her hair, pulling her deeper into a sea of desire.

"Is your plan to distract me with kisses to postpone giving an answer to my proposal?" Andy asked against her lips, his deep voice sending shivers down her spine.

"It wasn't, but perhaps now it is," Katie replied, kissing him again.

He pulled back a moment later, his hands skimming down her arms as he looked at her. "I know I don't possess the vast wealth of a gold mine, but I can provide for you."

Did he truly believe the gold mattered to her? "The only gold I need is here." She reached up and traced the arch of his brow with a finger. "I can feel the glow of it every time you look at me."

His eyes narrowed on her. "Does that mean you'll marry me? You've yet to answer, you know."

"We *would* have a nice life together," she mused with a bite of her lip.

"We would go for rides together and work with the horses in the day, and in the evening you could practice the bagpipes while I sit by the fire," he supplied.

"Don't forget dinners together where there may or may not be forks."

"I think I would like a future without forks..." He grinned.

She knew what she must say, and it couldn't wait any longer. "Andy, I have to be honest with you. If we're to build a life together, we have to begin with the truth. That much of life I learned from my mother."

"What is it?" He grew still beside her, waiting.

"I know you don't feel the same, but I want you to know that I love you. I hope someday you can return the sentiment. However, if you can't, I will continue to love you all the same."

He gave a small shake of his head. "Do you think I would want to spend the remainder of my life listening to you play bagpipes before the fire *every* evening if I didn't already love you?"

She wrinkled her nose and hit him on the arm. "You wouldn't enjoy listening to me play the bagpipes?"

"Ouch!" he exclaimed with a laugh. "Is that really the part of my statement you're going to dwell upon?"

She grew still. "You...you love me?"

"Katie, I think some part of me always loved you. It's the same wild part that likes to race horses— perhaps not through the streets of London like a certain hoyden I know, but it's a part of who I am that I'd forgotten existed until I met you."

"Does that mean you won't be racing me when next I'm in town? That would mean I would win by default. But, since I would win anyway..." She broke off with a shrug of her shoulder.

He sighed. "I can't very well forfeit to a lady. If we're racing through London, we must do it properly."

"There's a proper way to race someone through London?"

"As Lord and Lady Amberstall, of course."

"I think for once I would like to do something in the proper fashion," she replied.

"And I think while we're alone in this hayloft I would like to do something quite improper."

His lips met hers in a kiss that held the promise of a lifetime of adventures at his side. With him, life would be imperfect, improper, and impossible not to enjoy. She had a feeling she would like being the not-so-proper Lady Amberstall—forever.

Acknowledgments

When I was eighteen years old, I spent the summer in Ormesby, England. At the time, I had no idea the impact that trip would have on my life. I hopped on an airplane partly because it was an exciting adventure for the summer, and partly because my new boyfriend's parents lived there and I thought he was pretty cute. This is to say, at that age my mind was certainly not on books. But, as it happens in life, I fell in love—with the North Yorkshire Moors and the cute boy. This story is set in that place I love so dearly, just down the road, at the base of Roseberry Topping. Therefore, I want to thank my parents for allowing me to venture to a foreign country with a family they'd only met once over dinner, my (now) in-laws for inviting me to visit for the summer, my (now) husband for still being cute years later, and my son because his feelings get hurt if I don't include him in the acknowledgments.

A giant thank-you goes to Mary Altman for her editorial vision over this book and for her encouragement during the long hours spent at my computer. A huge thank-you goes to Michelle Grajkowski for her amazing support and belief in me throughout this process. I would also like to thank the entire Sourcebooks team who made this book possible, as well as my friends/critique partners/blog partners Heather McGovern, Jenna Patrick, Lori Waters, Jeanette Grey, and Sidney Carroll for being awesome. Finally, I thank you for reading this long-winded thank-you note, and for allowing me to share this story with you that's been eighteen years in the making. Thank you!

~E. Michels

About the Author

Elizabeth Michels blends life and laughter with a touch of sass into the Regency era. This flirty, fun-loving author turns ballrooms upside down, and challenges what lords and ladies are willing to do to get what they most desire. She lives in a small lake-side town in North Carolina with her husband, "Mr. Alpha Male," and her son, "The Little Monkey." Elizabeth is furiously typing away at her next novel while dinner burns in the kitchen. She loves to hear from her readers. Please visit her website at www.elizabethmichels.com.